THE SOUND OF MURDER

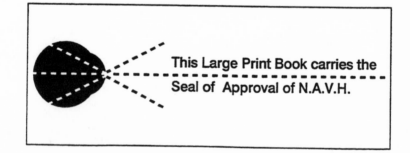
This Large Print Book carries the
Seal of Approval of N.A.V.H.

THE SOUND OF MURDER

Patricia Matthews
with
Clayton Matthews

Thorndike Press • Thorndike, Maine

Published in 1995 by arrangement with
Severn House Publishers, Ltd.

This book is a novel. No resemblance to actual persons living
or dead is intended.

Thorndike Large Print ® Basic Series.

The tree indicium is a trademark of Thorndike Press.

The text of this Large Print edition is unabridged.
Other aspects of the book may vary from the original edition.

Set in 16 pt. News Plantin by Rick Gundberg.

Printed in the United States on permanent paper.

Library of Congress Cataloging in Publication Data

Matthews, Patricia, 1927–
     The sound of murder / Patricia Matthews
          p.   cm.
     ISBN 1-56054-335-3 (alk. paper : lg. print)
     1. Large type books. I. Title.
     [PS3563.A853S65   1994]
     813'.54—dc20   94-33231

THE SOUND
OF MURDER

CHAPTER ONE

The night air had a bite to it, but Casey Farrel considered the coolness a welcome change from the blazing heat of the Phoenix summer.

She was riding with Josh Whitney, Phoenix Homicide Officer and her best friend and lover. Josh was a big man, well over six feet, with the heft and grace of a linebacker. He had a strong face with a large nose, and dark brows over intelligent gray eyes. At the moment he was attempting to maneuver his Camaro through the traffic along Thomas Road. It was just before eight of a Saturday evening, and Phoenix was jumping.

And Josh was grumbling. "I'll never understand what anybody sees in Country-Western music. Most of the singers have whiny voices that set your teeth on edge, and the subject matter . . ."

He shook his head and gave her a sidelong glance, looking for her reaction. "Unfaithful wives and lovers; lost wives and lovers; my sweetie done done me wrong; my man done left me; and my truck broke down! It's enough to turn a man's stomach."

Opening his mouth, he began to sing. His voice was not unpleasant, but the melody was doubtful. "I've got tears in my ears, from lyin' on my side, cryin' over you."

Casey gave him a look. "Not half bad. Maybe we can get you a second job. You'd look pretty cute in tight jeans and a Stetson."

Josh grunted. "Fat chance."

"My, aren't we grumpy tonight, Detective Whitney." Casey laughed. "Look, the evening will go much better if you'll just relax and *try* to enjoy it."

"Yeah, right."

"At least I don't insist you take me to the ballet or the opera. You should be grateful."

"Oh, I am. I am, but I still don't see the attraction."

She shrugged. "While I was in Prescott, down on Whiskey Row, I heard a lot of it and became intrigued. Besides, the music is fun, and I like the dances, the rhythm."

"Mmmmm." He gave her a sly look. "I might have known it, it's the Indian in you coming out, all those primitive genes."

She laughed. "That must be it, the influence of my Hopi ancestors."

She gave him 'the look.' "And your aversion must come from *your* genetic make-up."

"What do you mean?"

"Well, it's common knowledge that Anglo-Saxons don't have any rhythm."

Josh grinned and lifted his right hand from the wheel. "Okay. I surrender. I'll be good."

"Of course you will," she said, patting his knee.

He grunted. "But one night you have to come with me to someplace where they're playing swing, or jazz."

She nodded. "Sure. I'm game. Unlike some people, I'm open-minded and willing to try new experiences."

Josh was silent as he swung off the boulevard into a parking lot that was already nearly filled with parked vehicles. At the far end of the lot was a low, barn-like structure. Atop the building was a large neon sign depicting a couple in Western clothes, dancing. Below the couple, in flowing neon script, were the words: OKAY CORRAL.

"Well, there it is," said Casey, as Josh hunted for a parking space, "the Okay Corral."

Josh groaned. "Oh, come on!"

Casey smiled. "I think it's kinda cute, myself."

Josh wheeled the car into an empty space. "This'll have to do."

"It's fine."

Casey opened her door and got out of the

car, smoothing her short denim skirt down over her hips. Above the skirt, she wore a fitted, scoop-necked tee-shirt, and a studded denim vest. A slender woman in her early thirties, with short, black, curly hair, high cheekbones, and expressive brown eyes, she had a face that bordered on beauty. Her body was athletic, but nevertheless nicely rounded. She knew that she looked good in the Western clothes. That knowledge was verified by the look in Josh's eyes as he came round the car and took her hand.

"At least you look great in the clothes," he said. "Come on. Let's do it!"

Entering the wide door with Mexican carvings, they had their hands stamped by a sullen, bull-necked cowboy, while another behemoth looked on. Inside, the bar was alive with sound and movement. The huge room was crowded with dancers, drinkers, and just plain watchers.

A four-piece band — two guitars; keyboard and drums — was playing on a balcony that stretched across the back of the room. Fastened to the balcony railing was a large banner: "This Week Only, The Pickups, and Billy Joe and the Boilermakers!"

On the wooden floor below, rows of dancers, wearing everything from elaborate, pseudo-Western outfits ornamented with

10

rhinestones and fringes, to cut-off denims, tee-shirts, and cowboy boots, moved in unison to the foot-stomping music.

Josh raised his eyebrows. "Looks like a square dance," he said.

Casey smiled. "Well, not exactly. It's line dancing. A big fad now."

"The music's awful loud." He rubbed his ear.

"This is nothing. You should have been with me down on Whiskey Row. Now *that* was loud. Do you see any empty tables?"

Josh pointed to a couple just leaving a table for two, along the right wall, as he quickly maneuvered through the crowd to claim it.

Just as they seated themselves, the music ended. "Just in time," Josh said. "If I'm going to have to listen to this stuff, I at least want to be comfortable."

Casey shook her head. "Get over it, Josh. We're here to have a good time."

The microphone buzzed, as one of the guitar players spoke into the mike. "We're going to take a short break, folks. When we come back, be ready to welcome Billy Joe Baker and the Boilermakers!"

Cheers and shouts greeted this announcement.

"Well, it looks like we're just in . . ." The appearance of a waitress interrupted Josh's sentence. He stared at her askance. She was wearing a red fringed skirt that barely covered her crotch, and a matching blouse so low-cut that it barely covered her nipples. Oxblood cowgirl boots completed the outfit. "What'll you have, folks?" she asked. She looked tired.

"A couple of gin martinis, okay, Casey?"

Casey nodded. "Sure."

When the waitress left, Josh said, "So how's it going with the Governor's Task Force on Crime?"

Casey shrugged. "Things have been pretty quiet since I got back from Prescott, and I'm glad for the rest. The crime rate seems to be down."

"It always drops when the cool weather hits. The homicide rate is down twenty percent from what it was back in August. The only thing on my plate right now is a holdup killing in a convenience store two nights ago. We should nail the perp soon. The stupid bastard didn't spot the surveillance camera and we got a clear shot of him. Probably drugged out and thinking only of the money he'd need to make a buy. The owner wasn't too smart either. Came up with a gun from under the counter and got blown away."

Casey shook her head. "Every now and then I get overwhelmed by the stupidity of it all. I begin to wonder if we're worth saving, as a species that is."

"Hey!" He put a large, warm hand over hers. "That's not like you."

Casey squeezed his hand. "Yes it is — a part of me anyway, but I'll get over it."

They looked up to see the waitress bringing their drinks. As she leaned over the table, it appeared that the upper portion of her anatomy might fall out of her blouse. Josh, getting his money out of his wallet, carefully looked away. Casey smiled as the woman took the money and left, swinging her hips.

Josh caught Casey's eye and his face reddened. He was about to say something when the lights dimmed, and a bright spot focused on the balcony. Casey could see that a different group of musicians was on stage now.

The sounds from the bar patrons quieted as a man stepped into the circle of light, then swelled as he touched the brim of his black Stetson, and ducked his head. His voice, when he spoke, was deep and soft, with slurred edges. "Good evenin' folks. How y'all doin'?"

He stood there smiling as the crowd cheered and yelled. A medium-sized man dressed in black Levis and a white shirt, he projected a nice mixture of strength and humility. The illusion was heightened by the easy way he held his well-proportioned body, and the expression on his handsome, boyish face.

13

Josh grunted. "Got the whole nine yards, hasn't he, corn-pone accent and all."

"Well, he *is* from Tennessee. What do you expect?"

"Well, we've got a few songs for you to-night. Hope you'll like 'em. This here is a new one, just finished it this mornin' on the plane. It's called 'Smoky Mountain Woman', and I dedicate it to my mama, back home in Tennessee."

The band lit into the music, and the crowd quieted as Billy Joe began to sing. His voice was deep and resonant, and he pronounced the words lovingly:

"High on the side of old Smoky Mountain,
In a little old pine wood shack,
There lives a pretty-faced, brown-skinned
*   girl,*
Yaller hair hangin' down her back.
Though for a while I been forced to
*   wander,*
Through no fault of my own.
Never seen nothin' neither here nor yonder,
Like that yaller-haired gal back home.

"Oh, Smoky Mountain woman,
Lay the fire and sweep the floor.
For I'm free to go,
And in an hour or so,

14

I'll be knockin' at your door.

"Up by that shack on old Smoky Mountain
Is a little ol' piece of earth,
Never grew much but some greens and
  chickens,
But I can't tell you what it's worth.
Right by the porch there's a ramblin' rose,
That just covers the roof with flowers.
With the help of fate, if the train ain't
  late,
I'll be home in a few more hours.

"Oh, Smoky Mountain woman,
Turn the lantern wick up bright.
Though the path is dark,
I will see the spark,
And be in your arms tonight."

As the music faded, roars and yells of approval filled the room. Casey leaned over to shout in Josh's ear, "You see? Not a pick-up, not a truck, not a betrayed lover in the whole song."

Josh grunted. "It wasn't bad. Folksy as hell, but not bad. Nice tune."

"And clever words?" Casey prompted.

"Well, if you discount the countryisms, I guess so."

Casey hugged his arm. Such an admission,

from Josh, was tantamount to total agreement.

On stage, Billy Joe half-turned to indicate the band, and the applause rose in volume. The singer then turned back toward the audience and two things happened almost simultaneously: his face assumed an expression of surprise, and he staggered and fell backward, crashing into the drum set-up, and then to the floor.

There was an instant of stunned silence, then an eruption of sound and movement as the audience gave vent to their feelings of surprise and shock.

Casey and Josh were on their feet almost at once, exchanging glances. Neither was surprised when they heard the shout from the stage: "Good God! He's been shot!"

"Go to the front entrance," Josh said to Casey. "See that no one gets out that way. Get the doorman to help you. I'll get the rear exit blocked, and get up there before they track up the scene. See that someone calls Homicide."

Casey nodded, and began pushing her way through the patrons, toward the door. Behind her she heard shouts, and then the sound of weeping.

Casey held her identification out to the two men on the door. "Casey Farrel, Task Force Investigator. Seal these doors, don't let anyone in or out except the police and the ambulance attendants."

The two men looked at one another uncertainly.

"Do it!" Casey snapped. "Now!"

CHAPTER TWO

Fortunately, the first patrol car responding to Casey's call arrived within five minutes, adding the reinforcements needed to keep the crowd within the club.

When enough police had arrived to man the two exits and help with the crowd, Josh led Casey over to the body.

Casey, looking down at Billy Joe's mortal remains, thought, not for the first time, how pitiful a human being appeared in death; smaller, somehow, as if death had drained the body not only of life and color, but of physical mass as well. Billy Joe Baker lay on his back, one knee bent, his arms flung out to the side. His black Stetson lay at his feet, and his face bore an expression of shocked surprise. There was an ugly, dark hole, surrounded by a flower of blood, on the left side of his clean, white shirt. Blood from the exit hole framed the upper body, and dripped from the drums and the wall behind them. The coppery smell of blood mixed with body wastes hung heavy in the air. Casey turned away, fighting down nausea. She hadn't seen so many murder victims that she was able to view them with equanimity, and she doubted that she would ever be able to do so. The area had been roped off, and was being guarded by four uniforms.

"Can't do any more till the coroner gets here," Josh said.

Casey looked around at the milling, noisy crowd. "The natives are getting restless," she said.

He nodded. "I know. I'm going to have a couple of the uniforms begin checking their I.D.s. I want to talk to the people who knew him. Want to sit in?"

She nodded.

Josh set up a checkpoint at one end of the long bar that ran almost the length of left wall, leaving two uniforms to get the names and addresses of the general patrons.

As he turned away, a man in a dark suit, tie askew, glasses halfway down a long, pointed nose, approached. He was carrying a black bag.

"Body's over there, Doc. See me when you're finished. I'll be over there." Josh pointed to three tables along the right side of the room, where a number of people were congregated. The doctor nodded and moved toward the stage.

As Josh and Casey approached the group

at the tables a stunning blonde woman, apparently in her mid-twenties, left her chair and came toward them. She was obviously furious, and it was clear that she had been crying.

When she reached Josh, who was slightly in the lead, she grasped his arm. Josh's face tightened, but the woman was too upset to notice his displeasure.

"Who's in charge here?" she asked. Her low voice was either naturally raspy, or her vocal chords were thickened by crying.

"Are you in charge here?"

Gently but firmly, Josh removed her hand. "Yes, I am. Sergeant Josh Whitney, Phoenix Homicide. And you are?"

"I'm Joanna Baker, I'm Billy Joe's wife. They won't tell me anything. They won't let me see him. He's my husband, for God's sake, and I don't know for sure if he's alive or dead!"

Josh's face had softened. He took the woman's arm and led her to one of the chairs. "You'd better sit down, Mrs Baker . . ."

She lifted her hands to her face — her nails were long and blood red — and her shoulders moved. Her voice, from behind her hands, was muffled. "Oh God, he's dead, isn't he? I knew it."

Josh put his hand on her shoulder. "Yes,

Mrs Baker, he's dead. I'm sorry."

"Oh God!" She removed her hands from her face, which was wet with tears. "When can I see him?"

Josh hesitated. "Are you sure you want to? Perhaps it would be best if you . . ."

She shook her head violently. "No. I have to see him."

Josh nodded. "When the coroner is through, then. Before they take him."

"What do you mean, take him?"

"They'll take his body to the police morgue, Ma'am. It's procedure. I'm sorry, but there'll have to be an autopsy."

"An autopsy?"

"Yes. Like I said, it's procedure in a case like this. You'll be staying in town for a time, I suppose? That will be necessary anyway, at least until the preliminary stages of our investigation are completed."

She blinked back her tears, spreading her hands. "Yes, I'll be here."

"Now, Mrs Baker, I realize that this is a bad time, but do you feel up to answering a few questions? The sooner we start asking questions, the sooner we'll start getting answers."

She nodded. "I'll do whatever I can to help find out who the bastard was who did this."

"Well, let's sit down then." Josh led her

over to a vacant table, and Casey quietly followed.

"Now, you were sitting where when the shot was fired?"

She frowned. "Why, right there." She pointed to the table next to them.

"And what did you see?"

"You mean when it happened?"

"Yes. Start with the period just before the shooting."

She thought for a moment. "Billy had just finished 'Smoky Mountain Woman'. People were clapping and whistling, some got up, and we couldn't see, so we stood up too. Billy Joe smiled, and he turned to introduce his band, then he staggered, and I wondered what was wrong, and then he was falling, and I couldn't see him anymore . . ." She buried her face in her hands again, and Josh looked at Casey and shook his head. This part was never easy, even for seasoned cops.

Casey looked away, and saw the medical examiner approaching the table. She touched Josh's arm, and he turned. "Doc! What have you got to tell me?"

The doctor looked pointedly at Casey and Mrs Baker. He seemed tired, and looked rather rumpled.

"It's okay, Doc. This is Casey Farrel from the Governor's Task Force on Crime. Casey, this is Doctor Ted Martin from the Medical Examiner's Office."

He turned back to Joanna Baker. "If you'll excuse us for a moment." She nodded, hands still covering her face. Josh stood, and led the doctor and Casey away from the table to a quiet spot along the wall. "So, what did you find?"

The doctor pulled a large, white handkerchief out of his pocket and wiped his face. "He died almost instantly. The slug was either a cross-point, or something like it; it tore the hell out of the inside of his chest and his back. Probably a .38."

Josh nodded. "Well, the gun should still be in the building. We sealed the place off right away. Now all we have to do is find it."

The doctor put the handkerchief away. "Well, lots of luck. Me, I'm for home and bed. My wife is beginning to think I'm a stranger."

"Autopsy tomorrow?"

Martin nodded. "Sure thing. Call me in the afternoon."

By the time Josh and Casey returned to the table, Joanna Baker was somewhat more composed. Casey noticed that she had touched up her make-up, women's defense against the world.

"Are you all right?" Josh asked the woman. "Can we go on?"

She nodded. "Yes. I'll try not to break down again."

"It's understandable," Josh said softly. "Now, you were sitting there at the table. Was anyone with you?"

"Yes, Edgar Pace, Billy's business manager."

"Anyone else?"

She shook her head.

"Did he leave the table at any time?"

She thought for a moment. "Yes, he left once to make a phone call."

"How long was he gone?"

"I wasn't really paying attention, but not long. About ten minutes, I guess."

"When did he leave? Was it during Billy's song?"

She hesitated, then nodded. "Yes. Yes, it was."

Josh and Casey exchanged glances, then Josh said,

"Do you know of anyone who might have had a reason to kill Billy Joe?"

She hesitated again, then shook her head, slowly. "Not really. I mean there were some people who didn't like him. He was successful, and there were people who were jealous, that sort of thing. But to want to kill him? No,

24

I can't think of anybody."

"Have there been any threats against his life, any hate mail, or mail from obviously disturbed fans?"

Again she hesitated before she spoke. "I don't usually see his fan mail, so I can't say for sure, but I don't think so. At least Billy hasn't said anything. You'll have to ask Millie, Billy's secretary, she's the one who takes care of all of that."

"What's her last name?"

"Hanks, I think. Nobody ever calls her anything but Millie."

Casey put a hand on Josh's arm, signaling with her eyes. He nodded.

Casey leaned forward. "Mrs Baker, I know this is personal, but I have to ask it. Were you and Billy Joe getting along? Was there any problem between you?"

Joanna Baker's perfect face sagged for just the briefest of moments. "Not really. Oh, we disagreed now and then, as all couples do, but things were fine between us. Why do you ask?"

"It's just routine," Casey said, sympathetically. "I know some of our questions will seem cruel, but we have to ask them."

Josh, taking on the next hard question, said: "Has there ever been any problem with other women?"

Joanna looked up, and anger sparked in her green eyes. "Other women?" She hesitated. "Well, other women have gone after Billy; that's par for the course in this business. It's funny about success isn't it? Even a little of it improves a man's sex appeal one hundred percent! After Billy's first hit record there were girls all over the place, willing, eager, and aggressive as hell; but Billy was a pretty sensible guy. He knew it wasn't really him they were after, but his fame. As far as I know, he didn't play around. Is that what you wanted to know?"

Casey gently shook her head. "Again, I'm sorry."

The fire faded from Joanna's eyes. "Hell, it's not your fault. It's just that it hurts to talk about it. Can I go now?"

Josh answered: "But you understand that you're not to leave town?"

She nodded. "Of course."

Watching her walk away Casey said, "There's a woman who's really hurting."

Josh raised his eyebrows. "Yeah, I agree; but it still doesn't mean that she might not be responsible for having him killed. Jealousy is a great motive, and I'm not sure I believe her story about his not fooling around. After all, most wives don't want to admit that they can't hold their husband's attention."

26

Casey shrugged. "You're a cynic, Detective. Well, what now?"

Josh sighed. "First we hear what the forensics men have to say then we talk to the band and the entourage."

"Entourage?"

Josh grinned. "Sure, with performers of any stature there is always an entourage."

"I was just surprised that you knew the word."

"Now that hurts me, deeply."

"Where are they, the 'entourage,' that is?"

Josh pointed to where a group of people sat on chairs that had been arranged near the stage. "Up there."

Casey looked around. The crowd had thinned appreciably, and the line at the checkpoint was quite short.

As they neared the stage, a tall man in plain clothes came toward them, waving a plastic bag. Josh hurried toward him. "You found the slug?"

The forensics man nodded. "In the wall behind the drums, hardly embedded at all."

Josh took the envelope. Casey could see the slug — a shapeless wad of lead — considerably flattened.

"Cross point?"

The forensics man nodded. "After it tore out his chest it hadn't much force left."

"Well, now all we need is the gun."
"We're still looking."
"Let me know when you find it."
The man nodded and turned away.
"Now," said Josh, "for the entourage!"

CHAPTER THREE

The people gathered near the stage looked up as Josh and Casey approached. Casey saw in their faces their various attitudes — dismay, boredom, anger, curiosity. They were certainly a mixed lot.

Josh waded into the center of the group. "I'm Sergeant Whitney. I'd like to talk to you briefly, then you can go."

"It's about time." This came from skinny man with lank, red hair. When Josh turned to look at him, he appeared abashed. "Well, I mean there's nothing we can do for him now, is there? Hanging around here sure isn't going to help him, and as far as I'm concerned, I want to get out of here!"

There were murmurs of agreement from some of the others. Josh raised his hand. "I know that you're tired, and upset; but I need to ask you a few things before you go. Let's start with you." He pointed at the skinny redhead.

The man blinked. He was tall, with jumpy gray eyes.

"What's your name and your position here?"

"Me? I'm Toby Green, bass guitar."

Josh turned to the rest of the group, and Casey listened carefully as they gave their names and functions: Wesley Keyes, first guitar: close to thirty; dark, squatty, hirsute as a monkey. Ken Woodrow, drums: blond; blue eyes; thin and wired. Jeff Stone, keyboard: apparently the oldest of the group; balding; with lively brown eyes and a quirky, cynical smile. Jack Stover, soundman: looked close to forty with a round, soft face; going to fat; black eyes like raisins sunk in dough. Edgar Pace, agent: fifty-ish; tired; jowly, bloodhound face; small, dark eyes that missed nothing.

Pace said in a scratchy voice: "I'm Billy Joe's business manager and attorney, and if you're looking for suspects you can eliminate me, Sergeant. Billy Joe was my meal ticket. I'd sooner have sliced my own throat than hurt that boy."

Josh nodded. "I'll bear that in mind. Mr Pace, Joanna Baker told me that you were sitting at her table when Billy Joe came on stage, is that right?"

Pace said warily, "That's right."

"She also said that you left the table during Billy Joe's number."

"Before he began his song, actually."

jerk you around, Sergeant; she's being delib-
erately misleading. A lot of singers take credit
for songs they don't write. The fans like to
think the songs are personal, and so the singer
lets them think so. But the writer has to agree
to it. It's not like the singer's stealing the
songs."

Josh turned to Michelle. "Is that true?"

Michelle shrugged. "That's one way of
looking at it."

Carol stepped forward, her eyes snapping.
"You wouldn't dare talk like that if Billy Joe
[were] here. Billy didn't need your songs to make
[him] famous; it was him, his voice and per-
[sona]lity! He could have made anybody's songs
[sound] good!"

[Mi]chelle gave Carol a condescending smile.
"[The]n why did it take him so long to make
[it? He] wasn't going anywhere until he started
[doing] my songs. Check the dates!"

[Carol] turned away, cheeks blazing. Josh was
[silent for] a moment, watching Michelle's face.
[She co]uld see that the scrutiny was making
[the wom]an nervous; but she felt that Michelle
[deserved] it, with that attitude. It was also good
[techniqu]e; people often said more than they
[meant] when they were nervous.

[Then] Josh spoke. "How long have you
[been writ]ing music for Billy Joe?"

[Michelle] seemed less cocky now, and an-

"To make a phone call."

"That's right. To make a phone call. Business managers do that a lot, you know. Billy
Joe used to say that he was surprised I didn't
have a phone growing out of my ear."

Josh raised his eyebrows. "And the phone
you used is where?"

"Up front, at the end of the bar."

"Did you get your party?"

"Nope. Got his damned answering ma-
chine."

"Did you leave a message?"

Pace shook his head violently. "Can't stand
the damn things."

"Do you mind telling me who you called?"

"Can't see why you want to know, but it
was Tate Johnson, an old friend in Nashville."

Josh looked down at his pad. "Let's see,
that shouldn't have taken you more than three
or four minutes. Mrs Baker says that you were
gone close to fifteen."

Pace frowned. "Billy Joe had just begun his
first song. I didn't want to spoil the mood
by tromping in front of people. I intended
to wait there at the bar until the number was
over, but then . . ." His voice trailed off.

Josh turned a page in his notebook. "I'll
be getting back to you."

He turned to a tall brunette in her early
twenties. Pretty, in a flashy way, her looks

were marred by eyes red from recent tears.

"And you, Miss, what's your connection here?"

The woman swallowed, and Casey could see that her hands were trembling.

"I'm . . ."

"A sexual connection, what else!"

Casey turned her head to see a slender, strong-featured woman with shiny red hair and intelligent brown eyes. The corners of her lips were lifted in a small, superior smile.

The brunette glared. "You total bitch!" she spat out. Her voice showed traces of the South. "Why'd you have to bring that up here, with Billy Joe lyin' there dead . . ."

"It's the truth, isn't it?"

The brunette sniffed. "You make it sound . . . well, it wasn't the way you make it sound. Billy and I were in love. It wasn't just some cheap affair."

She looked as if she was about to go for the other woman's eyes, and Josh quickly stepped between them, taking the brunette by the arm. "Now, now, just cool it, Miss. There's been quite enough violence for one night. What's your name?"

Still glaring murderously at the red-head, the brunette said in a low voice, "Carol. Carol Lloyd."

Josh gently but firmly led her back to her seat, placing himself between her and the r[ ] head. "Now, back to what I asked you?"

Carol looked confused, then her [ ] cleared. "Oh, yes, well, as a friend of [ ] I was here for his opening night, that'[ ]

"You from Phoenix?"

She shook her head. "No, Fort W[ ]

"Okay, Miss Lloyd, I'll get back[ ]

He turned and looked at the l[ ] group, the red-haired woman. ['] ma'am, who might you be?"

She was of average height an[ ] though her features were a bit [ ] beauty, she had an attractivene[ ] to center in the large, intellig[ ] that regarded Josh with so[ ] "Me? I'm Michelle Tatum. I[ ]

"I beg your pardon?"

"What part of it are y[ ] with? I write the songs, th[ ] like the song Billy sang[ ]

Josh frowned. "If I'm [ ] Billy Joe stand up ther[ ] tell the audience he [ ] bus today."

Michelle nodded. [ ] right; but it was m[ ]

Jeff Stone, the k[ ] ward. His expres[ ] ance with the son[ ]

swered sullenly, "Like I said, for the past year."

"And during that year, Billy Joe's career flourished."

"Yeah. That's right."

"Am I to take it that you had a problem with this?"

The brown eyes were suddenly wary. "What do you mean, problem?"

"Which part are you having trouble with? You know, a problem, a difficulty, a difference, a conflict! Had you argued with Billy over the credit for the songs?"

Michelle flushed. "I guess I deserve that. I apologize."

Then she sighed. "I know this may sound odd, after what I just said, but no, there was no problem. I can't say that I was crazy about Billy, like these other two." She gestured at Joanna Baker and Carol Lloyd. "He had an exaggerated opinion of himself, but then most performers do, and I do think he owed a lot of his success to my songs; but, on the other hand, he made me a buck or two singing them, although he could have paid me better. Billy was a little cheap."

"Wrong again, Michelle," Joanna said indignantly. "It's true that he was careful with his money, but that's because he was dirt poor for most of his life."

"And he never could quite lose the fear that everything he had built up would come crashing down," Edgar Pace said, "and he would be poor again. It's a common enough story, I'm told. But to be fair, Michelle, I never once heard Billy Joe complain about what we paid you. And I may add that I consider what we paid you very generous!"

Michelle nodded. "Conceded. I was just shooting my mouth off, Sergeant. It's the way I react to pressure. I hope you'll forgive me."

Josh nodded slightly, but did not speak. In the silence that ensued, Casey turned to the bass man, Toby Green. "Mr Green, as Billy Joe began his song, you suddenly put down your instrument and hurried off-stage. I don't remember seeing you come back."

Green's thin face reddened, and he cleared his throat. "I had to go to the john. Something I ate today, I guess. I got kind of a nervous stomach."

The other band members snickered, and Green's face grew redder still. "It's, it's something of a problem, sometimes."

"Yeah, I guess so," said Jack Stover, the rotund sound man. "Billy Joe was getting pretty tired of it, too. Once or even twice, okay, but every God-damned performance . . ."

"It wasn't every performance, Jack," said Jeff Stone, putting his arm over Green's narrow shoulders. "The boy can't help it."

Stover shook his head. "That don't make it any better. It disrupts the performance, and, like I said, Billy Joe was getting pretty tired of it."

Josh looked speculatively at Green. "Were you upset about that? Did you talk to Billy Joe about it?"

Green shrugged. "No, we didn't talk about it, but I knew how he felt. I didn't blame him."

Suddenly, his face whitened. "Hey! You don't think that I . . . ? Lord, I'd never hurt Billy Joe! He gave me a job when nobody else would."

Josh waved a hand disparagingly. "Coming or going, did you see anything unusual, anything suspicious?"

Green shook his head. "I was on my way back to the stage, about halfway across the room, when I heard the gun-shot."

Josh's gaze swept over the faces of the others. "How about the rest of you? Did you see anything out of the ordinary, anything suspicious?"

When no one responded immediately, Pace said, "I'd put my money on a celebrity killer, Sergeant."

"It's possible, of course."

"Sergeant!" The voice came from across the

37

room, and Casey glanced over to see one of the suits beckoning.

"Be right there!" Josh looked at the group. "Don't any of you leave yet, I'm not finished with you."

Josh and Casey crossed over to the detective.

Josh said, "What is it, Gary?"

"We found the murder weapon, at least we found a .38 automatic with a silencer. Been fired once!"

Josh's expression brightened. "Must be it. Where did you find it?"

"In the men's room, hidden in the paper towel dispenser."

Both rest rooms opened off a small alcove just off the dance floor. Casey paused for a moment, looking toward the balcony stage. The stage was clearly visible from one corner of the alcove. Anyone standing there would have a clear shot at a range of about sixty feet. He or she would also have been partially sheltered from the general view, and at the time of the shooting all eyes had been focused on the stage.

Casey turned away and followed the men into the men's room, where Gary and Josh stood in front of an open towel dispenser.

Josh stepped aside so that Casey might see. The paper towels had been removed, and Casey could see the weapon in all its trim and lethal efficiency, taped to the back of the unit.

"He just took out some of the towels, and taped it to the back," Gary said. "We found the rest of the towels in the trash."

"Well, bag it, and get it to the lab."

Gary nodded. "Sure thing."

Casey interrupted, "Josh?"

"Yeah?"

"Toby Green?"

Josh shrugged. "That would be too easy, but yeah. I'll light a fire under his butt and see if he yells."

Expectant faces greeted their return. "What is it?" Pace asked. "Did your men find something?"

Josh nodded. "Yeah, as a matter of fact they did."

He turned to Toby Green, and Green's eyes flickered nervously.

"Mr Green, you said you were in the john just before Billy Joe was shot?"

"Ye . . . yeah."

"And you said . . ." Josh flipped open his notebook. "You said that you didn't see anyone else in the room."

Toby swallowed and shook his head. "That's right. Everybody was out watching Billy Joe."

"Well, we just found what we believe is the murder weapon. It was in the men's room."

Josh waited expectantly while Toby swallowed again. He seemed to be having difficulty with his voice.

Finally the words squeaked out: "But I told you, I had already left the john. When Billy was shot I was halfway to the stage!"

"But we only have your word for that."

Toby began to wave his arms. "Ask the other members of the band, they'll tell you that I was on stage seconds after Billy was shot."

Josh glanced at the other band members. "Is that true, boys?"

Wes Keyes said slowly, "Yeah, I think he's right. I couldn't swear to it, there was a lot of confusion, but I remember that Toby was there when we all gathered around Billy's body."

Josh turned to Ken Woodrow. "What do you say?"

The drummer squinted his blue eyes in thought. "Same here, I guess. It took me a little longer to get to Billy than it did Wes, but I seem to recall Toby running up within seconds after Billy fell."

"Mr Stone?"

The piano player shook his head. "I'm sorry, Sergeant, but I plain don't remember just when Toby showed up. It all happened pretty fast, and things were pretty confusing.

All I can be sure of is that when we were all gathered around Billy Joe, and it became clear that he was dead, I looked around, and Toby was there."

Josh nodded. "All right. That's good enough for now, but I'll want to talk to all of you later. Of course you all will be expected to stay here in town, and to make yourselves available."

They all began to move, and Josh raised a hand. "But first, one more thing. Did any of you happen to be looking at that alcove there," he pointed, "just before, during, or after the shooting?"

Casey watched their faces as they all shook their heads, or murmured no. "All eyes were on Billy Joe," said Michelle Tatum; her tone mocking.

Josh gave her a cold glance. "Some of my questions may seem obvious to you, Miss . . ." he glanced at his notebook "Tatum, but it is required that I ask them."

She shrugged, and turned away. Casey saw Josh's face redden, but he said nothing further.

When the group had dispersed, Casey said "Josh, it's late. I have to go. The neighbor who has Donnie tonight must be getting worried."

"Okay, I'll have a cruiser run you home. I have to stick around a while longer."

41

He leaned forward and kissed her cheek. "I'll call you tomorrow. Who knows, we might get lucky and nail the bastard tonight!"

Casey hesitated before she spoke. "Josh, you know it might not be a man. Many of the women here, including Michelle Tatum and Judy Lloyd, are wearing jeans. With all the attention focused on the stage, and the lighting dimmed in the rest of the room, anyone could have slipped into the men's room from that alcove."

Josh looked at her sourly. "Jesus, babe! Don't complicate things any more than they are already, okay?"

CHAPTER FOUR

Casey wakened slowly, stretching luxuriously. One perk of her job was the fact that, unless she was involved in a case, she did not have to come in to the office early.

She lay for a few moments longer, her thoughts moving back to last night and the murder of Billy Joe Baker. There was one similarity between this case and the case she had just completed in Prescott. In both cases, the victim had been killed in front of many witnesses; only in the Prescott case the weapon had been poison, a much more silent, less visible means. Of late Donnie had taken to naming the cases in which she was involved; the Prescott case he had tagged the Rodeo Murders.

She smiled. But this, thank heaven, was not her case, and was not likely to be. The Governor's Task Force on Crime was only called in when there was a question of jurisdiction, or if the case was being improperly handled. Since the crime had been committed within city limits, and since Josh was considered one of the best homicide men in Phoenix, there should be no reason for the task force to be involved.

The sound of the toilet flushing, down the hall, alerted Casey that her son, Donnie, was up and stirring. She had better rouse herself. Although she might not have to be in the office early, she still had to make Donnie's breakfast and drive him to school.

As she poured orange juice and made a pan of oatmeal, her thoughts focused on Josh. Ever since she had met him, two years ago, he had been gently trying to nudge her into marrying him. With quiet logic he pointed out that they were in love; they were lovers; and, although Casey was the legal adoptive parent of Donnie, in actuality they shared much of the care of the boy. Wouldn't it be much more convenient if they also shared Josh's comfortable home on the North edge of Phoenix?

But no matter how logical Josh's proposal, Casey resisted. She had been involved in a messy affair before she met Josh, resulting in heartbreak and, in the end, an abortion. She still didn't feel she was fully ready to commit herself again.

"Good morning, Casey," sang out a voice behind her.

She faced around and gazed fondly at Donnie. Eleven going on thirty, with a tumble of blonde hair and bright blue eyes, it made her happy just to look at him. When she had taken him in, two years ago, he had been so small, thin and undernourished; but two years of good food and loving care had added inches to his height and muscle to his frame. He was rangy now, instead of wiry, and showed promise of one day growing into a big man.

"Good morning, kiddo," she said affectionately. "You're disgustingly cheerful for so early in the morning."

He grinned slyly. "It's not so early. Usually you've had your morning run by this time. I guess you and Josh were up pretty late last night, huh?"

Casey gave him "the look." Ever since the three of them had met, during the Dumpster Killer case, Donnie had worshipped Josh. His dearest desire was that Josh and Casey should marry. He already looked on Josh as his father, but he wanted the security of the legal tie. Casey felt the pressure, and the fact that she could not take the step made her feel guilty.

"Yes, I was out with Josh, true, and I was late getting in." Donnie's grin widened. "But that was because there was a killing committed at the club where we were."

Donnie's eyes widened. "A killing! And you were there?"

Casey sighed. Since she and Josh were both

45

in crime investigation, Donnie had decided that he wanted to be a cop when he grew up. He always pestered her to death for details about any investigation she was involved in.

"Yes. Why don't you run out and bring in the paper? It's sure to be on the front page."

"Wow!" A flash of surprisingly large sneakers, and Donnie was out the door.

Casey turned off the oatmeal, and reached for the box of raisins sitting on the counter top.

As she placed two bowls of oatmeal on the table, the door slammed, and Donnie came charging back. Plopping into a chair, he opened the paper. "Wow! Billy Joe Baker! Is that the one?"

Casey put a pitcher of milk on the table, and took a chair. "Yep. That's it."

"Wow!" For a moment all was silent, as Donnie read. At last he looked up, and put down the paper. "It mentions Josh's name. How come they don't mention yours?"

She pushed his orange juice toward him. "Because it's not my case. I was just a bystander."

He considered this for a moment, not sure this was acceptable. "Well, okay. But tell me what happened."

"I will, if you start in on your breakfast. And, if you say wow one more time, I may dump my oatmeal on your head!"

He looked at her with that sideways look of his, the one that proclaimed that he just might say the word to see if she would really do what she said.

She gave him a stern glare, and he grinned. "Okay. I promise. So, tell me what happened."

Casey took a sip of her coffee, then briefly outlined the events of the previous night. Donnie listened intently, his bright gaze seldom leaving hers.

When she was finished, he said excitedly, "You going to solve this one, Casey?"

"Nope, kiddo," she said with a laugh. "Sorry to disappoint you, but this is Josh's case, not mine. The task force won't be involved in this one."

To Casey's dismay, when she arrived at her office later that morning, she learned differently. The first thing she saw was the memo on her desk: "Farrel: Call me the instant you get in. Wilson."

Bob Wilson was the head of the task force, and her immediate superior. He was a political appointee, who had been a big help in getting the present governor elected. Ambitious and competitive, Wilson hoped that this job was a big step toward helping him claw his way up the ladder to the seat of power. He was intelligent enough, but when he saw a chance to advance himself, he would run over his own grandmother if it would gain him an advantage.

The offices of the Governor's Task Force on Crime were located on the third floor of an old building near the State Capitol. The location was supposed to be temporary, until better quarters could be found, but now, two years after the task force's inception, they were still there. Most of the offices, including Casey's, were little more than closets. The only exception was Wilson's office, which was decently roomy and adequately furnished, with a nice view of the capitol two blocks away. Snide office gossip had it that Wilson had his sights on the ninth floor of that building, the floor where the Governor and other elite of the State Government had their offices.

Wilson had placed his large walnut desk at an angle, so that he could always have the capitol in view. He was behind that desk now, when Casey knocked and entered at his "Come in!"

He glowered at her. "Farrel, it's about time! We do keep office hours here, you know."

Casey sat down across from his desk and said composedly, "They're flexible, Bob. Isn't that what you always say? Last week I worked several eighteen-hour days on the Hampton case. Now, that's finished, and I have nothing on my plate, so I figured that it wasn't important for me to be here at the crack of dawn."

"Well, as of right now, you *do,* as you so quaintly put it, have something on your plate. I have a hot one for you," he said smugly.

With a habitual nervous gesture, he raked long fingers through the thinning brown hair on his narrow head. "I understand that you were on the premises when this one occurred."

Casey tensed. "What are you talking about?"

"The shooting last night at the Okay Corral. Billy Joe Baker!"

Casey felt a great wave of dismay. "Oh, come on now, Bob. This isn't anything that would involve the task force. The crime occurred within city limits, so there's no squabble over jurisdiction, and a homicide sergeant was there at the scene. You know Josh Whitney; he's one of the best around."

Wilson nodded. "That's all true; but there's more to it than that."

Casey sighed, "What?"

"Does the name Jonas Lester mean anything to you?"

Casey frowned. "Jonas Lester, it rings a faint bell. Isn't he the one who has that chain of fast-food restaurants? Lester Burgers. That's it."

Wilson nodded. "That's right. He built the first one here in Phoenix, now they're nation-wide."

"But how does he fit into this?"

Wilson leaned back in his chair, and Casey braced herself. He had that look on his face, the one that told her he was about to spring something he thought would shock or surprise her.

He smiled smugly. "Well, Lester is Billy Joe's father."

"Then why the different last name?"

"According to what Jonas told me, he and the boy's mother have been divorced for twenty years. Maybe the wife took back her maiden name. He didn't tell me, and I didn't ask."

"Did Jonas keep in touch with Billy Joe?"

Wilson shrugged. "He didn't say."

"And you didn't ask," finished Casey.

"That's right. I can only tell you that Billy Joe was Jonas' only child, and he is very in-terested in seeing the boy's killer caught and punished."

"Doesn't he think that Phoenix Homicide is capable of doing that?"

Wilson shrugged. "I don't think that's the problem, its just that Jonas wants all investiga-tive agencies possible involved in the case, to achieve a speedy solution."

"That sounds like a quote."

Wilson shrugged again, and Casey stared at him searchingly. "I notice that you refer to Mr Lester as 'Jonas.' I take it you are personal friends?" She paused, then snapped her fingers. "Wait a minute, now I remember, I've seen Lester's name listed as a heavy political contributor, and supporter of *your* party. Getting on his right side could be very helpful to your ambitions toward the Governor's Office."

Wilson did not even have the grace to be embarrassed. "So? That's the way politics works, *quid pro quo*. To think it works anyway else is naive. Any other questions?"

Casey fought down a smart retort, which, she knew, would not help the situation. "Yes, do you really think it's wise to put me on this case? Josh Whitney will be in charge, and, as you know, we are personally involved."

Wilson smirked. "Yeah, so I hear. *Very* involved, is the way I hear it."

Again, Casey managed to keep from taking the bait. "That's right," she said calmly, "and that's the reason I shouldn't be involved. It's sure to cause conflict."

"If you can't stand the heat, Farrel, you shouldn't be in the kitchen." He leaned across his desk, scowling blackly. "When push comes to shove, Farrel, remember that I'm the boss, and you're the underling. I know that you're the media's darling, but you still take orders from *me*. Are you turning down this assignment?"

Casey desperately wanted to do just that. On the other hand, she well knew that Wilson, resenting her high profile, would gleefully welcome the opportunity to discharge her.

She sighed and said, "No, of course not. But I don't think it's a wise move."

"I'll make a note of that," he said sarcastically. "Now, I want you on the case as of this moment. Understand?"

Casey nodded, and made a snappy salute. "Yes, Sir!"

Turning smartly on her heel she began to march out.

"Farrel!"

She stopped, turning back. She had never been able to satisfactorily define what the word "leer" meant; but the expression on Wilson's face, must, she thought, surely meet the definition.

"You should be happy, Farrel. Now you can be with your boy friend all the time, without anyone thinking twice about it. Hey, maybe you can even sneak off for a quickie during your lunch hour. I don't mind, as long as you don't get caught, and do your job."

Casey, very close to losing it, took a deep breath. She would not lose her temper. She. Would. Not. Give. Him. The. Satisfaction!

With her last ounce of restraint, she kept her voice calm. "Did anyone ever tell you what a vulgar-minded toad you really are?"

His raucous laughter followed her out of the office and down the hall.

CHAPTER FIVE

Josh was growing increasingly frustrated with Toby Green. He had Green in the interrogation room at the station, and for all he was learning, he might as well have been talking to someone who didn't understand the English language.

"Tell me again, Toby," he said wearily, "how it went down at the Okay Corral last night."

Green squirmed feverishly, running stubby fingers through his reddish hair. His gray eyes jumped like loose marbles. "I already told you and told you, man," he said in a whining voice.

"Tell it to me again."

"How many times do I have to tell it?"

"As many times as I want!" Josh snapped. Then he modulated his tone somewhat. "I know it's a bore, Toby, but there's a reason for it. Often telling and retelling a story brings out things that the teller has forgotten. Okay?"

Toby sighed. "Okay."

Once again, Green told of having to leave the stage for a quick trip to the john during

Billy Joe's performance, and of seeing Billy Joe stumble and fall, from the sidelines.

"What did you think when you saw him fall?"

"I just thought the booze had suddenly hit him. I saw him putting it away pretty good before he came on."

"Did he often do that, drink before a performance?"

"Once in a while." Green squirmed, nibbling at a thumbnail. "Seemed like he was belting them down heavier than usual during our last two or three performances."

"You know of any reason he should have been doing that? Any trouble that you knew about? Any threats, anyone strange hanging around?"

"Man, I don't know nothing about anything like that!" Green whined. "It ain't like we were buddy-buddy or anything. Hell, I hardly saw him except on stage and during rehearsals."

Josh let out a deep sigh. "You know, Toby, if you're lying to me, I'll have your ass." Josh stared at the other man sternly. "I ran your sheet this morning, and you've got some bad marks against you: drug possession; driving while under the influence; pushing; and you're a user, Toby."

Green twitched, and blinked his eyes.

"Man, that was a bad rap, that pushing. I wasn't convicted, you saw that. Just happened to be in the wrong place at the wrong time, that's all. The only time I've ever served was six months for possession; and that's all in the past, man. I've been clean now for over a year."

He took a swipe at his nose with the back of his hand, a habit he'd had so long that he couldn't break it. "I swear I'm telling the truth. Give me a test if you want to."

"I may just do that if you aren't being straight with me."

"I'm telling you everything I know, I swear. I sure didn't pop Billy Joe, and I don't have a clue as to who did. You have to believe . . ."

A knock on the door interrupted Toby's words. He gave a start, poised on the edge of his chair, as though about to take flight. Josh glanced at the door in annoyance.

He got up, batting a hand at Green. "Just stay right there, Toby. I'll be right back."

Josh opened the door and found himself face to face with Casey. "Casey, what are you doing here?" He stepped out into the corridor and closed the door behind him. "Is anything wrong?"

She gave a lopsided smile. "That depends on how you look at it." Her glance fell away.

"They told me you were questioning some-one."

"Yeah, Toby Green."

"Learn anything?"

"Yeah, a little. It seems that Billy Joe had taken to hitting the bottle pretty heavily recently. From what Toby says, this wasn't usual. And Toby has a rap sheet, nothing major, just penny-ante stuff."

Casey nodded. "Well, I know I shouldn't have interrupted you, but I thought it was important enough . . ." She broke off with a gesture, and met his gaze fully, smiling wryly. "I'm stalling, aren't I?"

Josh raised his eyebrows. "I'd say so, yes."

Casey took a deep breath. "I had an audience this morning with Bob Wilson, the total bas-tard! Josh, the task force is stepping into the case."

"And you've drawn the assignment?"

"You've guessed it. I'm sorry, Josh. I tried to avoid it, but he left me no choice. You know I'm on the bubble with him. He's just aching for an excuse to fire me, and if I refuse the assignment . . . Well, you can guess the rest."

Josh shook his head and scowled. "Well, it can't be helped, babe. It's out of our hands. Don't sweat it. We'll work it out."

He touched her cheek gently. "He knows it's my case?"

"He knows."

"And of course he knows about us." He smiled grimly. "Appears to me he's hoping to stir something up between us. Well, we'll just have to make sure he doesn't succeed. I think that we're adult enough to work together without going at one another's throats. But the big question I have is why? Why involve the task force at this stage of the game? It's not the usual procedure. Correct me if I'm wrong."

"You're not wrong, Josh. I tried to tell Wilson that the intervention of the task force carries an implication. To some people it might look like the Governor doesn't think the local police can handle it, and that's not fair on you! You're the best homicide detective on the force!"

"Thanks, I appreciate that."

"But he wouldn't listen. I finally got him to admit the real reason he's being so insistent. It's political pressure. Big time. Does the name Jonas Lester mean anything to you?"

"Jonas Lester? Oh, yes, Lester Burgers. Big bucks, big influence, big political contributions."

"Right, well brace yourself, Billy Joe Baker is Lester's son!"

Josh stared. "What?"

"It's true. Billy Joe is Lester's son, and the old man wants his boy's killer found, pronto!"

"And good ol' Bob Wilson is eager to help him out."

Casey nodded. "Of course the fact that Bob has his eye on the Governor's chair, and that Lester supports Bob's party, has nothing to do with all this."

Josh grinned ruefully. "Of course not."

"I have a strong hunch that Lester promised to contribute to Wilson's war chest in a big way if Wilson would put the task force on this case. At any rate, we're in, and I'm stuck with it."

Josh scratched his nose. "One thing puzzles me. Why was Billy Joe's last name Baker?"

Casey shrugged. "Wilson doesn't know. From what Wilson said, I gather that Lester didn't keep in close contact with Billy, even though Billy was his only child."

She shook her head. "People are really strange."

"You're right on that score. If what you say is true, it seems very odd that Lester is so hot to find the killer of a son he mostly ignored; but, like you said, people are strange. And, after all, we don't know how he really felt about his son."

Casey nodded. "Well, I'm going to try to

find that out. When I leave here I'm heading out to Lester's 'palatial mansion' as the papers put it. I wanted to let you know. I don't want to be stepping on the toes of Phoenix Homicide!"

Josh grinned. "Ask away. If you step on my toes, I'll let you know."

"Yeah, I thought you would."

He put his arm around her shoulder. "Besides, I figure that it's about time that we worked on a case together. And maybe we *will* solve it faster. Two heads, you know."

His gaze went past her, and he lowered his voice. "Here comes a hot one now. Good. This will save me a trip."

Casey turned. Edgar Pace, Billy Joe's business manager, was coming down the corridor toward them. He looked rumpled and pale; his obvious fatigue making him look even more like a bloodhound than he had last night.

He stopped in front of Josh. "Sergeant Whitney? They told me up at the front that I'd find you back here."

"Well, here I am. What can I do for you? You remember Miss Farrel? She's going to be working on the case with me."

Pace nodded perfunctorily, his eyes flickering over Casey's face. "Hello, Miss Farrel." He turned back to Josh. "Look, Sergeant, I need to get a fix on things here. Some of the band members and the soundman have called me. They need to know how long they'll have to stay in Phoenix. With Billy Joe dead, they need to look for other jobs. And I have to get out of here soon as well."

Josh looked at him thoughtfully. "Well, that's an honest question. As soon as I get statements from everyone, and talk to each of them again, you all will be free to go — that is, unless we find that one of you is the killer."

Pace's sad face paled. "I don't think that's funny, Sergeant, and it's cruel besides."

Josh nodded. "I wasn't attempting to be humorous, Mr Pace."

Pace looked shocked. "Do you mean to tell me that you suspect one of us, one of Billy Joe's friends and coworkers?"

Josh sighed. "At this point, Mr Pace, we don't know who to suspect, but it's also true that we can't discount anyone. So just stay cool, and let me do my job. Okay? The faster I do it, the sooner you'll all be out of here."

He looked down at the notebook he had in his left hand. "In fact, if you have the time, I'd like to talk to you now . . . well, in just a few minutes, when I finish with Mr Green. Will that be convenient?"

Pace thought a moment, then nodded. "That would be fine. Is there anywhere nearby where I can get a cup of coffee? I haven't had breakfast yet."

"There's always a pot brewing down the hall. Should be some sweet rolls as well. Help yourself."

"Thanks," Pace said, and began to turn away. Casey's voice stopped him.

"Before you go, Mr Pace," Casey said. "Did you know that Billy Joe's father lives here in Phoenix?"

He turned and looked at her fully for the first time. "Yes, I knew that."

"Do you know Mr Lester?"

"Not really. I knew of him, of course; but he and Billy Joe hadn't been on speaking terms for years. That applies to Billy's mother, Arlene, as well. The parents have been divorced for . . . what? A good twenty years anyway."

"Do you know the reason for the breakup?" Casey asked.

"I can tell you what I've heard. They say that Jonas was working day and night trying to get his burger chain off the ground. According to his wife, he had no time for his family, and she simply got tired of it. She went back to Tennessee with Billy Joe, and filed for divorce."

"Was it a bitter divorce?"

"If you're asking if the divorce caused the bad feeling, I gather not. That happened later, inches, and a dark, suspicious eye peered out at her.

Casey offered her card. "I'd like to see Mr Lester, please."

The door opened a few more inches, and Casey saw that the eye belonged to a middle-aged Hispanic woman of around fifty or so, with a stoic *India* face. The woman took the card, looked down at it, and then back at Casey's face, shaking her head. "*No es posible*," she said in a husky voice, "*Señor* Lester no see visitors."

"*Por favor*. It has to do with the death of his son, *El muerto de hijo!*"

The woman nodded, then closed the door in Casey's face.

Casey waited patiently. The air was dry and cool, filled with the scent of newly-mown grass and flowers. The sky was a deep blue, broken only by a few piles of fat white clouds. It was one of those days that made Phoenix bearable.

After nearly five minutes Casey heard footsteps again, and the door slowly opened. This time the woman stepped aside and nodded at Casey to enter. "*Señor* Lester, he will see you," the woman said.

"Thank you," Casey said, and stepped inside.

The interior of the entrance hall was high-

when Mrs Lester found out that Billy Joe could sing, and started pushing him. When Lester heard about it, he hit the roof. He was well on his way to being a rich man then, and he wanted Billy Joe to come into the business with him. Both Arlene and Billy refused to have any part of it. The old man is stubborn, I hear, and when they wouldn't go along with him, he cut them off. As far as I know, Billy never saw his father again."

"A sad story, Mr Pace. Thanks for your time."

"Well, I'll see you later, Sergeant," Pace said, and headed down the hall.

As Pace left, Casey said, "Well, I'm off to Lester's place." She put her hand on Josh's arm. "Thanks for not resenting my nosing in. You're a heck of a guy, Sergeant."

Josh looked left and right and, seeing no one in sight, quickly kissed her on the nose. "You're right again, babe. You're a woman of discernment. It'll be okay!"

And yet, as Josh watched Casey walk away from him with that easy, seductive stride of hers, he had to wonder just how okay it would be. They were both used to doing things in their own way, and they were both competitive. Casey was being placating and deferential now because she felt guilty about being thrust into his case; but he knew her well enough to know that once she got the bit between her teeth, the competitive side of her nature would come into play. He knew himself well enough to know that this applied to him, too. He had an uneasy feeling in his gut that warned of tense times to come.

CHAPTER SIX

Jonas Lester lived in Scottsdale, in a residential area where the homes, Casey judged were in the million dollar range. The hous was a Spanish-style stucco set on a one-ac lot. There was a high stone wall enclosi it.

As was her custom, Casey had not ca ahead; she had learned that catching a wit or suspect by surprise often gave her an e Of course she always ran the risk of not fin her subject at home, and, for a moment feared that might be the case here; bu iron gates set in the high, stone wall open, and she drove right in.

As she took the curving driveway l up to the house, she saw the probable for the open gates — a gardening servic was parked to one side of the drive, men were working on the lawn.

Casey parked the Cherokee in fror entrance steps and got out. She hac the doorbell twice before she heard t of footsteps. The door opened or

ceilinged and rounded. Casey got a quick glimpse of thick, cream-colored walls, and arched niches cradling what appeared to be pre-Columbian sculptures. The only light came from a domed, stained-glass skylight that spilled rich pools of color over the marble floor. Casey only had time for a quick look, before the woman turned and led the way through an arched doorway into a long, rather dark corridor.

After walking for what seemed to be a considerable distance, the woman finally stopped at a closed door at the end of the hall. Raising a solid, brown fist, she rapped briskly upon the door, elicited a muffled "Come in" from inside, and motioned to Casey to enter.

Casey did so. After the dimness of the hallway, the room seemed very bright; sunlight streamed in through wide windows. Two walls were covered by floor-to-ceiling bookcases, full of books, photographs, and plaques. A beautiful, large wooden desk sat some feet back from the windows, and sitting behind the desk was a man. The man rose as Casey moved into the room.

At first, with the strong light behind him, it was not easy to make out his features; but as Casey's eyes adjusted she could see that he had a shock of well-styled gray hair, a rather florid face with full lips and a Roman nose, and piercing black eyes. It was an imposing face, clearly that of a man used to giving commands and having them obeyed; but at this moment it bore a look of resigned sadness.

"Miss Farrel?" The voice matched the face, authoritative and brusque.

Casey moved a step closer. "Yes. I'm Casey Farrel. Thank you for seeing me."

He nodded, studying her face. "You're the woman from the Task Force."

"I am."

He frowned. "You look younger than your pictures."

"Is that good or bad?"

He sighed. "Excuse the prejudices of a foolish old man. I've followed your career. You seem to get things done."

"Well, thank you. I've been lucky."

He grunted. "I suspect that it is a matter more of hard work and intelligence than luck. Did Wilson tell you that Billy Joe was my son?"

Casey nodded. "Yes. I'm very sorry."

Lester looked into her eyes as if to judge the sincerity behind her statement. He seemed satisfied at what he saw. The slap of his hand on the desk caused Casey to jump. "I want his killer found, Miss Farrel, and I want him brought to justice. Nothing can bring Billy back, but at least I want that, to see his death avenged!"

"I'll be honest with you. Miss Farrel. Billy and I had not seen each other in some time. There were some problems between us, but I feel sure that they were about to be worked out. Then this . . ."

Lester's facade trembled for a moment, and she glimpsed his great pain. It made her ache inside.

This was one of the hardest parts of her job, dealing with the pain and hurt of a victim's families and loved ones. No matter how hard she tried to separate herself from it, it always got to her.

"I understand," she said softly.

"Billy called me when he knew that he was coming to Phoenix. We were to have dinner together — this very evening, in fact." His voice cracked, and he looked down at his desk.

Casey cleared her throat. "I know this is difficult for you to talk about, Mr Lester, but there are some things I need to know."

He lifted his head. "Go ahead."

Casey took out her notebook and opened it. "During this phone conversation, did Billy Joe mention that he was in any kind of trouble?"

Lester shook his head. "No. We didn't talk long."

"Well, what did he say?"

Lester paused, thinking. "He said he knew that his call must be a surprise, but that he was coming to Phoenix, and he wanted to see me. He said that he wanted to talk things out with me."

"And you were agreeable?"

"Hell, yes! I've wanted to clear this thing up for a long time, but I was too proud to make the first move. And now it's too late! The only thing I can do for Billy now is to see that his death is avenged."

Casey made a note in her book. That was what it usually came down to, wasn't it? The victim, or the victim's family, might speak of justice, say that they wanted the attacker off the streets so that he or she could commit no further crimes; but almost always what they wanted in their gut was the old *quid pro quo*, an eye for an eye, a tooth for a tooth, a death for a death.

And were they wrong? When a terrible injustice is committed against you, how do you deal with it? How do you finally put it away and get on with your own life? If you're a saint, you forgive the perpetrator and leave him or her to heaven. But few people are saints, and almost all humans hunger for what they perceive as justice.

"Is there anything else?"

70

Casey looked down at her notes. "Yes. I really need to know something of the background here. How long have you been separated from Billy Joe's mother?"

"Twenty years."

"Did your wife file for divorce at that time?"

"About a year later."

"On what grounds?"

He frowned. "I don't know how that will help you, but it was the usual; irreconcilable differences." Lester sighed, shrugging. "I was just starting my business, working eighteen hours a day, and away from home a lot of the time. I tried to tell Arlene that it was all for her and the boy, but she couldn't see that. And she had some crazy idea that she could sing. She wanted to be a country-western star."

"Did she have any talent?"

He shrugged again. "A little, maybe; but everyone knows how hard it is to make it in the music business. I reminded her of that. I asked her to be patient for a year or so, that in a little while I'd be bringing in real money, but she wouldn't listen.

"Next thing I knew, she had filed for divorce. I thought about fighting it, but I didn't have the time. She didn't ask for anything, just custody of Billy Joe. I didn't want to subject the boy to a long custody fight, so I agreed.

71

And, at the time, to be honest, I didn't have the time to look after him. I guess I thought that after a little time had passed she would cool down, and I'd be able to take a greater part in Billy's life."

"And did that happen?"

His lips thinned. "No. I'm sorry to say it didn't."

"So you didn't see Billy Joe very often."

He nodded. "That's right. Arlene moved around a lot, trying to make it on the country-western circuit, and she took Billy with her. It took me a few years to get the business going, and by the time I finally was able to pay some attention to the boy, it was too late."

"Did you contact her and Billy then?"

"Yes, but Arlene had turned the boy's mind against me. And then he went into that redneck country music. What a career to choose! He could have come into the business with me, made something of himself. When I first heard about it, he was still in his teens, not legal age. I thought of hiring somebody, a private detective, to kidnap him, bring him home to me. But my lawyer advised against it. Since my ex-wife had legal custody, I'd be breaking the law. I did have a detective find out where he was performing, and left messages for him. When he didn't call back, I said to hell with it."

"And then he finally called."

"Yes. And now this!" He waved a hand helplessly.

"Do you know if your son left much of an estate?"

Lester shook his head. "I've no idea, although I doubt it. I understand that he was becoming popular, but that was a recent thing, and I don't think he'd begun to earn the big money yet. Ask his mother or that wife of his, one of them ought to know."

"I will. But tell me, was Billy Joe your legal heir, Mr Lester?"

He stared. "Of course. Who else would I leave it to? He's my only living . . ." He stopped, cleared his throat. "He was my only relative."

"And if Billy pre-deceased you?"

Lester thought for a moment, his face sad. "I never thought that would happen, but my lawyer said that I had to arrange for all eventualities." He shook his head. "The will states that the money would then go to any children Billy might have, and if there were no children, then to several charities."

"And there are no children?"

"None that I know of. I guess I'll need a new will now. Hell! I spent all those years building a fortune for Billy, and now I've no one to leave it to!"

Casey smiled sympathetically. She truly felt for the man; he was hurting. Still, she couldn't help thinking that he was, to some extent, fooling himself. It was such a cliché: "I did it all for you, dear, for you and the kids!" when all the wife and children really wanted was a hands-on father; one who was there, one who spent some time with them and shared their lives. Was there ever a man or woman who really did it all for somebody else? Casey didn't think so.

She looked up from her note-pad. "Will Billy Joe be buried here, or back in Tennessee?"

He shrugged. "I was going to call his mother about that today. I'd like to have it here, but I suppose Arlene will want him to be buried in Tennessee." He bit his lip. "I won't fight her on it. We're both going to be hurting enough without that."

"Of course there's his wife. She'll have to be consulted."

He scrubbed a hand over his face. "I suppose so."

"Have you met her?"

He shook his head. "I don't know that I want to. From what I've heard about her, she's something of a bitch, and from the way Billy talked, I had the feeling things weren't going well between them. Why?"

74

"No particular reason." Casey closed her notebook. "If the funeral's in Tennessee, will you be going back there?"

"Damn right. He's my boy. Even Arlene can't keep me from seeing him buried."

CHAPTER SEVEN

Josh found Edgar Pace to be very cooperative: the man answered all of his questions freely, with apparent openness. In fact, he was so open that Josh mistrusted him.

"About this phone call you made just before Billy Joe was shot. You said that you didn't leave a message?"

Pace nodded. "That's right. I hate those damned things!"

"So there would be no record of your call. That's too bad."

Pace's bloodhound eyes flickered. "You mean that a record of the call would prove I was where I said I was at the time Billy was killed?"

"That's it."

"So, you see me as a suspect." Pace sighed. "Look, I told you that Billy was my bread and butter. He was the only client I had that was making real money. His death will cost me big bucks. Why on earth would I kill him?"

Josh did not answer this question, but, looking down at his notes, asked another. "How long have you known Billy Joe?"

Pace sighed again. "Let's see . . ." His mournful face contorted with thought. "It's been almost ten years now. Since Billy Joe was eighteen."

"Was that when he started singing professionally?"

Pace shook his head, and his jowls quivered. "Oh, no. Billy had been singing around, anywhere that he could, much earlier than that."

He smiled slightly. "I heard him at that time — it was one of those country music contests — but I must confess that I didn't think much of his chances. He was a gawky kid, and awkward on stage. It was Arlene — that's Billy's mother — who had faith in Billy Joe. She never gave up during all those years he struggled to get a toe in the door. She didn't have any real job skills; but she worked at whatever job she could get to support them while he made the rounds."

"So, you didn't take him on as a client until he was a success?"

Pace shook his head. "That's not quite true. I started handling him about three years ago. He was doing better by then. He'd gained a small following and was getting better gigs." He smiled, and his hound-dog face was almost attractive. "You know that commercial that Orson Welles used to do? The one where he said that they wouldn't sell any wine before its time? Well, performers are a lot like that wine — you can't sell them to the public until they're ready. They have to put in their time learning their trade; they have to pay their dues. Well, Billy had done that, and he was almost ready. He only needed a little polishing and some guidance."

"Sounds reasonable, and practical. So now you thought the boy had a chance?"

Pace smiled again. "Well, I'd like to say that was the only reason for taking him on; but I'll have to admit there was another. You see, I've known Arlene for several years; I met her at one of the places Billy was performing. I was there to see some other talent."

He paused, then looked Josh straight in the eye. "To put it plain, Arlene's a damned attractive woman. I fell for her, hard; even asked her to marry me. But she said she had one failed marriage, and that she didn't want to risk it again. She just wanted to devote herself to Billy Joe's career."

Pace shrugged. "So, I figured that if I agreed to manage Billy Joe, it would keep me close to her, and maybe, in time . . . who knows?"

"And did it work?"

Pace's smile this time was a touch sly. "Oh, she appreciated my taking him on, and she showed her appreciation. That's all I have to say on that subject. But as for the boy, I found that I had done a smart thing. I got better gigs for him, got him some publicity, got him some good songs, and his career really began to take off."

Josh could not quite repress a small smile. "Sort of like casting your bread on the waters, huh?"

Pace shrugged. "It worked out well for me, I'll admit; that is, until last night."

"What about Billy Joe's relationship with his wife?"

"I can't tell you much about that. Billy wasn't one to talk about his personal life, and I didn't press it. I'll have to admit that I was strongly opposed to the marriage; I felt that it was bad timing, that it would hold him back."

"How did Arlene feel?"

"She was even more set against it than I was." He shook his head. "I think it was the only time that Billy Joe really went against his mother's wishes. It hurt her, I know."

"Was it because she didn't like the girl? Was that why she was against the marriage?"

"Well, I don't think she cared much for Arlene personally, but mainly it was for the same reason I disapproved. When a performer is on the road a lot — and at this stage Billy was — it's not good for a marriage. In the beginning Joanna went along with him, and tried to be a part of it all. The rehearsing and the trade talk bored her. Then she saw all the women, and how they threw themselves at Billy Joe — that didn't set well. I guess she began to feel shut out, not really a part of things. That's when she started staying home.

"Then, of course, the inevitable happened. Billy Joe was a normal hot-blooded young man, after all."

Pace again looked Josh in the eye. "It's pretty hard for a red-blooded man to refuse all that free sex when it's offered to you night after night — pretty girls who tell you how wonderful you are . . ." He sighed. "It should happen to me."

"So Billy Joe played around?"

"You might say that."

"His wife says different. She says that he was a faithful husband, and that they got along very well."

Pace snorted. "Well, of course she does. Whatever else Joanna is, she's proud; and what proud woman wants to admit that she's not enough woman to keep her man happy."

Josh wrote briefly in his notebook. "So, Billy Joe had a lot of fans. Were any of them the insistent sort? Do you know of any enemies he might have had?"

Pace shook his head. "Can't think of a one. Billy was a likeable man, a little complicated, maybe, but not mean or arrogant like some performers. I can't help you there, I'm afraid."

"Did Billy leave much of an estate?"

Pace's eyes flickered. "I can't really tell you that."

Josh frowned. "Why? You're his business manager. Who would know better than you?"

Pace held up a hand. "I know, but I only handled company business. Billy handled his personal finances himself, with the help of Arlene. I can tell you what he took in from his performances, the gate receipts, that sort of thing; but as for how much he spent, and how much he kept, and what he did with it? Well, that's another story. Billy was very secretive about such things. It was just his way."

"Do you know who gets his estate?"

Pace shook his head. "Chris Waters, in Nashville, is Billy's attorney. If Billy left a will, I suppose Chris would have it."

"And you can't think of any reason why anyone would kill Billy?"

Pace scratched at his right eyebrow, a thick, dark tangle. "Maybe it *was* some loony; there are a lot of them around. Maybe a fan with a few loose connections who wanted to keep Billy Joe for herself."

Josh closed his notebook. "That may be one theory, but it's not mine. I think it was someone who knew him. In a homicide you have to look at three things: means, opportunity, and motive. The opportunity was available to all the people in the club last night. The means, the gun, we have found. The motive we have yet to uncover, and that's usually the most important of the three. Depend on it!"

When Casey returned from her interview with Jonas Lester, she found Josh alone at his desk. She sat down with a sigh. "Learn anything from Pace?"

Josh leaned back, pulling on his nose. "A few odds and ends. I don't know how important they are, but they fill out the picture a bit. One interesting part; Pace is involved with Billy Joe's mother."

Casey smiled, and Josh shook his head. "I know, I never would have figured Pace for the great lover, but . . ." He lifted his hands.

"Also, it seems like neither Pace, nor Arlene — Billy's mother — approved of Billy's marriage to Joanna. What did you find out from Lester?"

Quickly, Casey told him what she had learned. Josh frowned. "God, that is sad, isn't it? Alienated from his father for all these years, and just when they were about to make it up . . ."

"Yes, the old man is pretty shaken up. Billy was his only relative, his heir. Now Lester has all this money, and no one to leave it to except charity."

Josh frowned again. "Now, if it had been Lester that had been killed we'd have a motive. He must be worth a bundle. Well, at least that would seem to eliminate Joanna. No matter how mad she got at Billy Joe, the thought of all that money he'd inherit some day should have kept her from doing anything final."

"Maybe not. It would depend on how much she wanted the money. Maybe she's one of those people who aren't greedy."

Josh looked doubtful. "Babe, I've met a lot of people on this job, and learned a lot about human nature, and there's one thing I'm sure of. Where large sums of money are involved, almost everyone is greedy."

Casey leaned back and stretched. "Well, maybe you're right. Anyway, it's a moot question now, isn't it? Have you run a check on Billy Joe yet?"

"Yes." He reached for a manila folder and opened it. "There's nothing helpful. A couple of arrests when he was a kid, a DUI — got off with a fine — and assault and battery." He grinned. "It seems that our Billy was something of a homophobe. Claimed that some guy made a pass at him, and beat the shit out of him."

Casey raised her eyebrows. "Not exactly politically correct, but not all that unusual. The country-western crowd is pretty aggressively macho. How about the murder weapon? Anything on that yet?"

"Yeah. It was registered to a man named Herman Brown, and was reported stolen from his car in Fort Worth, over a week or so ago. Without the silencer."

He glanced at his watch. "Well, on to the next. What say we talk to Wesley Keyes and Michelle Tatum? They're both staying at the same motel."

"Okay. Who gets whom?"

He grinned. "Let's do it together. We can play good-cop-bad-cop. You never know, we may prove to be a better team than Abbot and Costello."

Casey said with a straight face, "Which one is Costello?"

"We'll figure that out when it's over."

CHAPTER EIGHT

Wesley Keyes, lead guitarist, was staying at the Fountain Suites on Greenway. Josh and Casey found him at the pool, seated at an umbrella table, a tall glass at his elbow. He wore only a pair of red, flowered shorts and a pair of wrap-around sun glasses. His broad, squat body was covered by a mat of thick, black hair.

Stretched out beside him on a deck chair was a tall, voluptuous blonde wearing two skimpy strips of cloth, one across her ample breasts, the other barely covering her crotch. It was difficult to see her face behind the huge sun glasses, but her deeply tanned body was spectacular.

As Casey and Josh approached the other couple, Keyes reached out a stubby-fingered hand and casually stroked the blonde's sleek flank. She did not stir.

Josh said, "Mr Keyes?"

Keyes removed the dark glasses and blinked up at them. His dark eyes were bloodshot. "Yeah?"

"Remember us from last night, Sergeant Whitney and Casey Farrel?"

"Yeah, sure." Keyes smiled, showing large, white teeth. "Looking into Billy Joe's murder, ain't you?"

"That's correct."

"Pull up a chair," Keyes said. "This here is Janice . . ." He patted the woman's bottom, "What is your last name, honey?"

The woman muttered something unintelligible. Keyes smile widened. "Janice is just a little bit out of it today. But she wouldn't be able to help you anyway, I only met her last night, in the bar."

He tilted his head to one side. "So you're here to toast me on the grill, right?"

"I wouldn't put it quite that way," Josh said easily. "But we do have a few questions."

Keyes replaced his glasses, and settled back in his chair. "So ask."

Josh and Casey both pulled out their notebooks. Josh said, "How long have you known Billy Joe?"

Keyes clasped his hands behind his head. "Oh, me and Billy Joe go back a long way. He was just a kid when we met, and I wasn't much older. I was playing the small clubs around Nashville, and Billy would hang around hoping to get a chance to sing. Our band didn't have a real singer, so we were

86

happy to have him do a number now and again, especially after we found out he was pretty good. He was raw as green wood, but he was a natural."

"So you became friendly."

"In a way, but I only saw him now and then in those days. Months would go by when I didn't see him at all. See, I drifted from band to band in those days, knocking around other towns, other states. It wasn't until . . . let's see . . . a few years later, anyway, that Arlene — that's Billy's mom — got enough money together so that Billy could hire his own band. He got in touch with me then and asked me to play with them. We played together for about a year, then we broke up. We just weren't making it. For the next couple of years I saw him off and on. We kept in touch."

"And when did you start playing with his present band?"

"A year ago. Edgar was handling Billy then, and he got Billy a contract to cut a record. Did pretty well, too. It was a good song, 'Back Home Again', one of Michelle Tatum's numbers.

"After that things just got better and better, and so the band stayed together. We recorded another number of Michelle's; 'King of the Honky-tonks'. That one ran right up the charts like a kitty-cat after a mouse. That led to the tour, and . . ." He spread his hands, grinning hugely. "The rest is history!"

"Do you know Michelle Tatum well?" Casey asked.

"Can't say that I do," Keyes said. "Billy was the only one of the group who did. She came to a recording session once, but she didn't say much. We were all surprised when she showed up in Fort Worth to join the tour. I guess she and Billy were working on some things."

"Did Billy Joe do any original songs in the early years?"

Keyes smothered a yawn. "Yeah, some stuff he said that he wrote; but later I heard rumors that it was someone else, some guy I never heard of."

Josh said, "How well do you know Arlene Baker?"

Keyes grinned. "Anyone who was around Billy for very long got to know Arlene pretty well."

"What kind of woman is she?"

"Depends on where you're coming from. If you're on Billy Joe's side, she's on your side. She's always felt that Billy Joe made the sun come up. I never knew a woman to dote on her son so, except maybe Elvis's mama."

"Would you say it was an unhealthy attachment?"

Keyes thought for a moment, then shook his head. "Nah, nothing like that; just mother love for her only chick."

Casey said, "We've heard that she didn't approve of Joanna. Is that your fix on it?"

"Oh, you've got that part right. But I don't think it was because Joanna was Joanna, if you get my drift. It would have been the same with any woman. Arlene was determined that Billy Joe was going to make it big, and she thought a wife — at this time anyway — would be in the way. She said that there were plenty of pretty little heifers out there for the milking, and that when getting free milk was so easy, why buy a cow?"

Casey frowned. "She used those words?"

Keyes laughed. "She sure did. Arlene usually acts like a lady, but she can be downright plain-spoken when she wants to make a point. She's a tough lady, but I don't know how she's going to take this." He shook his head. "It's going to be hard to face her, I can tell you that. Learning that Billy Joe was killed must have been like having her heart torn out."

"Mr Keyes," Josh said, "let's move on to something else. The band, being up on that stage last night, had a good vantage point from which to see what was going on. Did you notice anything unusual in the audience?"

Keyes stared. "Are you kidding, Sergeant? Have you ever been up on a stage?"

Josh shook his head.

"Well, during a solo performance, like Billy Joe was giving last night, the only lights are on *you*, right in your face! If the audience is dancing it's a different thing; then the house lights are up; but during a solo turn like Billy's, everything past the edge of the stage is pretty much a black hole."

Josh nodded a trifle sheepishly. "Tell me this, then . . . you've known Billy Joe a long time, did he have any enemies?"

"I suppose a few people didn't like him," Keyes said with a shrug. "He could be kinda thorny when he wanted something done a certain way, and he didn't much care what other people thought of him; but hell, as far as I ever saw he never gave anyone reason to hate him enough to kill him."

"No one?"

Keyes hesitated, his glance sliding away from Josh's face. He picked up his glass, drained it, and held it up to Casey and Josh. "Where are my manners? Would you guys like a drink?"

"No, Mr Keyes," Josh responded. "We're working."

"You mean that bit is true? You can't drink on duty?"

"Mr Keyes," Josh said impatiently, "are you avoiding my question?"

Keys rubbed a hand over his chin. "Okay, okay!" he sighed.

"I don't like saying this, but there is someone who might have a had a reason to kill Billy Joe. *Might,* mind you."

Casey said, "Who?"

"Edgar Pace."

"Pace?" Josh frowned. "What motive could he have had? From what I've been given to understand, Billy Joe was his meal ticket."

Keyes sighed again. "That's right. Billy Joe was the first of Pace's clients in a long time to earn some real money; but last week Billy told me that he thought Pace was stealing from him."

"Stealing?"

"Yeah. It's not hard for a manager to steal from his clients. A buck here, a buck there; it mounts up."

"Did Billy Joe say what he intended to do about it? Did Pace know of Billy Joe's suspicions?"

"Billy said that he was going to talk to Pace about it before we left for Phoenix, so I guess that Pace knew."

Casey and Josh exchanged looks. Josh nodded slightly, and got to his feet. "Excuse me for a few moments, Mr Keyes. I have to make a phone call."

Keyes turned to Casey. "Going to put out a . . . what do you guys call it, an APB, on old Edgar?"

"Nothing that drastic, I'm sure," Casey said.

Keyes looked sadly at his empty glass. "I hope that I ain't got the old boy in trouble; he never did me any harm."

"You've been very helpful, Mr Keyes," Casey cleared her throat. "In checking into Billy Joe's past, we discovered that he was once arrested on an assault and battery charge . . ."

Keyes looked alarmed. "Hey, you guys do a check on me, too?"

"It's standard procedure for anyone involved in a homicide."

Keyes raised his eyebrows. "You know, you guys sure use some peculiar language. I wasn't *involved* in a homicide, I just happened to be there when it happened. It would be truthful to say I was a witness, but I sure wasn't *involved!*"

Casey felt herself flush. "You're right," she said. "Technically, anyway. It's the jargon; but you should understand that, you use a lot of it in your business too."

Keyes grinned. "Yeah, you're right on

about that. Anyway, look into my past all you want. I've never done anything really criminal."

"So, as I was saying: Billy Joe was arrested on this assault charge, and let off with a fine. Do you know anything about that?"

Keyes shook his head. "Nope. But I'm not real surprised; Billy Joe has . . . had a short fuse, especially when he was boozing."

"Billy Joe told the arresting officer that the man he assaulted had made homosexual advances toward him."

"Oh, man, that would have ticked old Billy off, all right," Keyes said with a laugh.

"Billy Joe had a problem with gays?"

"You might say that. Billy Joe was straight as a ruler about sex. He thought anything aside from the missionary position was kinky, perverted. As for sex between men . . . Well, you can imagine."

"Do you know of any other such incidents?"

"Nope. Didn't know about that one 'till you told me."

Casey saw Josh returning, and got to her feet. She studied Josh's face, but it gave away nothing. He stopped beside her. "Mr Keyes, I must ask you to keep quiet about what you just told me about Edgar Pace."

Keyes flipped a hand at him. "No problem. Hey, who am I going to tell? Janice here wouldn't be interested."

At the sound of her name, Janice sat up, snatching away her dark glasses. "What?"

Keyes smiled at her. "Hey! She's alive! Wasn't talking to you, sweets. Talking to the Sergeant here."

"Sergeant?" Janice blinked startled green eyes at Josh.

"Sure. Where you been, sweetheart? These two are cops."

"Cops?" Janice squealed and jumped up. Casey noticed that the ample bosoms didn't bounce. Inserts, she thought to herself, a trifle smugly.

Janice scurried away, as the others stood watching. The boobs might not bounce, but the derrière did. It was quite a sight.

With a straight face Casey said, "Sorry, Mr Keyes, if we frightened away your friend."

"What the hey," Keyes grinned slyly. "Like busses, you know; another one will come along in a few minutes."

As they walked away, Casey said to Josh, "Too bad we can't nail *him* for the killing. I don't like Mr Keyes."

"Not the most likeable guy I've ever met."

"What about Edgar Pace? Is he still in Phoenix?"

"The desk clerk at the motel said he checked out around noon."

94

"Do you think what Keyes told us is the truth? Do you think old Edgar has been raiding the cookie jar?"

Josh shrugged. "It's possible, but we'll need more than secondhand hearsay from Keyes. The desk clerk said that Pace reserved a room for later in the week, so he'll probably be back, as long as he doesn't suspect we're on to him."

"That's assuming Keyes is telling the truth."

"Yeah. Assuming. I almost hope it's true. At least then we'd have someone with a solid motive."

Josh had taken a small notebook out of his pocket as they walked toward the motel lobby. "Michelle Tatum is in Room 210. Hope she's in and receiving guests."

CHAPTER NINE

Room 210 was the last room at the end of the hall. At Josh's knock a voice called out, "Who is it?"

"Sergeant Whitney, Miss Tatum. We met last night. I'd like to ask you a few questions."

The door opened, and Michelle Tatum stood in the doorway. She was wearing jeans and a loose-fitting blouse. Her long, narrow feet were bare. Her glance went immediately to Casey. "What's she doing here?"

Josh said, "Casey Farrel, special investigator for the Governor's Task Force on Crime."

Michelle raised well-plucked eyebrows. "The Governor's Office is interested in the case? Looks like Billy Joe is more important in death than he was in life. Come on in."

The hotel room was attractive, furnished with a king-sized bed, a table and two comfortable chairs. A large television sat on a long cabinet. Sheets of scribbled music were scattered across the bed and on the table. A guitar was propped up against one chair. Past the table were sliding glass doors opening onto a small balcony.

"Sorry about the mess," Michelle gestured. "Since I'm stuck here for a few days, I'm working on a couple of songs. When I'm working, I tend to be messy."

She moved the guitar away from the chair and onto the bed, motioned for Casey and Josh to sit down, then perched on the edge of the bed. At the scene of the crime things had been too hectic for Casey to really get a fix on anyone, so now she studied the woman. A bit taller than Casey, Michelle Tatum was on the thin side, with strong, long-fingered hands and high breasts. She had an interesting face, long and narrow, with large, slightly protuberant brown eyes, a rather prominent nose, and well-modeled, if thin, lips. An overly strong chin and a certain coolness of expression kept her from being, in Casey's estimation, entirely attractive; but it was a face with possibilities. Her thick straight hair was a light, coppery red, and hung to her shoulders.

Casey said, "Perhaps I can explain why Billy Joe's murder is getting special attention. His father lives here in Phoenix, and it seems he's a very important man."

Michelle's slight smile looked, Casey thought, more like a sneer. "With connections in high places."

Casey shrugged. "You know how it is."

Michelle folded her legs, yogi fashion. "Oh, yes. I know how it is."

Her brown eyes studied Casey with interest. "I didn't even know Billy had a father, at least not a living one. He sure didn't show up around Nashville. So he's a mover and shaker, huh?"

"Have you heard of 'Lester Burgers?' "

Michelle nodded. "Sure, who hasn't? You mean . . ."

"Jonas Lester is Billy Joe's father."

Michelle Tatum whistled softly. "So Billy Joe's old man has the bucks, huh? That is a surprise."

"He has the bucks and the political influence, and he wants Billy Joe's killer found. That's why the task force is involved. How about Billy Joe's mother? Do you know her?"

"Heard of her, but never met her. I gather she's the ultimate stage mom. A lot of people say that Billy Joe would never have made it without her."

Casey sat back, looking over at Josh, who nodded, and said: "Miss Tatum, we understand that you wrote some of Billy Joe's music. We've been told that two of your songs helped put Billy Joe into the big time. We were also present last night when Billy Joe told the audience that he wrote 'Smoky Mountain

Woman'. How do you feel about that?"

Michelle Tatum's thin lips formed a cold smile. "If you're asking whether I resented the fact that Billy took credit for my work, well, you're right. I did and do. But I have only myself to blame. I agreed to it, in writing."

"But why?" Casey asked.

Michelle shrugged. "A matter of survival. If you're not in the business, you can have no idea of how hard it is to get a song sold, or recorded. There are millions of would-be songwriters out there, and some of them are damn good. The competition is wicked. I don't have a name yet; I need to get my stuff out there. This was one way to do it. So, if you're trying to imply that I had a reason to kill Billy Joe, you're way off track. I'll have to admit, after 'King of the Honky-tonks' became a big hit, I wished that I had insisted on getting public credit. But I went into it with my eyes open, and, to be fair, without Billy Joe, my songs might never have gotten air time. Anyway, my contract with Billy Joe was only for a year which is almost up — and if 'Smoky Mountain Woman' is the hit I hope it will be, I'll be able to dictate my own terms, and write under my own name."

"Going back to last night . . ." Josh took a folded piece of paper from his pocket and smoothed it flat on the table. "I've drawn a rough sketch of the interior of the club."

He tapped the paper with the end of his pen. "Can you show us where you were seated at the time of the shooting?"

Michelle unfolded herself and rose from the bed. Leaning over the table, she studied the drawing in silence. "It's a little hard to tell from this, but I think it was here." She tapped a long finger on one of the rough circles.

"Were you alone?" Casey asked.

"Yes, I was. I arrived a little late, and the tables were all filled; but when Billy Joe came on stage, the couple sitting at this table got up and moved to stand on the dance floor. I suppose so they could see better. Anyway, I took the table."

"What time did you arrive?"

"It was about fifteen minutes before Billy Joe was scheduled to perform."

"Did anyone you know see you?"

"Nope. But then I'm new in Phoenix. Edgar Pace and Joanna are the only people in Billy's group that I know, besides the band members, and they, of course, were on stage."

Josh studied the drawing for a moment. "You were seated on the left side of the room; the rest-room alcove was about thirty feet from your table. Did you happen to look that way at any time; or did you see anyone standing in that alcove?"

"No. When the house lights went down it was pretty dark, and a lot of people were standing."

She shrugged. "Personally, I was tired, and I didn't need to see Billy Joe. I know what he looks like. I just wanted to hear my song, and to see how it went over with the audience."

Casey said: "How about enemies? Do you know of anyone who had it in for Billy Joe?"

Michelle looked at her blankly, and Casey went on: "Did you ever see or hear of any obsessive fans, for instance? Or, I understand that Billy Joe was homophobic. Do you know if he was in the habit of attacking gays?"

Michelle blinked rapidly, her expression one of surprise. "How in heaven's name would I know that? I know nothing about Billy Joe's personal life, I haven't known him that long, and our relationship was strictly business."

Casey nodded. "How about Edgar Pace? Were he and Billy on good terms?"

Michelle shrugged. "I suppose so; at least they seemed to be pretty friendly."

"Did Pace manage Billy's affairs well?"

Exasperation hardened Michelle's face. "You do ask the damnedest questions. How on earth would I know that?"

"I only want your impression. Did you ever

overhear anything that Billy Joe, or anyone else, said regarding Pace's competence?"

Michelle hesitated before she spoke. "From my balcony, I saw you talking to Wesley down by the pool. Did he say anything about Pace?"

"I'm sorry," Casey said, "but I can't discuss that."

She waited, as Michelle twisted a strand of hair around her finger. Finally Michelle said, "Let me put it this way, I don't have any direct knowledge that Edgar Pace is a thief; but it wouldn't surprise me to learn that he was."

Casey leaned forward. "Oh! Why is that?"

"You said you wanted my impression; well that's it. Anyway, you ought to talk to Arlene Baker about Pace. If anyone should know what goes on with him, it's her."

Josh closed his notebook. "Anything else, Casey?"

Casey shook her head. She said, "Thank you, Miss Tatum. We'll get back to you."

She stood up, and Josh followed suit. As they headed toward the door, Casey turned back. "Will you be attending the funeral, Miss Tatum?"

Michelle Tatum rose from the bed and pushed back her hair. "I'm not sure. I may or may not."

Josh said, "Maybe you should. Maybe it'll

give you an idea for a song."

"I don't think so," Michelle said composedly. "Songs about the death of a lover, a faithful dog, a horse — even a pick-up truck — might be saleable; but a song about the death of a country-western star wouldn't go over very well with the fans."

Going down the hall, Casey said, "That was a rather nasty remark, Detective, unworthy of you."

Josh grunted. "You said that you didn't like Keyes; well, I don't like Michelle Tatum. Something about her sets my teeth on edge."

In the parking lot, Josh glanced at the lowering sun and then at his watch. "Well, that didn't take long. We still have time for another chat, two if we split them up."

They had come in different cars, parked side by side. Casey leaned against the Cherokee. "Hmmm. I seem to remember that only a few minutes ago you suggested we talk to the witnesses together. What's the matter, can't you stand the competition?"

Josh looked sheepish. "Aw, Casey, give me a break. It worked fine; but if we split up, we can get two more done, and that's two less we'll have to tackle tomorrow. Besides, I'm hungry, and I'd like to have dinner *sometime* tonight."

Casey patted his arm. "I know. I'm just giving you a hard time. Who do you want me to talk to?"

Josh fingered his lip. "Why don't you take Mrs Billy Joe — and I'll take the girl-friend."

Casey smiled, and Josh raised a hand. "Now don't say anything you'll be sorry for. It's just that I think maybe you'll get more out of the Mrs than I will — woman to woman, you know."

"And you'll get more out of the bimbo — man to woman, you know. I understand."

He gave her a sharp look. "Okay, smart-ass. Meet me back at the station in an hour and a half and we'll compare notes, then we'll pick up Donnie and go and have dinner."

"Yes sir, Mr Detective."

Casey was grinning as she climbed into the Cherokee.

Joanna Baker's hotel was situated next to a large mall.

Handy, Casey thought, as she parked the Cherokee.

Joanna wasn't in her room, but Casey finally tracked her down in the hotel restaurant, having a late lunch. When Casey found her, the woman was alone in a booth, staring down at an apparently untouched salad, her expression gloomy.

As Casey approached, the woman glanced

up, her green eyes cloudy with thought. She blinked rapidly, then said: "Miss Farrel, isn't it? With some kind of task force?"

"That's right. Sorry to intrude on your meal, but I have a few questions to ask you. May I sit down?"

Joanna nodded, and Casey slid into the booth.

As she settled herself, she studied the other woman's face. Upon close inspection, she was still beautiful, with that clear, fine-grained type of complexion usually referred to as "English". The green eyes were striking, the features even and well defined, the hair salon-perfect. Even the brooding expression flattered her. Casey sighed.

Joanna pushed away the unfinished salad, and Casey's stomach reminded her that she had eaten no lunch. She turned her thoughts back to the matter at hand. Joanna, she thought, seemed much less aggressive than she had appeared last night.

"I thought Sergeant Whitney was in charge of the case," Joanna said.

"He is. I'm working with him."

Joanna nodded. "Well, you might as well get on with it; nothing can make me more depressed than I am."

"I'm sorry," Casey said. "But it has to be done."

Joanna leaned forward. "Do you know when Billy Joe's body will be released? I've called several times, but they keep putting me off."

"In another day or so, I expect. I understand the body is being taken back to Tennessee for burial."

Tears welled in Joanna's eyes. "Yes. Nashville is home. It's what his mother and I both want, and Billy Joe would want it too."

"What about his father?"

Joanna looked up, her eyes suddenly hard behind the tears. "His father? Why should he have any say? He's a father in name only. Jonas Lester hasn't seen Billy Joe in years!"

"Mr Lester told me that he was supposed to have dinner with Billy Joe tonight. Did you know about that?"

"No, I didn't, and I flat out don't believe you. Billy Joe would have told me about it."

"Why should Mr Lester lie?"

"Why does anyone lie? He was trying to make you think he was on better terms with Billy than he really was, would be my guess. The man's a phony through and through."

"Then you've met Mr Lester?"

Joanna shook her head. "No. And I have no desire to; but I know what I've heard."

"But you do know Billy's mother?"

"Of course. I've known Arlene for years."

"How do you get along?"

Again Joanna's eyes sharpened. "We get along just fine. Why, what have you heard?"

"It's a standard question, Mrs Baker. So you're saying you got along well?"

Joanna hesitated. "Well, perhaps that's putting it too strong, but we got along most of the time. It was only when she thought I was interfering with Billy's career that she got a bit huffy."

"And how did you interfere, or how did she think you interfered?"

"It was nothing really, just that any time I tried to give a word of advice, she got on her high horse."

"For instance?"

"Well, once a songwriter submitted a song to Billy Joe, and I thought it was a dog, so I advised Billy not to use it. Arlene thought the song was great, and Billy took her side."

"And who was right?"

"Oh, she was. She always was. The song did very well, and got Billy some notice."

"Was the songwriter Michelle Tatum?"

"No. It was some guy I never heard of before."

"Speaking of advice, since Edgar Pace is Billy Joe's business manager, didn't he make all the business decisions?"

"Most of the time; but the final word always

belonged to Arlene. If she disapproved of any decision Edgar made, she simply quashed it."

"I've been told that a problem had come up recently between Pace and Billy Joe; that Billy suspected Pace of stealing money from him. Is that true?"

Joanna grew still. "Where did you hear that?"

"I can't tell you that, but the sources are reliable. How about it, is it true?"

Joanna shook her head vehemently. "No! I don't particularly like Edgar, but I've never seen anything that would lead me to believe that he was crooked. I've always gotten the impression that he was devoted to Billy, and I *know* he's devoted to Arlene. Why, she'd *kill* him if she thought he was up to anything . . . Oh, Lord!" She paled, and covered her hand with her mouth. "I didn't mean . . ."

"I know," Casey said. "People say it all the time, we all do. It takes something like this to bring home to us what we're really saying. Don't worry about it."

Joanna moved her hand and took a deep breath. "What I mean is, in addition to other considerations, I don't think Edgar would ever risk displeasing Arlene."

"And Billy Joe never discussed such a thing with you?"

"No. Billy rarely discussed business with

me; and, as I told you earlier, I haven't seen too much of him lately."

"Do you think he might have discussed it with his mother?"

"Heavens, no! I've just told you how she'd probably react. Besides, she hasn't been very well lately; that's why she didn't come on tour this time."

Casey looked down at her notebook. "Did Billy Joe leave a will?"

Joanna looked at her sharply. "You may not believe this, but I don't know. It wasn't only business that Billy Joe didn't discuss with me. He also didn't discuss money. I never knew how much we had, or didn't have. He and Arlene took care of all that."

"But his mother would know."

"Yes, I'm sure she would."

Casey looked at her watch. "Just one more question. About Billy Joe's personal life — how did he feel about gays?"

Joanna looked confused. "Gays? Homosexuals? Why on earth do you want to know that?"

"Because we have a report that Billy has done a little gay-bashing. Have you ever seen him, or known him to show hostility to gays?"

Joanna frowned. "I've never seen Billy around any gay men, so I can't answer that. I know he didn't *approve* of gays. Whenever the subject came up, in conversation, or in the papers or on television, he would say something. He said that they chose that way of life, and that it was perverted. I guess he felt pretty strongly about it, but I've never known him to *do* anything about it. Besides, what could that have to do with his murder?"

Casey closed her notebook. "Probably nothing. Thanks for your time and cooperation. Let us know when you leave town."

Joanna nodded. "As soon as they release Billy Joe's body, I'll be taking it back to Nashville."

The words hung in the air, sad and very final. Casey turned away, feeling tired and a little depressed. It's probably low blood sugar, she thought. In an attempt to lift her spirits she turned her thoughts to Donnie and Josh, and the nice dinner she soon would be having.

CHAPTER TEN

After only a few minutes with Carol Lloyd, Josh reached the conclusion that she was completely self-involved. She appeared to be one of those people that he encountered all too often nowadays; people whose only goal in life was immediate gratification.

She received him in her small motel room, wearing a robe, her black hair wrapped in a towel. "I just got out of the shower," she said in a voice that Josh imagined she thought was sultry. She sprawled back in one of the chairs, carelessly — or perhaps not so carelessly — exposing long, shapely legs well past mid-thigh.

Josh tore his gaze away from the leg show and sat down across from her in the room's other chair. "Sorry, I should have called ahead, but I was close by, and thought I'd drop in. I only have a few questions."

"How long am I going to be stuck here?" she asked petulantly. "I can't afford to stay much longer. I've already had to move out of the room in the hotel."

Josh nodded. "I suppose Billy Joe was paying for that?"

She shrugged. "Sure. But now . . ." She spread her hands.

"I understand. Is there a job you have to get back to?"

She flicked him an incredulous look. "Do I look like the kind of girl that has to work? I live with my daddy. He's in oil."

"Then I don't understand why you need money."

She sighed. "Well, Daddy doesn't, didn't, like, approve of me and Billy Joe; and he won't pay for me to stay here. I've already called him, and he'll only send me money when I'm ready to come home."

Josh decided to rattle her cage a little. "Did you kill Billy Joe, Miss Lloyd?"

Her pretty — but rather weak — mouth fell open. "How can you ask me that?" She leaned forward and her robe fell open, exposing heavy but well-shaped breasts.

Tears welled in her eyes, as she sat back. "I loved Billy Joe. I don't know what I'll do without him."

"How long had you and Billy been . . . ?"

"Sleeping together?" she said coyly. She giggled, and Josh felt a wave of disgust. He never would understand people like this. Never!

"Well, we've been together since Houston; that's about four months."

"Did his wife, Joanna, know about this?"

Carol shrugged. "Yeah. It wasn't any big secret."

"I imagine that she wasn't happy about it."

Carol shrugged again. "I suppose not, but who knows what that cold bitch thinks."

Josh changed direction. "How well do you know Edgar Pace?"

"Hardly at all. I've seen him around, of course, but who wants to know him? He's an old man."

"How about Billy Joe's mother, Arlene?"

Carol shook her head. "Never met her."

"Did Billy Joe ever mention any threats on his life, or that he had any enemies?"

She thought for a moment, a frown corrugating her forehead. "Not that I remember; but then we didn't do a lot of talking, Billy and I." She looked at Josh, waiting for his reaction. He kept his expression noncommittal.

She smiled coquettishly. Is she trying to come on to me? Josh thought. Nah, couldn't be. After all, I'm an "old man." He said, "Then you wouldn't have any idea who would want to kill him?"

"No. Ugh." She wrinkled her nose. "I don't even want to think about it."

113

He stood up with a sigh. "Thanks for your time, Miss Lloyd. As far as I'm concerned, you can go back home to Fort Worth. Just leave us an address where we can reach you if necessary."

Her expression brightened. "Thank you. You know, you're not a bad guy, for a cop, and . . ." She cut off, but he finished the phrase in his mind, "for an old man," and sighed.

When Josh returned to the station, he found Casey at his desk, reading over the notes she had taken during her interview with Joanna Baker. She was drinking a cup of the terrible coffee made at the station.

She glanced up as Josh slid into his chair behind the desk. "Learn anything from Lloyd?"

"Nada," he said in disgust. "There's very little in that brain of hers, aside from worry about when she's going to get laid next."

She cocked her head. "Tickle your gonads a little, did she, Detective?"

"Nah." Then he grinned. "Well, maybe a touch. She's a sexy broad, but I prefer my women with a least a modicum of mind."

"Oh? I thought that all macho men preferred their women dumb but willing."

He grunted. "Come on, Casey. Don't tell

114

me you've never run across a man or two who were hunks, but vacant between the ears?"

"Once or twice, yes," she admitted. "But I was never really tempted by them."

"Nor was I by Carol Lloyd. Depend on it." He leaned across the desk. "What did you find out from Mrs Baker?"

"A few tidbits of interest." Succinctly, she sketched in the high points of the interview.

Josh scrubbed his hand across his chin. "It appears she was a little disturbed by the news that Edgar Pace might have been stealing from her husband's estate. Of course as his widow, she *would* have an interest."

Casey took another sip of the bitter coffee. "Yes. But we don't know yet if there is much of estate, or who will get it. Although Joanna denies it, it seems obvious that she and Billy Joe weren't getting along all that well; and she told me that she didn't know if Billy left a will. Also, Arlene seems to be pretty much in control of things — maybe most of the money is in her name; after all, she financed Billy for years. We need to find out, first, if there is a will, and second, who gets his money. If he left a large estate, that could be our motive."

Josh stretched. "Speaking of Mrs Billy Joe, she'll be able to pick up the body in the morning."

"They've finished the autopsy?"

He nodded.

"Did they find anything we didn't know?"

"Not much. He was killed by a shot to the heart, and his blood alcohol content was close to the point of legal intoxication."

"So, where do we go from here?"

"Talk to the rest of his troops; and one of us should probably go to Nashville and talk to his mother and to his attorney. We need to know who profits financially by Billy's death. And there must be someone among his Nashville friends and acquaintances who knows something. I think you should be the one to go."

Casey looked at him sharply. "Oh. Why me?"

He smiled. "Because you can probably do a better job with his mother, and because, as a Governor's Task Force member, you can probably get travel money. Homicide is reluctant to send its investigators out of state unless it's absolutely necessary. The rule is, do it by phone."

Casey thought for a moment. "A few days out of state does appeal to me, I must admit. And since Bob Wilson is under pressure, he'll probably be amenable to forking out the money for the trip. You're sure you don't want me to go so I'll be out of your hair for a few days?"

"I hadn't thought of that," he said, dead-pan, "but now that you mention it . . ."

"You'll have to take Donnie."

"That's no problem. He'll be in school most of the day, and I can get Mrs Martinez to come in after school. He'll be cool."

"Okay then. It's a done deal. Now let's get Donnie and eat; I'm starving."

CHAPTER ELEVEN

It was 6:00 A.M. Quietly, Casey set about putting on her running togs, trying not to waken Donnie.

Donnie's dog, Spot II, came trotting out of the utility room, eyes bright and stubby tail wagging.

She reached down and scratched behind his ears, hushing him gently. He watched eagerly as she lifted the bag of dog kibble down from the cupboard, and filled his dish. While he was eating, Casey scribbled a note for Donnie and left the apartment, locking the door behind her.

The morning was clear and cool. She started out at a moderate pace, easing into a steady rhythm. The past two mornings she had missed her run, and felt the worse for it. She liked to jog, not only for the physical well-being that it brought her, but also because the physical exertion enabled her to clear her mind of problems and concentrate only on the movement and her immediate surroundings.

The canal bank path where Casey usually

jogged was a popular route for runners, joggers and walkers. Early as it was, there were already others out and about; but she ignored them and closed her mind to everything but the feel of her feet hitting the hard-packed earth, and the rhythm of her breath.

She ran for about forty minutes. By the time she returned to the apartment, her shorts and tank top were wet with sweat, but her muscles were loose and she felt marvelous. After a brisk shower and a good breakfast she would be ready to face Bob Wilson, and brace him about the trip to Nashville. She wasn't looking forward to it. There was no way to foretell his reaction.

As she opened the front door of the apartment, Donnie was there to greet her. His eyes were red, and he looked angry and upset. "Casey! Old Mr Ralston says we have to get rid of Spot. It ain't fair!"

"Isn't, not ain't," she corrected him automatically. "Now suppose you calm down, kiddo, and tell me what this is all about."

She led him to the couch, sat him down, and sat down facing him. Spot, looking downcast, sat beside Donnie, wet nose nudging the boy's hand. Absently, Donnie rubbed the animal's head.

Casey said, "What happened? Did he get out?"

"No. When I got up he wanted out, so I took him."

"On his leash?"

"No, I didn't think . . . He only wanted to do his business."

Casey sighed. "Donnie, you know I told you never to take him out without his leash." She waved a hand. "What happened?"

"I was taking him out to the street, but he stopped on the way and did his business in the flower bed. We had just started back when Mr Ralston met us halfway up the walk, and he . . ." Donnie broke off, wiping at his eyes.

"And?"

"He said that I couldn't keep Spot here any longer. He said that Spot was doing his business on the lawn and flower beds, and the neighbors were complaining." Donnie swallowed and stared at her with pleading eyes. "Gee whiz, Casey, what are we going to do?"

Casey reached out and pulled him into her arms, hugging him fiercely. She knew very well the anguish he was feeling. Another dog, Spot I, was responsible for her meeting Donnie; and the death of the little dog at the hands of the so-called "Dumpster Killer" had been extremely traumatic. The loss of Spot II would open up many old wounds that Casey had been trying very hard to heal.

"I'll have a talk with Mr Ralston before I

leave for work." She got to her feet. "Right now, I need a shower. Can you fix your own breakfast, kiddo?"

He nodded. "Sure, Casey. Do you think you can talk Mr Ralston out of it?"

"I'll give it the old college try, kiddo." She rumpled his hair. "Now have your juice and cereal and get ready for school while I shower and change."

After showering and putting on her work clothes, Casey hurried into the kitchen. She didn't have much time if she was going to talk to the super before she left. She had a cup of instant coffee, a glass of orange juice and a slice of toast while Donnie went to say good-bye to Spot II.

As she stood at the sink finishing a second of cup of instant, she heard Donnie in the utility room: "Now, Spot, you behave yourself. Don't bark or make any big noise, or Mr Ralston will come get you. No telling what he'll do!"

Casey sighed, shaking her head. She rinsed out her cup and called: "Get a move on, kiddo! Time to go."

Outside, she sent Donnie on to the Cherokee and headed down the hall to the manager's apartment.

Chuck Ralston reminded her of Mr Wilson in the *Dennis the Menace* comic strip. He was a portly man in his late fifties, with heavy jowls, a balding head and a perpetual scowl. Beneath his gruff, grumpy manner, there beat the heart of a constant worrier.

At her ring he answered the door, carrying a cup of coffee. His scowl darkened when he saw who it was. He held up a staying hand. "Now, I know what you're here for, Miss Farrel. I'm sorry for the boy, but I have no choice."

Casey took a deep breath. "Mr Ralston, you can't know what that dog means to Donnie. There are circumstances . . ."

He waved his hand. "It's out of my hands, Miss Farrel."

"But you have no rule against pets!"

"No, not unless they make a nuisance of themselves; I told you that when you rented."

"But Donnie usually keeps Spot on a leash when he takes him outdoors."

"That may be, but he didn't this morning, and it's happened before. The other tenants are complaining. And then there's the matter of his barking."

"But Spot isn't a barker. I've never heard him bark unnecessarily."

Ralston's smile was grim. "That's because he barks when you're away. Dogs are pack animals. They get lonely. He's probably not used to being confined to an apartment, is he?"

Casey sighed and shook her head. "No, he isn't."

Ralston shook his head. "I'm really sorry, Miss Farrel, but the owners have given me an ultimatum. Either the dog has to go, or you and the boy have to find another place to live. They'll give you to the end of the month to come to a decision."

The door closed behind her as she turned away. It was a very final sound.

A mixture of emotions washed away the good feeling engendered by her run: anger at Ralston, although she knew he was only doing what he had to do; anger at Spot, for causing the problem; pity for Donnie; anger *at* Donnie for letting Spot go out without a leash! This being a single parent was not an easy job. The end of the month was only two weeks away, and now, in addition to the strain of the Billy Joe Baker case, she had the distraction of not knowing what to do about the damned dog!

Her thoughts were dreary as she trudged out to the Cherokee. As far as she could see she had three choices: get rid of the dog; find another apartment that would accept animals; or move herself, Donnie, and Spot into Josh's house on the north edge of Phoenix.

The first option was beyond consideration. After having lost Spot I in such a horrible way, she was not certain if Donnie could survive the loss of Spot II. As for option three, well, it would certainly make Josh happy; it was what he had been asking her to do for some time, but it was a commitment that she still wasn't sure she was ready to make. That left option two, find another apartment, or maybe a house. She had been thinking of buying a condo, or maybe a small house; but even if interest rates were lower than they had been in some twenty years, she simply didn't have the money for a down payment. Her job with the task force paid well, but the added expense of raising a child had been more than she had anticipated; and she had not been on the job long enough to save any money.

Josh had money saved, and he would probably loan it to her, but he had already done so much for her, and she hated to feel indebted to anyone, even Josh.

In the Cherokee, Donnie greeted her with a hopeful smile. "Did you change his mind, Casey?"

Casey sighed. "I'm afraid not, kiddo. He said that either we have to get rid of Spot, or we have to move."

She started the Cherokee and moved out as Donnie gave her a stricken look. "What are we going to do, Casey?"

She reached over to grip his knee. "Well, we're not going to get rid of Spot, that's for sure. For the next few days you and Spot will probably be staying with Josh, anyway. I have to go to Nashville for this case I'm working on, that is if my boss approves."

Donnie's face lit up. "Say, maybe we could move in with Josh for good. I know he'd like that. Why don't we . . . ?"

Casey shook her head. "Hold it, kiddo; don't start the cart before the horse is hitched. I don't think I'm ready for that quite yet."

It was almost nine o'clock when Casey got into the office, so she went directly to see Wilson. As Casey went into his outer office, Kathy Condon, Wilson's secretary, glanced up from her computer. "He's been asking for you, Casey."

"So what else is new?" Casey said in a dry voice. "I didn't even stop at my office."

Kathy punched a button on the intercom on her desk. "Ms Farrel is here, Mr Wilson."

A voice bellowed through the closed door, "Well, send her in!"

Casey grimaced. "Sounds like he's in his usual good humor."

Kathy grimaced, then smiled, as she turned back to her keyboard.

Casey drew a deep breath, and opened the door to the inner office.

Bob Wilson looked up from the papers on

his desk, then scowled. "Where's your report? I expected to see it on my desk this morning."

Casey sighed. "Good morning, Bob. Yes, I'm fine this morning, thanks."

Wilson's scowl deepened. "Cut the crap, Farrel. Tell me what's going on."

Casey sat down in one of the chairs in front of his over-size desk. "Now listen, Bob, about that written report, well I've only been on the case one day, and that day was very busy, and very long. As to what's going on? Well, if you'll give me a minute without shouting, I'll try to tell you."

Wilson's scowl grew darker still, but he kept silent as Casey briefly sketched in the events of the previous day.

"So, you haven't got anything definite yet."

"Like I said, it's only been one day. I think we did pretty well."

"We? I suppose you mean you and your boy friend."

"If, by 'boy friend', you mean Sergeant Whitney, the answer is yes."

Wilson snorted. "You sure you spent all your time working?"

Casey leaned forward. "Bob, do the words 'sexual harassment' mean anything at all to you?"

He flushed, and quickly changed the subject.

"How did you get along with Lester?"

Casey shrugged. "Fine, as far as I could tell. Don't tell me he didn't call you and give you a report."

Wilson's lips twisted in what might have been a smile. "Yeah, as a matter of fact he did. He said that . . ." He broke off, his face a study in conflicting emotions, and Casey suppressed a smile, knowing the reason.

"Well, that doesn't matter. He seemed to find you capable."

"I'm very pleased." said Casey sweetly. Compliments from Bob Wilson were few and far between, and this one was all the sweeter for being given grudgingly.

"Just be certain that you don't step on his toes," Wilson went on. "Jonas is an important man in Phoenix."

"I'll try not to," said Casey primly. "By the way. Sergeant Whitney believes that it would be useful if I were to go to Nashville and talk to Billy Joe's mother, and his friends there. They will all be there for the funeral."

Wilson looked at her sharply. "He does, does he? Well, what do you think?"

"I agree. Billy Joe's mother played a big part in his life and affairs, and she's not well. That's why she's back in Nashville. It's possible that she might be able to shed some light on his situation, give us a lead. Sergeant Whit-

127

ney thinks that since I'm a woman, I might get more out of her."

"Hmmm." Wilson worried the eraser on his pencil, and looked at her out of narrowed eyes. "It's possible, I suppose. Anyway, it's worth a try. All right, you can go, but don't stay any longer than you have to, understand?"

Casey nodded. "I'll be as quick as I can. I'll need travel and expense money."

Wilson made a note. "All right, I'll get you a voucher. When do you want to leave?"

"I'd like to leave in the morning."

"Okay, but I'll expect nightly reports by phone or fax. Understand? And don't take too long!"

"Only as long as it takes," said Casey.

In her own office, Casey called the travel bureau and made her reservations. She had no sooner hung up, then her phone rang.

"Morning, babe," Josh drawled.

"Josh!" She leaned back, smiling. "I was going to call you in a bit."

"Two great minds," Josh said. "I've got news. I just talked to Jeff Stone, Billy Joe's keyboard player. Guess what he told me?"

"Why don't you just tell me, Mr Detective?"

"He's been around a long time, you know, and has played for Billy Joe off and on in the past. He also knows Jonas Lester by sight, and he says that he saw Lester in the Okay Corral about fifteen minutes before Billy Joe was shot. How do you like them apples?"

Casey frowned. "But how can that be? Lester's name isn't on the list that the uniforms made. How do you explain that?"

"Well, I can think of two possible explanations. One, he left before Billy Joe was shot; or two, he got out right after Billy Joe was shot, before we had the exits barred."

"Have you talked to the men who were on the doors?"

"They're next on my list."

"I think we should talk to Lester first."

"I'm ahead of you there, but he's already left for Nashville, for the funeral."

"Then I guess it's up to me. Wilson approved the trip, so I'm on my way in the morning."

"How long will you be gone?"

"I don't know. Wilson said to make it as quick as possible, but it will depend on what I turn up. I'd say at least two or three days, maybe more. Look, are you sure you'll be able to pick up Donnie after school?"

"Depend on it."

"Josh . . ." She hesitated, reluctant to tell him about the dog, but Donnie was sure to tell him. "I had a run-in with the apartment manager this morning. He says that we have to get rid of Spot, or move."

"Why all of a sudden?"

"He claims that the other tenants are complaining. He says Spot barks during the day, when we're gone; and that he 'does his business' as Donnie calls it, on the grounds."

Josh whistled softly. "He won't bend."

She shook her head. "Nope. He says the owners have spoken!"

She waited, certain that he would use this opportunity to push for her and Donnie to move in with him; but he surprised her, saying only: "That's a bummer. What are you going to do?"

"Well, I haven't much choice, have I? I can't get rid of Spot; you know what that would do to Donnie; so I guess we'll have to move. He gave me to the end of the month."

Josh voice softened. "It'll be okay, babe. It'll work out. We'll talk about it when you get back. I have to go now; I'm being paged. Take care down there, you hear? And call me."

"I will, Josh," she said, but he had already hung up. Slowly, she did the same, a puzzled frown on her face.

CHAPTER TWELVE

The flight to Nashville was uneventful, interrupted only by a change of planes at Dallas-Fort Worth. Soon after Casey reached her destination she would be immersed in the details of the case again; but for the moment she could put it on the back burner. She didn't have enough data as yet to attempt to put the pieces into any sort of pattern; and it was useless to speculate upon what she might learn in Nashville. The time for constant obsession with the case would come later, when more information had been gathered.

Casey had already determined to find a few hours for herself in Nashville. She had never been there, and she intended to see at least some of the city, and to attend a performance at The Grand Old Opry. To this end, she had booked herself into the hotel in Opryland, U.S.A., and made a reservation for tonight's performance.

When the plane landed, it was late afternoon, and raining. Casey immediately noticed the humidity, uncomfortable after the dryness of Phoenix, and the incredible greenness of everything.

She rented a car at the airport, and after getting a map and direction from the car rental clerk, she headed for Opryland, a few miles east of downtown Nashville.

It was a bad hour for traffic, but she found the hotel easily enough, and was properly impressed. The building looked like something right out of *Gone With the Wind*, only much larger. A soaring dome connected the hotel to an attached atrium. Opryland was some distance behind the hotel.

The giant amusement park had opened in 1972, and had been an immediate success, attracting over a million visitors a year. The theme, of course, was country and western music. The main attraction was the "new" Grand Old Opry, which had been the prime reason for the building of the park. The original Grand Old Opry had occupied the Ryman Auditorium, in downtown Nashville, since its inception; but in the late sixties, the show had outgrown its quarters, and the area around it had decayed.

Casey checked in at the hotel desk, picked up her show ticket for the evening and went to her room for a quick shower and a change of clothing. She was hungry; the food on the plane had not been the best.

The atrium restaurant was huge and airy. The fading daylight filtering through the dome, high above, gave a softness to the room.

Casey dined leisurely and well, finishing with time to spare before the first performance started at The Grand Old Opry.

The rain had stopped, and she took the tram to the amusement park, and wandered around, taking in the sights. The country music motif was obvious, even blatant; there was a roller coaster called The Wabash Canon Ball; and performers dressed as hillbilly clowns and musical instruments mingled with the crowd.

In addition to the rides and games, there were any number of free musical shows throughout the park. Casey was surprised at their diversity; everything from bluegrass and folk music to Dixieland, rock, and a condensed Broadway musical. Some of the acts were very good, many mediocre. Watching some of the performances, Casey concluded that this was a place for talent on the way up, or the way down. She was disappointed to find that some of the acts stuck to watered-down versions of old country hits, parodies of true country music. But she supposed that she should have expected it: theme parks were, by their very nature, a bit corny; and catering to the masses seldom generated a quality product.

Also, from the accents she heard around her

in the crowd, most of the tourists were not from the South. Maybe the-powers-that-be assumed that the visitors didn't know much about country music, and thought that hoking things up was the best way to ease them into a better acquaintance with the sounds and songs. She hoped that the performance at the Opry House would be more up-to-date.

She wasn't disappointed. The audience was rowdy and noisy, but also appreciative, and she soon realized that there were more true country aficionados here than in the theme park. She was a touch disappointed that no stars were appearing that night — probably because the real tourist season was over. However, the performers were very good, clearly selected by someone who knew true talent.

Casey suddenly wondered if Billy Joe Baker had ever performed here. More than likely he had, since most successful country singers appeared here sooner or later.

She pushed the thought from her mind. It was the first time all evening that she had thought of the case.

She left the huge auditorium happy with what she had seen and heard, glad that she had made the effort to attend.

Back in her hotel room she found the message light blinking on the telephone. A few moments later she was talking to Josh.

"Why didn't you call us, Casey?" he growled. "Donnie and I thought something might have happened to you."

She smiled into the mouthpiece. "Now what could have happened to me?"

"I don't know, something! Anything! One of those singing cowboys might have carried you off!"

"Well, they didn't. I went downstairs for dinner, and I took in the show at the Grand Old Opry. I needed some time for myself, *with* myself. Can you understand that?"

"Yeah. I guess so."

"Well, don't get your knickers in a twist."

He sighed. "I *wish* you wouldn't use that expression."

She smiled again. "All right then, don't get your drawers in a bunch. Is that better?"

"Not much, but I guess I should be grateful for small favors. At any rate, I'm glad you're safe and sound. I guess you'll start making your contacts tomorrow?"

"Yes. I'm going to the funeral. Did you make any progress today?"

"Nah. I finally got a chance at those two doormen at the club; but both denied letting Lester out. They said that *no one* left the club after Billy Joe and his group came on stage. Of course they could be lying. They both have sheets, nothing serious, but I have the feeling

135

that they'd do just about anything for a few bucks.

"I also talked with the rest of the band members and crew. Nothing new."

"How about the rest of the customers?"

"We're about two-thirds down the list, but so far no one will admit to having seen anything out of the ordinary, before Billy was shot."

"So, how are you and Donnie doing?"

"The kid's fine. He and Spot rough-housed for a while, and now he's sacked out in front of the TV. Want to talk to him?"

"No, don't wake him. I'll call tomorrow night. Has he said anything about this business with Spot II?"

"Yeah, he mentioned it."

"Was he still upset?"

"No. He seems to think that you'll be able to fix it. He has great confidence in you."

Casey sighed. "I hope I deserve it."

"So, now you know about our evening, what about yours?"

"I told you. I went to dinner here in the hotel, and then to see the Grand Old Opry."

"Alone?"

"No. On the plane I was seated next to Alec Baldwin, and he insisted that we spend the evening together!"

"Now, there's no need to get testy."

"Well, there's no need for jealousy, either."

"Well, how do you know it's jealousy? Maybe it's just normal curiosity. I mean, you could have run into someone you know from Phoenix; maybe someone we've interviewed, and had dinner with them, all perfectly innocent, as innocent as my question."

Casey's cheeks warmed as she realized what he said was, technically, quite true.

"All right, Detective. I'm sorry. I don't, for a moment, believe anything you just said, but you've got me on a technicality."

"Just don't do it again."

His voice was dripping with sanctimony, and she had to smile.

"All right, Detective. You and Donnie have a good night."

His voice lowered. "It would be a better night if you were here. I'd . . ."

"Just hold it right there, bub. Just keep it till I get back."

"Okay. But it won't be easy. You take care now. Billy Joe's killer could be one of the people who will be at the funeral. Don't take any unnecessary chances."

"I won't, and I'll call you tomorrow night. Give Donnie a big hug for me, will you?"

"Depend on it. Good night, babe. We both love you."

"Same here, Josh. Good night."

Billy Joe's funeral was held at eleven the next morning. To Casey's surprise, the day was bright, sunny and cool; no sign of the gray, dripping skies that had greeted her upon her arrival.

The services were held at a small chapel, and attendance was limited to family and friends. Casey's credentials got her through the police cordon, which held a bevy of weeping fans at bay, outside the building.

She had arrived early, and she sat in the back so she could see the others who came in, and study their reactions.

Singly, in couples and small groups, she watched them arrive. The members of the band and their sound man came first, looking uncomfortable and depressed. They sat together just behind the area roped off for the immediate family.

Then several couples, the women weeping, the men stony-face but red-eyed, arrived and were shown to the family section. Casey didn't recognize any of them. Local relatives, probably.

Jonas Lester came in, walking stiffly in his expensive, dark suit, his eyes hidden by dark glasses, his mouth set in a grim, hard line. An usher seated him in the family section, away from the couples already seated.

Next was Edgar Pace, his bloodhound face

set in lines of grief; then Michelle Tatum, looking pale but composed, and surprisingly chic in a navy blue suit and hat.

Another bevy of people unfamiliar to Casey, and the small chapel was almost filled. The smell of the banks of flowers was almost overpowering, and the organ music, Casey thought, was too loud. She stirred restlessly. She hated funerals, always had. They seemed, to her, a barbaric and depressing rite.

Better just to hold a wake, or a memorial service, after the burial or cremation, where you talked about the good times and the good things you remembered about the deceased.

Casey was recalled from her thoughts by a buzz of conversation, and the movement of turned heads. She turned to see Joanna Baker and a plump, heavily veiled woman, enter the chapel.

Joanna's face was set in stern lines, and she appeared to be bearing much of the weight of the woman leaning against her. This was the mother, Arlene Baker, no doubt. Casey blinked. God, it must be hard to lose a child. For a moment, Donnie's bright face flashed across her inner vision; but she pushed it aside, concentrating on what she could see of the woman, which was not much.

An usher hurried up to take the woman's other elbow, and together he and Joanna helped the woman to a seat in the front row.

Slowly, the front door of the chapel began to close, and people re-settled themselves in their pews. Casey, going over a mental list, realized that Judy Lloyd was not present. Had the family kept her out, or had she decided that discretion was the better part of valor? Well, it didn't really matter. She wasn't a good suspect, anyway.

The sound of the organ faded, and the minister, managing to look smug and sad at the same time, stepped forward.

To Casey's relief, the service was mercifully brief. As most of the mourners filed past the open casket, Casey left the chapel. She had no intention of bothering Billy Joe's family and friends at his funeral, but she did want to have a word with Edgar Pace before the group left for the grave site.

She stood aside, watching, as the mourners left the chapel. At last she saw Pace lumber through the door. He looked preoccupied, and jumped when she touched his arm. "Mr Pace?"

He stopped, and blinked at her questioningly, until recognition came to him. He frowned. "Casey Farrel, isn't it? What are you doing here?"

"I need to talk to you, Mr Pace."

His frown deepened. "Here? Now?"

She shook her head. "No. However, I do need the name of the hotel where you're staying. Something came up before I left Phoenix, but we found that you had already left."

"Something you need to talk to me about?"

"Yes."

"Well, your Sergeant Whitney told me I could leave. I had business to attend to, and I also wanted to be here for Billy Joe's funeral."

"I understand that, and I'm not being accusatory. If you'll just give me your address here, we can talk later, tomorrow, perhaps." She pulled out her notebook.

He grunted softly. "I'm staying at a motel on Union. I'll be there for a day or two more."

He gave Casey the address; and Casey wrote it down, closed the notebook and put it back into her purse. "Thanks. Would tomorrow be all right? Say about nine in the morning?"

He nodded. "I suppose so. At least that way it won't break up my day, and . . ." He broke off at the sound of loud, angry voices, and both he and Casey turned to see what was causing the disturbance.

Arlene Baker and Jonas Lester were standing next to Lester's limo, which was parked at the curb. Behind them stood the members of the band, Michelle Tatum, and Joanna Baker. Arlene, her veil thrown back, was confronting Jonas Lester. She had a round, girlish face, relatively unlined, in which Casey could see the reflection of her son, and short curly, dark hair. She would have been pretty, except for the naked emotions twisting her features. She spoke in a high angry voice. "Why are you here, you bastard? You weren't invited! You have no right!"

"I have every right," Lester said evenly. "Billy Joe was my son."

"Not any more. You forfeited that right a long time ago."

Lester's lips tightened. "No matter what you say, Arlene, he *was* my son. You may have poisoned his mind against me, but . . ."

"Poisoned!" Arlene Baker's face twisted, and Casey thought that she was going to spit in her ex-husband's face. "*You* were the poison. I only told Billy Joe what was true!"

Lester tightened his fists, but remained relatively calm. "It may surprise you to know that Billy Joe called me before coming to Phoenix. We were supposed to have dinner together after his show, on the night he was murdered."

Arlene Baker glared at him. "I don't believe you! You're lying! He wouldn't do something like that without telling me."

Lester sighed. "Believe what you like, Arlene, but it's true. I think, I hope, that he wanted to mend fences. I loved that boy, Arlene, as much as you — although I know you won't believe that. In the beginning, I built my fortune for him and for you, but later, when you took him away from me, it was just for him; for the day when he'd come back to me. Now he's gone, and he'll never know."

Arlene sneered. "Money! Money was all you ever thought about. Well, it couldn't have made up for all the years of neglect. If Billy Joe wanted to see you, it wasn't about 'mending fences', or reconciliation."

Lester looked at her steadily. "You can't know that. You believe what you want to believe; but I feel in my gut that he wanted to make things right between us. And you can't stop me from believing that!"

Suddenly, Arlene seemed to deflate, all the fight leaking out of her. "Believe what you want," she said tiredly.

He held out a hand, as if to touch her, then drew it back. "There are a few things we should talk about, Arlene."

She turned away. "I have nothing to say to you."

He shrugged. "Well, if you should change your mind, I'm staying at the Embassy Suites. I'll be there any time after seven, tonight."

Arlene shook her head, and turned to Joanna, who was standing a bit behind her. "Joanna, maybe you should tell him."

Joanna stepped back. "No. No, Arlene. We agreed that I shouldn't."

Arlene sighed, and swallowed. "I know, girl, but I've changed my mind. There's no reason that others should suffer because of my bitterness. Tell him."

"Tell me what?" Lester demanded.

"It's nothing, Mr Lester. Nothing at all," Joanna said.

Lester stood for a moment, staring at her. Then he gave a shake of his head, turned on his heel, and got into the limo.

When Lester was out of hearing, Wes Keyes stepped forward.

"Joanna, what was that all about?"

Joanna glanced at Arlene.

"You might as well tell them," Arlene said. "It's not like they won't find out in a few months."

Joanna took a deep breath. "All right," she said. She lifted her chin. "I'm going to have Billy Joe's baby."

Her announcement was greeted by a stunned silence, and she went on: "That's why I went to Phoenix, to tell him. But I didn't get the chance. He died not knowing."

Edgar Pace said softly. "Well, I'll be damned!"

He started to move toward the group, whose members had now regained their voices, and were offering Joanna congratulations and condolences.

Casey watched as Pace approached Arlene Baker, leaning in to whisper something in her ear.

Casey saw the woman look toward her, and decided that it was time for her to leave. Yet she lingered for a moment, bemused by Joanna's startling revelation. Sometimes she didn't like the way that being a law enforcement officer made her think; but could Joanna's pregnancy have anything to do with Billy Joe's death? With Billy Joe gone, a grandchild might stand to inherit Lester's fortune. She had known murders to be committed for less.

With a touch of dismay, Casey saw that she had delayed her departure too long. Arlene Baker was coming toward her.

The woman halted before Casey, her dark blue eyes curious, her expression guarded. "Edgar tells me that you're investigating my boy's murder."

"Yes. I'm Casey Farrel," Casey replied. "I'm a special investigator with the Governor's Task Force on Crime in Arizona."

"You came here to see me?"

"Well, yes, among others. But that's not why I'm here today. I'll be in Nashville for a few days. Perhaps we could make an appointment."

Arlene was silent for a moment, studying Casey's face. Finally, she nodded. "We're having a sort of wake at my house this afternoon. Why don't you come out, and we can talk then."

Casey hesitated, then said, "I'm not sure I'd feel right about doing that. Are you sure you wouldn't rather wait until another day?"

Arlene gave a small, wry smile. "I'm still going to be hurting, no matter how long you wait. I want to see my boy's murderer caught and the sooner that happens the better, so come today."

"Well, all right," Casey said hesitatingly. "If you're sure you won't mind."

"Do you have something to write on? I'll give you the address."

Casey pulled out her notepad and pen and handed them to the woman, who quickly scribbled the information, and returned them.

"I will be expecting you," she said. With a nod, Arlene Baker turned and marched back to the group waiting for her, her head high.

Now there's a woman with great strength and determination, Casey thought. Today she had buried the main focus of her life, but she would manage to pull herself together and go on. As Josh would say, you could depend on it.

CHAPTER THIRTEEN

The address that Arlene Baker had given Casey was located in Belle Mead, an expensive section of older homes. The street was lined by huge oaks, just beginning to drop their autumn leaves. The Baker home stood on an acre of manicured grounds, well back from the street, with a curving, brick driveway. The house itself was a white, two-story building, with a columned porch, rather like a miniature version of the Opryland Hotel.

There were some twenty cars already parked along the wide drive and a parking area at the side of the house. Casey found a place for the Cherokee, and walked back to the front of the house.

She found the double front door open. Pausing a moment, she listened to the clink of glasses and the buzz of conversation from inside. There was a good-sized crowd, many of them clustered in the hall. Beyond this, she could see the portals of another, much larger room. A wide set of marble steps lifted this room a foot or so above the hall. To the right, a wide stairway climbed gracefully upward. It, too, was crowded with people. It would seem that Billy Joe had a great many mourners.

Casey stepped inside the hallway, and looked around, hesitant about which direction she should take. Then she spotted Joanna Baker near the staircase, talking to a tall man with the build of an ex-football player.

At the same moment, Joanna turned, and saw Casey. Excusing herself to the man she had been talking to, she made her way toward Casey. Her expression was non-committal.

"Miss Farrel," she said.

Casey nodded. "Mrs Baker. I'm here to see your mother-in-law."

Joanna frowned. "Today? Really! I should think that you might have waited. I . . ."

Casey interceded softly. "She asked me to come, Mrs Baker. In fact, she insisted. She wants Billy Joe's killer caught as soon as possible. I should have thought you'd feel the same way."

Joanna flushed slightly. "I do, I do, but . . ." She paused and took a deep breath. "I'm sorry. It's been a bad day for me. Arlene is upstairs. I'll take you to her."

"How is she holding up?"

Joanna sighed. "Better than you might suppose. Better than I am, anyway. You have to

148

understand about Arlene. She is a strong woman, with more guts than any other woman I know. Even though she's been sick, even with what happened to Billy Joe, she's tending to business. She's in her office. It's upstairs."

Joanna started up the stairs, and Casey fell in behind her, as Joanna made her way between the people on the stairway.

When they reached the top, Casey said, "I thought Mrs Baker would be downstairs, mingling with the guests."

Joanna shook her head. "Arlene's not very social. She said hello to most of them when they arrived, but then she left the hostessing to me and some of the other relatives. Here, this is her office."

Joanna stopped in front of a large, heavy polished door, with an elegant brass knob. Casey reached out a hand to stay her.

"Just one thing, Joanna. That was quite a surprise, about your pregnancy. Why didn't you tell Sergeant Whitney or me about it?"

Joanna looked at her coolly. "Why on earth should I have done that? It has nothing to do with you. Nothing to do with Billy Joe's death."

Casey raised her eyebrows. "How can you know that for sure? Also, you are apparently reluctant to tell Jonas Lester that he is about to be a grandfather. Why? Don't you think he has a right to know?"

Joanna gave Casey a cold glare. "I don't see why this is any of your business; but Jonas Lester abandoned Billy Joe and Arlene a long time ago. Billy Joe never thought of him as his father, and I see no reason to think of him as my child's grandfather."

Casey studied the woman curiously. Was she really as naive as this statement made her sound? She decided to push it a bit further.

"But I understand that it was Arlene who insisted on the divorce; and that she was the one who wouldn't let Lester see his son?"

A shadow slid across Joanna's green eyes. "I suppose you got that from him. Well, you should talk to Arlene. She has a very different story."

"But you've only heard her side. Have you ever stopped to consider that maybe it's a little slanted? Maybe there's some truth on Lester's side too."

Joanna's eyes flickered, and she hesitated.

Casey pressed on. "And hasn't it occurred to you that Jonas Lester could do a lot for your child? He has a great deal of money and an equal amount of influence. And now, your child may well become his only heir."

Joanna pressed a slender hand to her eyes. When she spoke her voice was shaking. "Look. I don't want to talk about this now. Why are you badgering me? My God, my husband has only been dead three days. How do you expect me to . . ."

Casey, feeling slightly ashamed, raised a placating hand. "I'm sorry; but it was necessary."

Joanna did not answer, but knocked on the door — rather harder than was necessary, Casey thought — then opened it and stepped aside so that Casey might enter.

Casey did so, and found herself in a pleasant, sunny room, furnished for business. Arlene Baker sat behind the larger of two desks. She looked up from the papers in front of her as Casey entered, the light reflecting from the glasses she was wearing. "Miss Farrel. Have a chair; I'll be with you in a moment."

Casey selected a comfortable chair, as Mrs Baker stacked the papers on which she had been working to one side, removed her glasses, and rubbed the bridge of her nose. Joanna stood disapprovingly to one side.

"It seems strange to me," Arlene said, "that Billy Joe is gone, but business matters go on. I wish I could just let it all go, but there are responsibilities . . ." She lifted a hand. "But that's not what you're here about, so let's get this over with."

"Arlene," Joanna said, "unless you need me, I'd better get back to the guests."

Arlene nodded. "Yes, sugar, you go back,

151

and Miss Farrel and I will have our little session." She stood, and walked over to Joanna, taking her by the arm.

Casey thought to herself that however Arlene had felt about Billy Joe's marriage to Joanna, now that Joanna was about to bear her son's child, she seemed very friendly toward her daughter-in-law.

As Arlene walked with Joanna toward the door, speaking softly with her, Casey stepped to the window and looked out. Below the house, children were playing, and small groups of adults were gathered around the ornamental iron tables which surrounded the large, guitar-shaped pool.

She turned, as Arlene stopped beside her. They both watched as the children ran between the tables, the sound of their voices light and bright as birdsong.

Arlene sighed. "Billy Joe loved children. He would have been so happy to know that he was going to be a father." She bit her lip, and turned away, moving back to her seat behind the desk. "Well, shall we get to your questions now?"

"If you're ready."

Arlene's head went back. "Ready as I'll ever be. Fire away."

Casey took out her notebook and pen. "All right. I gather that you've been closely involved with Billy Joe's career right from the beginning; is that correct?"

"Before, actually," Arlene said promptly. "When Billy Joe was just a little tad, he could sing. He learned all the lyrics from the radio, or from tapes, and he could get the melody after hearing a song only once or twice. I bought him a little guitar, and he taught himself to play by ear. He just had a natural aptitude."

She shook her head. "I've always wondered about that, how some people are born knowing how to sing, and learn to play instruments without anyone teaching them. Billy could sing like an angel, and play along with what he sang; but he couldn't read a note of music, and didn't want to. When he had a new song to learn, he'd just listen to it over and over until he had it committed to memory. Once he had it, he didn't forget it."

Casey looked up from her notepad. "I understand that some of Billy Joe's hits were written by Michelle Tatum."

"Yes, that's right. Michelle's songs seemed to suit Billy's voice. I knew they would, the first time I heard them. I always had good luck in picking songs for Billy. He always used to say what a good team we made."

For a moment, Casey was afraid that Arlene was going to break down, but the older woman managed to pull herself together. She was amazing, Casey thought. She quickly asked another question, not quite so close to the mark: "Did you ever feel that Miss Tatum resented Billy Joe's success with her songs? Did you sense any jealousy?"

For a moment, Arlene thought, then said slowly: "I never really saw much of Michelle after we bought the songs. I can't say I took to her; she's a cold sort of girl; but I never noticed anything out of the ordinary. She and Billy Joe seemed to get on well enough."

"Let's return to your son's career. People have told me that in a great measure, you are responsible for your son's success."

Arlene flushed slightly, and the color was becoming. She looked at Casey levelly. "I know what they say, Miss Farrel. I hear the stories: that I'm a typical 'theatrical mom', that I pushed Billy. Well, maybe they're right; but it's what helped get Billy Joe to the top; and I was always there for him. It's a hard life, being a performer, and there should always be somebody there to help a performer over the rough spots. That was my job; and I was happy to do it."

"It wasn't easy, was it? I understand that in the early years Billy Joe sang for his supper at honky-tonks all over the country."

"It's never easy. If it was, just anybody

could do it. Even your so-called 'overnight successes' don't really happen that quick or that easy. When you look into it, you usually find that they've been singing or performing for years; it's just that no one ever heard of them until they made good. It's been my experience that the good things of life usually have to be worked for, and that seems fair enough to me."

Casey nodded. The belief might not be entirely true; but it was a good, healthy philosophy; certainly better than the belief that the world owed you a living.

"Through all those years of working and striving, did Billy Joe make any enemies that you know of? Anyone who hated him enough to want him dead?"

Arlene's face suddenly tightened, and she looked every one of her years. "Not that I know about; and that's what's so puzzling. Billy Joe was a fine young man. I never knew him to knowingly hurt anyone!"

Casey pretended to write in her notebook. This was standard fare — what almost all parents in similar situations said about their children — even if the offspring in question was a proven axe-murderer. But in this case, Mrs Baker might be telling the truth. The profile of Billy Joe Baker, so far, showed a rather ordinary young man, with no really major vices.

Casey looked up, keeping her expression neutral. "Mrs Baker, when did Edgar Pace come into your lives?"

"Edgar? Why, we've known him for years."

Casey noted that the other woman's cheeks had grown pink again.

"And he's done well for you? You're satisfied that he's done well for you as a business manager?"

The blush deepened. "Why yes. Of course. Otherwise I would have fired him. Why do you ask?"

Casey took a deep breath, trying to think of a delicate way to phrase what she wanted to ask.

She leaned forward. "I have been given to understand that you have, or have had, a personal relationship with Mr Pace."

The other woman's eyes narrowed and their expression hardened.

"Where did you hear that? Who told you that?"

"A number of people, Mrs Baker. They seemed to consider the information common knowledge."

Arlene Baker's jaws tightened. "Well! I didn't realize that my friendships were such a popular subject for conversation. But for your information, yes, Edgar Pace is a friend of mine. A personal friend, if you will."

Casey nodded. "I see." She paused again, this one was going to be even harder. "And you have never had any reason to suspect Mr Pace of any irregularity in his handling of your son's affairs?"

Casey had thought that it was impossible for Mrs Baker's expression to grow any more tense, but she had been wrong. The woman glared at her now. "And just what is that supposed to mean? Irregularity? What are you driving at?"

Casey raised her palm placatingly. "It may be just a rumor, entirely false; but it's been brought to my attention, and I must ask the question. I have been informed that Billy Joe suspected Mr Pace of stealing from him, and that Billy Joe intended to confront Pace about the matter. Did you know about this?"

Arlene shook her head, her expression one of scorn. "Of course not. The idea is ridiculous! Do you think such a thing could happen and I wouldn't know about it?"

The telephone on the desk rang, and she scooped it up. "Yes?"

Casey listened for a moment — the conversation was about business — then rose from her chair. She wanted to give Arlene Baker time to collect herself.

As she walked around the room, she looked at the framed pictures and awards that covered most of one wall, surrounding the two gold records that occupied the place of honor.

She moved to look at the pictures more closely. All of them included Billy Joe: a very young Billy in what appeared to be a graduation picture, and singing in country-western bars; a boyish Billy with members of his band; an older Billy in friendly poses with various celebrities and/or friends and family. One picture in particular drew her eye. It was small, a snapshot, but the composition was good: Billy Joe and two other young men, sitting on the steps of a clap-board house. Billy and one of the boys — a slender, long-haired youngster, held guitars and were unsmiling. The third boy, taller and older-looking, grinned into the camera. Casey found something haunting in the young faces. It was so sad. Just three days ago this wall had been a tribute to a rising star; today it was a monument to a lost life.

She felt Arlene behind her, and turned. Arlene said: "I must apologize for losing my temper back there. I should be used to gossip and rumors by now." She sighed. "This business thrives on such things; but they still upset me."

Casey smiled. "No apology necessary. We have to ask some unpleasant questions, and I know it must seem like prying, but as I said before, the questions have to be asked. To finish the last one, I need to know if you're telling me that you know nothing about the possibility of Edgar Pace embezzling monies from Billy Joe's accounts."

Arlene nodded. "That's what I'm telling you."

"But would have been in a position to do so, right?"

Arlene hesitated. "That's true enough. An entertainer's manager has to have control of certain monies, in order to do business; but it would have been discovered sooner or later, and Edgar's no fool."

Casey nodded, and turned back to the picture wall. She pointed to the large group picture. "Is this Billy Joe's graduation picture?"

Arlene nodded.

"And the others? Billy Joe with friends and admirers? How about this one, for instance?" She pointed at the small photo of Billy Joe and the two other young men on the porch.

Arlene leaned forward. "Oh, that's Billy, Leland Thomas, and Buck Dewey. The three of them were best friends all through high school, and for a while after. Lee was very good with a guitar, and he played with Billy in the beginning. Then they all just drifted apart. The last time I asked Billy Joe about them he told me that Lee had disappeared, just dropped out of sight, and that he had heard that Buck was married and living in Nashville."

She shook her head. "They were so close."

"How about some of the others, his friends from the old days, does he keep in touch with any of them?"

"Not really. That's one of the sad things about success. When you get famous, a lot of your old friends become jealous, and you lose contact with them."

"Well, I'd appreciate it if you could give me some of the names and addresses of Billy Joe's friends, both new, and from the old days. I'd like to talk to them."

Arlene looked puzzled. "Why? They weren't even there when he was . . . when he died. How could they help you?"

Casey shrugged. "Maybe they can't; but there is always the possibility that one of them might have some little bit of information that could be important."

Arlene nodded. "I see. Like a piece of a puzzle. All right. I have Billy Joe's address book. I'll find what I can."

Casey smiled. "Thank you. I'd appreciate it. I'll be around for another day or so. I've bothered you enough for one day. Thanks for your cooperation."

Arlene managed an answering smile, and it

lit up her face, making her beautiful. "I'm happy to help."

Her expression darkened. "Like I told you before. I want the monster that killed my boy put away. No, more than that, I want him killed too; I don't want to have to think of him alive when my son lies dead. Catch him, Miss Farrel. Catch the murderer of my boy."

Casey reached out and gently touched Arlene Baker's hand. "I'm giving it my best shot," she said, and turned away before Arlene could see the pity in her eyes.

CHAPTER FOURTEEN

Downstairs, Casey hesitated in the foyer, debating whether she should stay for a while. Perhaps she might overhear something of value if she mingled with the crowd.

She recalled one of Josh's maxims: "No matter where you are, no matter what the circumstances, never avoid an opportunity to ask a question. The more unlikely the circumstances, the more likely you are to catch a suspect off guard."

Smiling to herself, she wandered around the large room in the rear of the house, where most of the guests were gathered. She saw the members of the band in one corner, grouped together as though for protection against the other mourners. All of them held drinks. As Casey watched, she saw Michelle Tatum walk up to the group, place a hand on the arm of Wesley Keyes, and draw him aside. They stood talking, heads together, Michelle gesturing expressively. Casey wished that she was close enough to overhear the conversation. It might be interesting.

She turned away, picked up a drink from the mahogany bar that covered most of the length of one wall, and went outside to where other guests were gathered around the wrought-iron tables.

Walking toward the huge, guitar-shaped pool, Casey spotted Edgar Pace sitting by himself at a small table at the edge of the pool. He had his arms on the table, and he was staring morosely into his half-empty glass.

Casey walked over, and took the chair across from him. He glanced up and scowled darkly.

"You again. What are you doing here?"

"Arlene invited me," Casey said equably. "She wants to help in any way she can."

Pace snorted. "You just be careful not to hassle that fine woman. Her only boy's been killed, and she's hurting bad."

He raised bloodshot eyes to Casey's, and his look was hard.

Casey sighed. "Mr Pace, I sometimes get the feeling that you don't think we're on the same side. I'm not here to 'hassle' Mrs Baker, or indeed any of you. I'm simply doing my job, which is to try to find out who killed Billy Joe Baker. Why do you seem to have a problem with that?"

Pace grunted, and lowered his gaze. "Maybe I'm overreacting."

He scrubbed a heavy hand down over his

face. "This has all been very . . . difficult."

"I understand; and I understand that it's been your job, for a long time, to protect Billy Joe, his reputation and his business. But Billy Joe is gone now, and if we're going to find his killer, we need to look for the truth. Do you understand what I mean?"

He nodded slowly. "I think so."

"So, can we talk now? It will save me some time."

He sighed wearily. "I guess so. I'll feel just as bad tomorrow."

Casey took a deep breath. "Well, some information came in after you left Phoenix, and I have to know if it's true."

He frowned. "So, what is it?"

"We have been told, by a reliable witness, that before his death, Billy Joe was about to confront you concerning certain monies that seemed to be missing."

Pace's eyes narrowed. "What? Money missing? What are you talking about?"

"We were told that Billy Joe thought that you were stealing from him," Casey said bluntly.

Pace's face reddened and swelled. "That's a goddamned lie! There's not a word of truth in it! Someone is trying to blacken my good name."

"You know we're going to investigate this

fully; so if it's true, it will be best if you tell me now."

"Not a word of truth in it," he said in an outraged voice. "Have you talked to anyone else about this — Arlene, for instance?"

Casey felt her own face flushing. It was at times like this that she didn't like her job very much. She said slowly, "Yes, I mentioned it to Mrs Baker. I needed to know if she knew about it."

Pace threw up his hands. "God, you're so arrogant! My reputation is at stake here. Do you think you can just make this kind of accusation and . . ."

Casey raised her hand placatingly. "I am not making an accusation, Mr Pace, only asking you a question, the answer to which might have a direct bearing on the case."

Pace's eyes flickered. "Oh, I can see where you're going, Miss Farrel. You may think I'm crooked, but I'm not stupid. If I had been stealing from Billy Joe, and was about to be discovered, that would make a pretty tidy motive for wanting him out of the way, wouldn't it?"

Casey nodded. "Yes, it certainly would."

Pace pushed his chair back with a squeal of iron on cement, and rose. He glowered down at Casey. "Any more questions from you, and I'll want my attorney present. And one word of warning. If this rumor is spread around indiscriminately, I'll sue you to hell and back."

As he stamped off, Casey, turning to watch him leave, gave a start. Just behind her stood a short, slightly plump woman of perhaps forty, wearing a black dress that almost brushed the ground. Her brown hair was cut short, framing a round face devoid of make-up. Small dark eyes shone behind thick glasses.

In a low, excited voice she said, "Don't you believe Edgar. It's all true. Billy told me himself that he was almost sure that Edgar was cheating him!"

Casey realized her mouth was open, and closed it. "And who are you?" she said.

"Oh, I'm sorry." The woman's hand flew to her mouth. "I'm Millicent Hanks. Everybody calls me Millie. I worked for Billy . . ." She choked, turning her face away.

Another woman in love with Billy Joe, Casey reflected, as she waited for the woman to regain her composure. Only this time she was pretty certain that there was not much of a chance that the feeling had been returned.

Millie Hanks faced Casey again, dabbing at her reddened eyes. Casey said gently, "I've heard your name mentioned. You were Billy Joe's secretary, right?"

Millie bobbed her head. "That's right, although actually Billy Joe liked to call me his assistant. He said it had more class."

"May I ask why you weren't with Billy Joe on the tour?"

Millie pulled a tissue out of her pocket, and blew her nose before she answered. "I was; but I had to leave him in Fort Worth and come back here for a few days to take care of some business. How I wish I had been with him. It might not have happened if I'd been there."

Casey felt both touched and amazed at the human animal's capacity for guilt. Or perhaps it was really ego. Did this little woman really think that her presence might have prevented Billy Joe's killer from doing what he or she had done?

Aloud, she said: "I don't think that it was something you could have stopped, Miss Hanks. You or anyone else, except the killer."

Millie Hanks sniffed. "I suppose not."

"And so you were here, in town, on the night that Billy Joe was killed?"

"Yes. I was here."

"Can you tell me exactly where, and who might confirm it?"

An expression of surprise appeared on the woman's face. "Why I guess so, let's see, I had finished with my work for the day, and was at home, watching television."

167

"And can anyone vouch for that?"

"Well, no, I guess not. I live alone, you see. Surely you don't think that I . . . I mean, you don't think that I flew out there and somehow . . . I mean, that's too . . ."

Casey raised a protesting hand. "Just routine. Nothing to worry about."

Millie's expression still showed surprise and disbelief, and Casey thought that she had better change the subject. "Now, about Edgar Pace?" she said. "You say that Billy Joe told you he thought Edgar was stealing from him?"

"Yes, just before we left on the tour."

"What, originally, made him suspect this?"

"The fact that money was disappearing, unaccounted for."

"Why did he think that Edgar Pace was responsible?"

"Because Edgar handled all the money that came in, and he also had the power to cash checks. Billy was incorporated, you know, and there were only two other people who could sign checks on the corporation; Mr Pace, and Billy's mother, Arlene. Billy knew it wasn't him — himself, that is — and he knew that it couldn't be Arlene."

"So that left Edgar."

Millie shrugged and raised her eyebrows.

"And you don't handle any of the accounts, or pay any of the bills?"

Millie's sallow face turned a blotched pink. "Well, I do, in a way; but I only type out the checks, put them with the bills, and give them to Edgar or Arlene to sign. There's an accountant who keeps the books. I had suggested putting the whole process on computer; but Edgar and Billy didn't take much to the idea."

She smiled wanly. "Some people are afraid of computers, you know."

Casey nodded. "About how long had this been going on, the losses?"

Millie cocked her head and Casey was reminded of a plump, brown wren. "Oh, about six months, I guess; from about the time that Billy Joe did a two-week gig in Las Vegas. Mr Pace was with him, and he lost a bundle gambling, something like fifty thousand. Billy said he thought that was when it started."

Casey whistled softly. "Gambling is definitely not a good addiction for someone who handles other people's money."

"That's what Billy said."

"And Billy told all this to you?"

Milly nodded. "He talked to me about a lot of things." She flushed again. "He said I was a good sounding board. I guess it was because I listened, but didn't give him advice, the way the others did."

"You know Arlene says that she knows

nothing about all this? And yet, I've been told that she and Billy were very close."

Millie gave her bird-like shrug again. "That's true, but she had been sick, and Billy didn't want to upset her. Besides . . ." she hesitated, "she and Edgar were . . . friends . . . you know."

"Yes, I know. So you know for a fact that Billy didn't tell her about this?"

"Well, he said that he hadn't."

"Yes. Well, by the way, can you tell me just what Mrs Baker's health problem is?"

"Oh, don't you know? Arlene had a heart attack a few months ago — only I guess they don't call them that anymore, they call it an episode, or something. Anyway, that's what it was.

"The doctor told her to change her diet, get plenty of rest, and put her on an exercise program. And he told her to cut down on the stress. She's recovering very well, even with . . ." She swallowed painfully.

"She seems to be a strong woman."

"Oh, yes. She is that."

Casey looked down at her notebook. "Millie, I presume that you handle Billy Joe's fan mail, is that correct?"

Millie smiled. "Oh, yes, and he got a lot of it, more all the time. I told him that pretty soon I'd need some help with it."

"Do you remember any particular letters? Were any of them threatening, or out of the ordinary?"

This time Millie reddened all the way down to her shoulders. "Well, some of them were real . . . personal . . . if you know what I mean. Those women . . . I never knew how they could write things like that. But, Billy Joe told me not to answer those, so I didn't."

"Answer them?"

"Oh, yes. Billy answered almost all of them, except the dirty ones; or, that is, he had me answer them. We made up some form letters that would fit almost any situation; and he always had me send a signed picture."

"Did Billy Joe sign all these letters and pictures himself?"

Millie gave Casey a small, superior smile — the smile of one on the inside, giving information to the uninitiated. "Oh, no. He didn't have time for that. We had a stamp made, and I used that. It looks almost like the real thing."

Casey made a note in her book: Check into Millie's alibi for the night Billy Joe was shot.

"And you don't recall any occasion on which Billy Joe was threatened or hassled by one of his fans?"

Millie shook her head. "No, I really don't."

Tears appeared in her eyes and threatened

to overflow. "I just can't think of anyone who would want to hurt Billy Joe. He was a good man, Miss Farrel — the best employer I ever had."

Casey closed her notebook. She said sympathetically: "I know this must be difficult for you, Millie. It's always a shock when someone close to you dies suddenly and violently. What are your plans now?"

Millie wiped her eyes with another tissue. "Arlene wants me to stay on. She says there'll be a lot to do; that Billy's records will sell really well now, and that he'd want us to carry on for him. Maybe . . ." She brightened. "Maybe Billy will become really famous now, like Elvis."

Casey smiled and nodded, keeping her reservations to herself. There was a great deal of difference between Elvis Presley and Billy Joe Baker, but if Millie wanted to cling to her illusions, well, maybe they would help her get through this.

She got to her feet. "I have to go now, but I may want to speak to you later, Millie."

Millie nodded. "Catch him, will you, Miss Farrel?" she said softly.

"I'll certainly do my best."

At the patio doors, Casey paused to glance back. Millie still sat at the table, a disconsolate figure, slumped in grief.

CHAPTER FIFTEEN

The office of Chris Waters, Billy Joe's lawyer, was downtown on Third Avenue, only a few blocks from the old Ryman Auditorium. It was a small office, with only a secretary in the reception area.

Casey had to wait only a few minutes after announcing herself to the secretary, then the door to the inner office opened, and a tall, skinny man of around forty stood framed there.

"Mrs Farrel?" he said in a deep, bass voice, incongruous in a man with so little heft to him. "Please come in."

Casey handed him her card as she stepped past him into the room.

He took it and nodded. "I know who you are. I talked to Arlene today at the house. Please have a seat."

The inner office was small. Book shelves lined the walls, and law journals were stacked on almost every piece of furniture, including the well-worn desk. The office was definitely untidy, yet there was a certain sense of orderliness about it, as though Waters could immediately locate anything he needed.

He went around the desk and lowered himself into the leather chair with a sigh, as Casey studied him. He was not at all a handsome man, but there was something attractive about him. His lank brown hair was receding, but the brown eyes behind the black, horn-rimmed glasses were bright and alert. Laugh lines crinkled the corners of his eyes, which were almost Oriental in shape. Now his wide mouth shaped a weary smile as he gestured with a long, thin hand.

"Please excuse the mess. Miriam, my secretary, is always at me to neaten things up, and threatens to do it herself; but I tell her that I'll throttle her if she does. At the moment, I know where everything is; if she straightens it, I'll never find anything. Now, what is it you want to know?"

Casey leaned forward. "First, exactly what legal matters did you handle for Billy Joe?"

Waters leaned back, his expression thoughtful. "Billy Joe had me on retainer. I handled all contracts for Baker Enterprises; gave legal advice and handled anything that required the services of an attorney."

"What kinds of things would those be?"

Waters shrugged. "So far, not much. But Billy Joe was becoming better known every day — in short, he was becoming famous. When a performer becomes famous, he or she becomes a target for litigation, particularly from people filing nuisance suits, hoping to get a quick settlement."

"The records show that some time ago Billy Joe was arrested for assault. Were you his lawyer then?"

Waters shook his head. "Nope. Never even heard about it. Truthfully, I'm surprised. I've never known Billy to be violent."

Casey nodded. "Well, he was younger then. Do you manage any of the corporate monies — advise on investments, anything like that?"

"No. I'm not into money management. Edgar Pace and Mrs Baker Senior handle the money."

Casey made a note in her book, then looked up. "Speaking of Edgar Pace, I have been informed by two reliable witnesses that Billy Joe suspected Pace of embezzlement, and was about to confront him concerning his suspicions. Did Billy Joe mention this to you?"

Water's lips drew into a thin line, and the dark eyes lost their twinkle. "I'm sorry, but I have no comment on that."

Casey frowned. "You won't talk about it? May I ask why?"

Waters leaned back in his chair. "I'd rather not talk about it at all, if you don't mind;

at least not at this time."

"Legal complications?"

"You might say that."

Casey sighed. "Well, can you at least tell me if Billy Joe left a will?"

Water's expression lightened. "Certainly. No, he did not leave a will, at least not through my office. I badgered him about it. I told him that if he didn't want the state to decide who got his money when he died, he'd better get on it; but he kept putting it off."

"According to the state, who will be his heirs?"

"Since he had no children, it all goes to his wife, Joanna."

"And if there was a child?"

"Then the child would share the estate with the mother."

"Did you know that Joanna says she is pregnant?"

His eyes narrowed. "No. Where did you hear that?"

"This morning, at the funeral. It came from Joanna, herself."

Water's long fingers drummed on the table. "Well, that is a surprise."

"Because of the fact that Billy was considering a divorce?"

He shot her a quick look. "And where did you hear that?"

"I can't say," Casey said. From Waters' reaction, she figured her guess was correct.

Waters grunted, seemed about to say something, then evidently thought better of it. Lifting his arm, he looked at his watch.

"Just a few more questions," Casey said. "Can you think of anything unusual that might have occurred recently, anything to do with Billy Joe?"

Waters closed his eyes briefly, then opened them. "I don't know if this is important, but perhaps I should tell you. The afternoon of the day Billy Joe was murdered, he called me. He asked me to fly out and meet him while he was in Phoenix. He said there was something he wanted to discuss with me."

Casey leaned forward. "A legal matter?"

"He didn't say. In fact, he refused to tell me anything at the time. He said he would explain when he saw me."

"Did he often do this kind of thing?"

Waters spread his hand. "Not often, but sometimes." He gave a meager smile. "You have to understand about Billy Joe, Miss Farrel. Most of the time he was a sweet guy. Other times, not often, he could be, well . . . demanding. But it's understandable. Being famous isn't all fun and games, you know. There are pressures, sometimes great pressures."

"I'm sure there are," Casey said. "So, he

wanted to talk to you about something important."

Waters shrugged. "Maybe. On the other hand, it might have been something that *he* thought important, but that really wasn't."

"Did he tell you that he called his father when he arrived in Phoenix, and set up a meeting with him?"

Waters shook his head. "He didn't mention it. Was this to be a reconciliation?"

"His father seems to think so."

"And Arlene. Did she know about this?"

"No. At least she says she didn't."

He nodded. "That rings true, all right."

Casey flipped closed her notebook, and rose from her chair. "Well, I think that about does it, for now.

"I'll be here for another day or so. I'm staying at the Opryland Hotel. You can reach me there if you remember anything else you think might be useful: or call me in Phoenix. Thank you for your time, Mr Waters."

It was not yet four o'clock when Casey emerged from Waters' office. At the funeral home, Jonas Lester had said he wouldn't be back at his hotel until seven; so she decided to do a little sight-seeing. The Ryman Auditorium was within walking distance, so she left the rental car where it was, and walked over.

At the Ryman, Casey had to wait a few minutes before she could join a walking tour of the Auditorium. Seeing the empty stage and rows of empty seats, it seemed a shabby memorial, but the sense of history gave it a touch of magic. The greats of country music had all performed here: Hank Williams; Patsy Kline; Johnny Cash; Roy Acuff; Ernest Tubbs; Loretta Lynn and countless others. Some were gone now and some were still performing; but it seemed to Casey as if something of all of them was still here; their essence permeating the old walls and the wooden stage.

The tour took about a half hour, and since she still had some time to kill, Casey returned to her car and drove over the Music Square to the Country Music Hall of Fame. Of course there were several other museums devoted to individual performers: The House of Cash; Twitty City; Minnie Pearl's Museum; Barbara Mandrell Country; but the Hall of Fame offered something for everybody in one place.

She found the Hall of Fame fascinating, and was only driven from it by hunger and the sense of limited time.

She had an ample, satisfying dinner at the Stock-Yard Restaurant, tidied herself a bit in the ladies' room and called Lester, asking him if it was convenient for her to see him. He said it was.

Casey arrived at the Embassy Suites Hotel about seven-thirty.

At the desk, she gave her name to the clerk and asked that he ring Lester's room. When she knocked on his door, a few minutes later, Lester called out, "Come in! Door's unlocked."

Lester was seated at a small table, finishing dinner. He was dressed casually, and appeared to be relaxed. "Excusing me for not getting up, but I ran a little late."

He gestured at the table. "Would you care for some dessert, or some coffee? Some left, still hot."

Casey nodded. "Coffee would be nice." She saw that a second cup and saucer sat near the silver coffee server. A thoughtful gesture that spoke of a nature used to careful planning and preparation.

"Cream and sugar?"

"No, black."

"Have a seat while I pour."

Casey took one of the comfortable chairs, facing Lester across the table, her back to the door of the suite.

Lester handed her the cup and saucer. The coffee smelled wonderful. After pouring another cup for himself, he leaned back in his chair.

"Well, Miss Farrel, any progress to report?"

Casey set down her cup. "I've collected quite a bit of information, and there are several possibilities; but there's nothing definite yet. I have a few questions I need to ask you."

Lester smiled grimly. "Don't you ever get tired of asking questions?"

Casey shrugged. "It's what I do. It's part of the job; in fact the *main* part of the job. If I didn't ask questions, I wouldn't get answers."

He nodded. "Fair enough. Ask away."

"First, someone saw you at the Okay Corral just before your son was killed. When I talked to you, you never mentioned that fact. Why is that, Mr Lester?"

He grew still. "Who told you that?"

"Who isn't important, Mr Lester. Were you there?"

He stared at her for a long moment, his expression unreadable, before he spoke: "Yes. I was there, for a short while."

"May I ask why? You told me that you hated country music."

"I do. But Billy Joe was my son, and I hadn't seen him in years. I wanted to see him, see what he was like now, before we had our meeting. I wanted to see him doing what he seems to do best, in context, you might say."

"When did you arrive?"

"About ten minutes before he came on stage. It was impossible to get a table, of course, so I stood at the bar."

"Why didn't you tell me that?"

He moved uncomfortable. "I didn't think it was important, and frankly, I was a little embarrassed."

Casey frowned. "Embarrassed, why?"

"Because I'm not the kind of man who does things surreptitiously. Normally, when I do something it's out in the open, for all the world to see; and here I was slipping in to see my own son, like some star-struck groupie."

"How long did you stay?"

Lester's face paled noticeably, and his mouth formed a tense, thin line. "Until . . ." He cleared his throat, his gaze turned inward. "Until he was shot."

Casey tried not to show the surprise she was feeling. "You left the club after Billy Joe was shot?"

Lester threw up a hand in an almost spasmodic gesture. "I didn't know he had been shot. I just assumed he was drunk, and had lost his balance. As I told you before, I've kept tabs on the boy, and had learned that lately he had developed a drinking problem. I didn't want to see him like that, and I certainly didn't want him to know that I had; so I left, quickly. I'll never forgive myself."

Casey looked down at her notebook. His pain showed on his face, and it looked very real.

"The men at the door told us that no one left after Billy Joe was shot."

Lester shook his head. "I was out of there a second after it happened, and they had moved away from the door to see what was going on. They evidently didn't notice me."

"When did you learn that your son had been murdered?"

"Later that evening. It was on the TV news." He looked at Casey, his expression agonized. "Look, don't you think I've cursed myself a hundred times for walking out like that? Maybe I could have spoken to him for just a moment before he . . ." Lester choked on the words, then his voice rose. "But I swear I didn't know."

Casey said softly, "It wouldn't have made any difference, Mr Lester. Billy Joe died instantly. If it's any consolation, he couldn't have suffered. It was very quick."

Lester shook his head. It was apparent that he was near the end of his considerable control. There was just one more thing. It wasn't her place to tell him, but he would have to know eventually, and perhaps it would comfort him.

She said, "There is something that I think you should know, Mr Lester."

He looked up, his face set.

"This morning, at the funeral, your daughter-in-law started to tell you something, and Arlene stopped her. But, after you left, she told some of the others. Joanna is pregnant. She is going to have your son's baby."

Lester flinched, as if he had been slapped. It wasn't the reaction that Casey had expected.

Slowly, Lester's face darkened. "She said that! That she was having Billy Joe's child?"

Casey nodded. "Yes."

Lester's hands tightened into fists. "Well, she's lying! If she's really pregnant, it's not by Billy Joe! My sources have told me how unhappy she made Billy."

Casey kept her voice and manner calm. "It will be easy enough to check. A DNA test will do it."

Lester shook his head. Casey felt compelled to speak out. "But how can you be sure the child's not Billy's? Billy wouldn't be the first man to sire a child during a brief reconciliation."

Lester's eyes widened. They were fixed on something behind her. He half-rose from his chair, and said, "What do you want here? What are . . ."

Casey, caught by surprise, put her hands on the arms of her chair, began to turn, and crashed into a painful darkness.

CHAPTER SIXTEEN

Casey surged upward into semiconsciousness. The bright lights hurt her eyes and she blinked painfully, trying to focus on what was happening. Before she could do so, she plunged back into darkness.

The next time she surfaced she heard a woman's voice say: "I think she's coming out of it!" She wanted to, but her head hurt so badly she didn't dare move, and her eyes weren't working properly. Peering upward, she saw a blurred figure in white looking down at her with worried eyes. She attempted to think, to put things together. It was very painful, and it took much longer than usual, but at last she realized that she must be in a hospital.

"What happened?" she said, and winced as the words jarred the pain in her head.

"Shhh," the nurse said. "You'll be all right. You have a concussion."

Casey closed her eyes against the pain. When she opened them again she saw a broad man scowling down at her. "What happened?" he barked.

She frowned at him. Hadn't she just asked that?

The nurse, who was standing next to the man, gave him a cold look. "If you please, Detective, this woman is in no condition to be questioned. You'll have to wait. Doctor's orders. She's not going any place. We'll be keeping her for a day or two, while we run some tests."

The man's scowl deepened, but he turned away. Casey felt grateful to the nurse. But who was the man, and what did he want with her?

She closed her eyes to ponder this question, and felt the nurse's hands on her arm. She felt a small prick of pain and then, as she thought about *this,* a warm wave seemed to wash the pain away, and she gratefully let it take her.

When Casey next awoke it was to full daylight, and to full awareness. She was in a hospital bed, that was obvious enough, in a private room, and she was alone.

As the events of the previous night returned to her, she reached up and gingerly touched the back of her head. It was exquisitely tender. She winced. Whoever had hit her had been serious about it. Or had it been the night before? For all she knew, she might have been out for days. She remembered the surprise on

187

Lester's face as he stared at someone behind her. She remembered being hit, and those were her last coherent memories.

But wait!

She sat up too quickly; and the room tilted slightly. She eased herself back down. There had been someone in the room, a hard-faced man asking her questions, very accusatory?

She frowned, and winced again. Probably he was a cop; but why the hostility?

She suddenly realized that she had a raging thirst. Her glance went to the bedside table. There was one of those little plastic hospital pitchers and a tumbler, but both were empty. Looking further, she found the call button and pressed it.

As she waited for someone to answer, she thought of Josh and her promise to call him last night. He would be worried, and undoubtedly furious . . .

The door opened, admitting a perky young woman in a crisp white uniform. She said cheerily, "Well, we're awake!"

Casey had to work moisture into her mouth before she could speak. "Yes. I'm very thirsty. May I have some water, please?"

The young nurse smiled. "Certainly, but Dr Roland said to call him the moment you woke up."

Casey lay quietly while the nurse made the

call, then took the pitcher and left the room. In a few minutes she returned with the pitcher full of ice water, and filled the tumbler. Casey was finishing her second tumbler when the door swung open again, and a tall and very young-looking doctor appeared. He looked alarmingly like Doogie Howser.

He picked up Casey's arm, his thumb on her pulse. "Well, young lady, how are you feeling this morning?"

Casey tried to smile. "Pretty good, I guess, considering."

He nodded. "Yes, well, you suffered a rather nasty blow to the head."

He put his stethoscope to her heart, then examined her eyes.

"Pupils appear normal this morning. Any dizziness, double vision?"

"No. Just a sore head."

"That should be better soon. Let's take a look at it."

The nurse handed him a pair of scissors, and he gently cut the band of gauze holding the bandage in place.

"The skin was broken," he said, "but the bleeding has stopped. You're going to be all right, young lady."

He turned to the nurse. "Re-bandage, and ice it down."

He smiled down at Casey. "That will help.

I want to keep you another night, just for observation. If no other symptoms show up, you will be able to leave tomorrow. Now, we'll need some information from you: name, address, insurance — all that."

Casey started to nod, but stopped herself. "Fine," she said, briefly wondering why they hadn't gotten that information from the contents of her wallet; but mainly wondering if Jonas Lester was all right, and what had happened in his room.

The young doctor turned to go, but Casey took hold of his sleeve. She was surprised at the weakness of her grip. "Doctor, I have some questions of my own."

He paused. "Just what do you remember of last night, Miss Farrel?"

So it *had* been last night. "I remember everything up to the time when I was hit on the head. I was in the hotel room of a business associate, Jonas Lester. We were seated at a table, having coffee. My back was to the door. Evidently someone came into the room behind me. Lester seemed very surprised. I started to turn to see who it was, and wham! That's about it, except for a few flashes of consciousness here in the hospital."

He nodded, his face grave.

"Is Lester all right?"

He hesitated. "I'm afraid not, Miss Farrel.

190

Mr Lester was brought in at the same time you were. He was dead on arrival."

Casey sank back onto her pillows as a cold wave washed up from her belly to her throat. The fear had been there since she had wakened, but she hadn't wanted to acknowledge it.

"How?" she said.

He shook his head. "I'm afraid I can't tell you that. You'll have to talk to the detective in charge of the case."

Casey frowned. "Was he here during the night? I seem to remember . . ."

The doctor nodded. "You weren't even conscious yet, and we told him he'd have to wait until you were."

Casey's frown deepened. "But why can't you tell me how Lester died? I'm a law enforcement officer myself. I'm here in town because I'm working on a case in which Jonas Lester was involved."

An expression of embarrassment made the young doctor's face look even more boyish. "I'm sorry," he said. "Do you feel up to talking to the detective now? He's very anxious to see you."

"Yes," Casey said brusquely. Something was not quite right here, and she wanted to clear it up as soon as possible.

The young doctor hesitated, then spoke:

"Look, if he gets too pushy, or you get to feeling faint or anything, ring for the nurse. Okay?"

"Okay," Casey said, wondering why the doctor thought that this detective would get aggressive with her; for that was surely what the doctor had meant. Well, she should soon find out.

Detective Harvey Woodson was in his middle forties around five-ten, with a muscular build. His triangular face looked hard enough to chisel rock, and his sour expression did nothing to soften it. His narrow gray eyes had a flat look that said that their owner had seen too much, and was tired of it all.

He pulled up a chair to the side of the bed, and leaned toward Casey. His breath was stale with cigarette smoke and the under-odor of chewing gum.

"Well," he said in a hoarse voice. "The doc said you were ready to talk. That right?"

Casey didn't care for the tone of his voice. She said quietly, "I don't think 'ready' is the operative word here. I'm *able* to talk now, if that's what you mean."

He grunted.

It was clear to Casey that his attitude was not friendly, and it puzzled her.

She took a deep breath. It made her head

throb. "Look," she said softly. "First I'd like to know what this is all about. I need some answers myself . . ."

He sliced a hand at her. "I'm here to question you, not the other way around."

Casey felt her anger rising. What was wrong with this creep? She bit back a short retort, and instead said resignedly, "Ask your questions, Detective."

Woodson hitched his chair forward, and she looked into his eyes. Their expression was cold and hard. "Why did you kill Jonas Lester?" he said.

Casey gasped. "What are you talking about?"

Woodson's lips twisted. "You can save us both a lot of trouble by telling me now."

Casey drew back into her pillows. Jonas was dead, God! And the killer had gotten away. She glared at Woodson. "How on earth can you be stupid enough to think I killed him?" she said angrily.

Woodsen barked a laugh. "Because, lady, we found two .38 slugs in Lester's chest, one right in the heart. And you, we found lying across from him, the thirty-eight in your right hand. I'm pretty sure that when we do the ballistics, we'll find it's the gun that fired the shots."

Keeping his eyes on her face, he reached

into a coat pocket and removed a note pad. "Now, what's your name?"

Casey frowned at him. "Haven't you checked my identification?"

He shrugged. "What identification? There was nothing on you."

"My purse," she snapped. "My billfold. My badge!"

His eyes narrowed. "We found diddly-squat. No purse, no I.D. Who're you trying to con here, lady?"

Casey's anger was fueled by the rising pain in her head. "I'm not trying to con anybody, detective. My name is Casey Farrel. I'm an investigator with the Governor of Arizona's Task Force on Crime. I am here because I am investigating a murder which occurred in our state, and many of the suspects are now in *this* state. Jonas Lester was the father of the murdered man, Billy Joe Baker; that's why I was talking with him. Satisfied?"

Woodson put down his notebook. His expression said that he didn't believe a word she had said. "Now let me get this straight. You *claim* you're an investigator from Arizona, investigating a murder. If that's so, why didn't you check in with us before you started nosing around? It's common procedure, not to mention common courtesy."

Casey sighed. "Truthfully, I didn't think of

it. My time here is limited, and I have a lot to do. Also, as I said, I'm not a regular officer. Mine is an unusual classification."

He grunted. "Hot shit. Well, it makes no never-mind. If you're legit, you should have checked in with us. Since you've no I.D., how do I verify this?"

"Call the Arizona Governor's Office, or the Phoenix Police Department — ask for Sergeant Josh Whitney. He can verify my credentials."

Woodson grunted again. "Okay. But if you're not who you say you are, your ass is in a sling."

He got up from his chair, and turned to go, then turned back. "Don't even think of leaving the hospital. I've got a man on the door, and he's a mean bastard."

Casey muttered an expletive under her breath. Talk about mean bastards . . .

Her heart was pounding, and she felt weak, tired and depressed. She closed her eyes, and must have dozed, for she was roused by the sound of the bedside telephone. Feeling groggy and unfocused, she picked up the receiver.

"Hello," she said hoarsely.

Josh's voice was loud in her ear. "Casey? Casey, is that you?"

Casey cleared her throat. "Yes. Josh. I'm

so glad to hear your voice."

"My God," he said. "Are you all right? Are you hurt badly? Some asshole of a homicide dick called and said you were in the hospital. The bastard seemed to think you were some kind of desperado; said Lester was dead, and you were suspect number one. He wanted verification as to who you are."

"Did he believe you?"

"I guess so. I gave him your office number, and the number of the Governor's Office too. Hell, Casey, how did you get into this?"

"Just doing my job. I was talking to Jonas in his hotel room, and the door was behind me. Someone came in — I never saw them — and sapped me good. I don't remember a thing until I woke up here."

"Jesus. How badly are you hurt?"

"I'm concussed, the doctor says, but it's not too bad. They're going to keep me another night just for observation."

"How do you feel?"

"Fairly rotten, but better since I've heard your voice."

Josh's voice softened. "Aw, Babe. God, I wish I could be there with you."

"Me too," she whispered.

"I'll call you again tonight."

"Good."

"But, in the meantime, did you learn anything yesterday that I should know?"

Casey marshalled her thoughts. "A couple of things. Edgar Pace denies that he stole from Billy Joe, but Billy Joe's secretary, Millie Hanks, says that Billy Joe suspected Pace. Also, I found out that Joanna Lester is pregnant with Billy Joe's child; at least she claims that it's his. Lester, before he died last night, said he didn't believe that. He became very angry and said he was going to change his will so that Joanna and her child could never inherit anything from *him*. He also admitted that he *was* at the club the night Billy Joe died; but said that he slipped out unnoticed just as Billy Joe fell. He said he didn't know Billy had been killed, that he just thought he was drunk, and he didn't want to see him that way. Maybe you ought to talk to Jonas' attorney and see who gets *his* money."

"I'll see what I can do."

Casey looked up and saw Detective Woodson reentering her room.

"Oh, God!" she said. "Woodson's coming back."

Josh grunted. "Don't let the bastard get to you. Tell him that if he hassles you he'll have me to answer to. Better yet, put him on the horn, and I'll tell him."

Casey managed a smile. "Oh, no, Detective. I don't want you to get into trouble with the

Nashville police. Who knows, you might need their help sometime. I can take care of myself. Good-bye. And thanks for calling."

Gently she hung up the receiver, quieting the sound of Josh's loud disagreement.

Woodson dropped into the chair he had recently vacated. His expression was grimmer than ever. "Well," he said, "it appears that you are who you say you are; but that still doesn't completely clear you."

Casey stared at him in disbelief. "Come on, Detective, you don't really believe that I killed Lester."

The word came out slowly, grudgingly, "No."

Casey sighed with relief. "Well thank you."

He grunted. "Then suppose you tell me about this murder in Phoenix. Your partner seems to think that the two crimes may be connected."

Briefly, Casey told him most of what she knew. When she was finished, Woodson nodded thoughtfully. "So most of Billy Joe's close friends were at the club the night he was killed, and now most of them are here in Nashville."

"All except for Judy Lloyd, Billy Joe's current girlfriend," Casey said. "She went home to Fort Worth, and as far as I know, she's still there. Sergeant Whitney and I have just about ruled her out as a suspect."

Woodson took out his notebook. "I want the names of those who were at the club and at the funeral."

"All right. Sergeant Whitney can fax you those, along with their addresses; and I'm sure Billy Joe's mother, Arlene Baker, can get you a list of those who attended the funeral and the wake."

He looked up. "Anyone in particular stand out in your mind as a strong suspect?"

Casey lay back. She was growing tired. "No. No one special; although there is one thing that might be worth checking out. As I told you, it appears that Billy Joe suspected his manager, Edgar Pace, of embezzling from him. I haven't had time to look into this yet, but the books were handled by an accountant, whose name I don't have. You might want to talk with him. Now, I'm awfully tired, and I think I need a pain pill."

Woodson had the grace to look chagrined. "Look, I'm sorry I came on so strong. But we didn't know who the hell you were, and it looked bad."

She raised her hand. "It's okay. I understand."

He stood up and stretched. He looked as tired as she felt.

"Wait," she said. "Before you go, I need

some *quid pro quo*. How was Lester killed? Who found us?"

Without sitting again, Woodson rattled off the facts. It was not a long recitation.

She looked up at him. "Not a lot, is it?"

He shook his head.

"So, I'm no longer a suspect?"

She thought he almost smiled. "I guess not. The paraffin test verified the fact that you had not fired the gun. We tested you and printed you while you were still unconscious. When do they let you out of here?"

"In the morning, I believe."

"I'll try to be waiting for you."

"To take me in, or what?"

He looked embarrassed. "It's been suggested that we work together." He waited for her reaction.

She tried not to show her surprise, and smiled. "Word from upstairs, huh? I guess they think that you will keep me out of trouble."

He almost smiled again. "Maybe. But I have to tell you that after talking with you, I've almost come to the conclusion that maybe, just maybe, you might know what you're doing; but don't quote me on that."

The door closed behind him.

CHAPTER SEVENTEEN

Josh called just as Casey was finishing her dinner.

"How are you feeling, babe?"

"Not bad, considering. I still have a headache and a very tender head, but otherwise I'm okay. I even ate the hospital dinner and almost enjoyed it."

Josh chuckled. "Well, that *is* a good sign, from what I know of hospital food."

"Well, this is the South. They put a lot of time and effort into their food. Is everything okay at home? How's Donnie?"

"He's fine, but he misses you. So do I."

She smiled softly. "That's nice to know. I miss you guys too."

"Do you feel up to going over what happened in Lester's room?"

"Sure, but what I told you before is pretty much it."

"Well, I'd like to hear it once more."

Casey went over the sequence of events yet again. Doing so depressed her.

"So you didn't see the person Lester spoke

to, and he or she didn't say anything?"

"That's right. Not a blinking thing. I had just started to turn, and that was it."

"Damn!"

"I know. It's really a bummer. There I was at the scene, and *nada!* Zip! Woodson filled me in after he called you. Lester was shot twice in the chest — one right in the heart — with a thirty-eight."

"Anybody hear the shot?"

"Evidently not. Maybe the shooter used a silencer."

"Could be. Sounds familiar, doesn't it? I wouldn't be surprised if it was the same person that took out Billy Joe."

"You won't get me to bet against that. But I feel like such an idiot. I'm supposed to be a trained law enforcement officer, and I let Jonas be killed while I was right there in his room!"

"You can't blame yourself, babe. And you did get some information from him."

"Yeah. What do you think? About that, I mean."

"Well, as far as the death of Billy Joe goes, I think that two suspects are at the head of the pack: Pace, and Joanna. Pace because of the embezzlement thing, and Joanna because Billy was apparently about to divorce her. I suppose that it's even possible that she shot

202

Lester. I imagine that her child would be in line to inherit Lester's fortune."

Casey sighed. "I don't know. I guess I find it hard to see Joanna as a cold-blooded killer. Pace? Well, that's another matter."

"Yeah. By the way, who found the body? I gather you didn't call it in."

"Hardly. According to Woodson, it was a couple who were returning to their room. They found the door wide open, and looked in. Not a very pleasant sight for them. They called the desk, and the man on the desk called the police, who were there within minutes."

"I suppose no one saw anything, or anyone coming out of the room."

"No such luck."

"Any physical evidence?"

"None. No fingerprints except mine and Lester's and the maid's. The room had been cleaned that afternoon."

"Does Woodson strike you as competent?"

"I think so. A little quick on the trigger maybe, but he seems to know his business. He's been around a while. I'll be talking to him again in the morning. What about your end, anything?"

He sighed. "Not much. We finished grilling all the customers who were in the club that night. What a job that was! Nobody saw anything, heard anything, or knows anything. I also talked to the doormen again. They finally admitted that it *was* possible that someone could have left the club during the few seconds after the shot, when their attention was on the stage, and they hadn't yet been told not to let anyone out."

"So Lester could have been telling the truth."

"Yeah. He could have."

"Well, it looks like you have found out everything you can. So I guess you'll be coming home tomorrow morning?"

"No, not tomorrow. Arlene has promised me the addresses of some of Billy Joe's old buddies, and I want to talk to her and Joanna again. Probably the day after."

Josh's replying grunt hurt her ear. "Look, Casey, I want you to get your tail on a plane and get back here as soon as you can. As soon as they discharge you from the hospital!"

"You want? Who appointed you my boss, Detective? I came here to do a job, and I intend finishing it."

Josh exploded! "Goddamnit, Casey, it's too dangerous! Don't you realize how close you came to being killed last night?"

"Danger is my business," she said lightly, then wished she hadn't as Josh shouted: "Don't get flippant with me!"

"Josh," she sighed. "I appreciate your concern, really I do; but, like I said, I have a job to do. Besides, if the killer is one of our suspects, I'll be in just as much danger in Phoenix."

Josh was silent for a few moments, although Casey was certain that she could hear him grinding his teeth. Finally he said resignedly, "You are without a doubt the most obstinate woman I've ever known. I should have known it would be a waste of breath, arguing with you. I always end up saying the same thing. 'Be careful, Casey'. I'm beginning to feel like your damn father! When *will* you be back?"

She thought for a few moments. "Depends on how much ground I can cover tomorrow. In a day or two at the latest."

"Promise to call me tomorrow night?"

"Depend on it, Detective."

"Yeah, right, like you did last night. Okay. I'll let you go now. That head of yours probably needs a rest."

"Good night, Josh," she said softly. "And give Donnie a big hug for me."

"Better if you were here to give it yourself," he said in a grumbling voice. "Good-bye, babe. Love you."

Casey was discharged at nine the next morning. Detective Woodson was waiting for her at the front desk.

"Here," he said, "I have something for you." He held out her purse.

"My purse! Where did you find it?"

"It was found in the hotel dumpster."

Casey opened the purse and searched through its contents. "Everything seems to be here," she said. "I was worried about how I was going to settle my bill. I wonder why the killer took it?"

"Probably to muddy the waters temporarily."

She looked up at him. "Did you get any prints off of it?"

He shook his head. "Only yours."

She looked at him. "That's right. You printed me while I was still unconscious, didn't you?"

He looked uncomfortable. "I told you, we had no clue as to who you were. In fact, the consensus at the time was that you were some bimbo Lester had picked up and taken to his room."

Casey's feelings teetered between amusement and anger. "So you think I look like a bimbo, Woodson?"

He looked at her and grinned a crooked grin. "Well, maybe a classy one. After all, Lester could afford the best."

Despite herself, Casey found herself laughing, and was happy to find that it hardly hurt at all.

He seemed pleased by her response. "Do you have transportation?" he asked. "I can drive you where you want to go."

"I forgot!" Casey slapped her forehead. "I have a rental car. It's still out at the Embassy Suites parking lot; at least I hope it is."

"I'm sure it is." He smiled at her. "Well, let's go get it."

As they drove toward the hotel, Casey said, "What did you find out?"

"All of Billy Joe's people have left town, except for the wife. She's still staying with her mother-in-law."

"Do Joanna and Arlene have alibis for the time of the Lester's murder?"

"They alibi each other, but it's far from iron-clad. Both of them said that they were worn out after the funeral and wake. They had an early dinner, together, and then retired to their separate rooms."

"How early?"

"At least an hour before the approximate time of Lester's death."

"So, it's possible that either of them could have slipped out without the other one knowing, driven to the Embassy Suites, knocked me out, shot Lester, and driven back."

"It's possible."

Casey drummed her fingers on her knees,

thinking hard. "They both have strong motives. Arlene has a long-time hate for Lester. But that would mean two killers instead of one. She worshipped Billy Joe; he was all she had, and besides, she wasn't in Phoenix during the time he was shot; at least not to my knowledge."

"And Joanna?"

"Well, there's Lester's money. As far as I can find out, Billy Joe's unborn child will be Lester's closest living relative, and should have some claim on his estate. Of course Lester denied that the child could be Billy Joe's; but, as I told him, a DNA comparison will settle the question. And, if it's Joanna, the motive for both deaths could be the same, as she and the child would be Billy Joe's heirs. What do you think?"

"It's possible, I suppose; but somehow it's difficult to think of a pregnant woman as a murderer. I've seen stranger things, mind you, but this just doesn't ring right. You know her better than I do; do you think she's capable of two cold-blooded murders?"

Casey shrugged. "My friend, the homicide sergeant you talked to yesterday, says that anyone is capable of murder if the motive is strong enough. But then Josh is a cynic."

Woodson grinned over at her. "Most cops are."

"How about Billy Joe's accountant; did you question him?"

"Yeah. Name's Kenneth Tildman. He was reluctant to talk, but I kept at him. He finally admitted that a great deal of money had come up missing over the past year, over fifty thousand bucks. He's the man who brought it to Billy Joe's attention. They thrashed it out together, and decided that Pace had to be the culprit. He apparently used all kinds of scams — padded bills, false billings, all the usual. Tildman said that Billy Joe had finally made his decision. Billy Joe figured that he owed Pace a lot, career-wise; and that was why he didn't go directly to the cops. He planned to face Pace down with what he knew, and give him a chance to pay the money back. If Pace would agree to do that, he'd let him resign without pressing charges."

"I wonder why he waited until Phoenix to confront Pace?"

"I gather that it took him that long to make up his mind. Tildman said that Billy Joe called him the night before Billy was killed, and asked him to fly to Phoenix and set up a meeting between the three of them and Billy Joe's lawyer."

"That explains one thing. Billy Joe's lawyer told me that Billy called him to fly to Phoenix, but Billy didn't tell him why."

She glanced over at Woodson. "It seems that this reluctant accountant really let loose when he got started talking."

Woodson laughed. "Often happens that way. When a suspect, or a witness, finally opens up, sometimes you can't shut them up. And Tildman was pretty upset. It seems that Billy Joe first suspected him! Anyway, he not only told all, but he dictated and signed a full statement. That should cause Pace some uneasy moments. I'll give you a copy, and you can slap him over the head with it."

"It might be worth a shot; but I doubt that Pace will be willing to trade an embezzlement charge for two murders."

They pulled into the parking lot of the Embassy Suites. Casey breathed a sigh of relief as she spotted the rental car. She pointed. "There it is, the fourth car down, the blue one."

Woodson parked behind the rental. He took a folded sheet of paper from his pocket and extended it to Casey. "Here you go, the accountant's statement. When are you leaving, Casey?"

"I'm not sure yet." She took a deep breath. "There are still some people I need to talk with; and I want to see Joanna and Arlene Baker again. I'll probably take a flight back late tomorrow."

He nodded. "Stay in touch, you hear? After all, Lester's murder was committed on our turf."

"I'll keep you up to date, Harvey, I promise."

Woodson gave an embarrassed grin. "And I'm sorry about the bad start we had."

She shrugged. "If our situations were reversed, I would probably have labeled you the prime suspect too; although I wouldn't have been so mean about it."

She watched him flush. "Yeah, well, I guess I'm getting a little sour in my old age. Anyway, I'm sorry."

"Apology accepted." She got out of Woodson's car, gave the detective a final wave, and unlocked the rental car. Her mood, as she drove away, was dark and pensive. The day, which had begun bright and sunny, had clouded over, threatening rain.

Casey felt that she had been spinning her wheels ever since she had been given the case. Every avenue she explored seemed to open up another can of worms. Usually, she delighted in difficult cases, cases that challenged her intellect. But this one bothered her; she seemed to be getting nowhere.

On top of this, Casey felt somehow responsible for the death of Jonas Lester. He had been killed with her right there in the room, for God's sake. What kind of law enforcement officer was she, anyway, to have let this happen? Maybe she was in the wrong line of work.

She shook her head, thinking of Josh's words on the subject: "The perp, babe, is responsible, no one else. Depend on it!" But in this case was that entirely true? Still, how could she have known, or guessed, that Jonas had been in danger? Well, it wouldn't help to torture herself over it. She only hoped that no one else was scheduled to die.

It was shortly before noon when she pulled into the driveway of the Baker home. Arlene answered the door wearing an apron over her dress. Arlene's color was better today, and the apron gave her a quaint, old fashioned look. When she saw Casey, she looked surprised and a bit flustered. She smiled, but it looked forced. "Miss Farrel! I heard about what happened to you. Are you all right?"

Casey returned her smile. "I think I'll survive."

"It's terrible, what happened to Jonas." Arlene shook her head in distress. "God knows I had every reason to dislike the man, but nobody should die like that."

"I know," Casey said.

"Well, come in, come in." Arlene stepped back from the doorway. "Joanna and I were about to fix some lunch. Would you care to join us?"

Casey hesitated, suddenly realizing that she was hungry; she had been so eager to make her escape from the hospital that she had skipped breakfast. "If you're sure it won't be any trouble."

"No trouble at all," the other woman said briskly. "We'd like to have you. Come along."

Casey followed Arlene down the hall and into the kitchen. Joanna, busy at the stove, gave a start at the sight of Casey, and Casey was sure that she saw a flicker of fear in the woman's eyes.

Arlene said, "Miss Farrel is joining us for lunch, dear. Isn't that nice?"

"I'm not so sure," Joanna said nervously. "You're here with more questions, I suppose?"

Arlene put her arm around her daughter-in-law. "Now, dear, don't get yourself all upset. It's her job to ask questions."

Joanna was still staring at Casey. "You just never give up, do you?"

"If I did, this case — or any case for that matter — would never get solved. You do want the murderer of Billy Joe found, don't you, Joanna?"

"Of course we want him found!" Arlene's eyes flashed. "I'll never be at peace with myself until Billy's killer is caught and punished."

Joanna sighed, and her shoulders slumped. "You're right, of course, Arlene."

Casey's gaze was on Arlene. "Do you feel the same about the killer of your ex-husband?"

Joanna looked up. "You think they are the same?"

"I do. Don't you?"

"I haven't given it much thought," Joanna muttered.

Arlene said, "Let's put lunch on the table before we talk. Would you care for a cup of coffee, Miss Farrel?"

"I would," Casey said gratefully.

"Then you just have a seat in the breakfast nook, and lunch will be on in a few minutes."

It wasn't until Casey was sitting at the table that she realized that Arlene hadn't responded to her question about her ex-husband.

For lunch they had a thick, pungent pea soup, and a delicious crab salad. Casey ate hungrily. Arlene also ate heartily, but Casey noticed that Joanna merely picked at her food.

As they were finishing the salad, Arlene said, "Ask your questions, Miss Farrel. Don't be bashful."

Casey put down her spoon. "Well, I understand from Detective Woodson that on the night of Mr Lester's death, you and Joanna both retired early. Is that correct?"

Arlene answered, "That's right. I hadn't slept a wink the night before, and I was worn out. I took a sleeping pill — something I hardly ever do — and was out like a light all night long."

"I suppose you're thinking that we can't alibi each other," Joanna said tartly.

Casey kept her tone level. "This is just part of the routine, Joanna, and it doesn't necessarily mean that we consider you a suspect. It's a way of narrowing the field."

Joanna gave her a cold stare. "But you do suspect me, don't you? Billy's lawyer has told me that as Billy's widow I, and the baby, will inherit his estate. I know how you people think!"

Casey looked at her coolly. "I doubt it. What you say is true, of course; but we realize that having a motive is not the same thing as committing murder."

Joanna slumped, all the fight gone out of her. "I just want this to be over, so I can get on with my life." She placed her hand on her slightly rounded belly and, for the first time, Casey felt she was being sincere.

Arlene put her hand on the younger woman's shoulder. "You should have let me tell him, Joanna. Much as I disliked the man, I can't help but feel sorry that he died not knowing he was going to have a grandchild."

Casey held up her hand. "That's not quite true. While I was with Mr Lester, I told him about Joanna's pregnancy, but he said he did not believe it. In fact, he said he was going to change his will so that there was no possibility of the child inheriting. Of course, he died before he could do that!"

Joanna sprang to her feet, her face livid. "How dare you? How dare you tell him about something that was none of your business! Of all the interfering, pushy . . ."

Arlene rose and put her arm around her daughter-in-law. "Now, now, girl. Calm down. He would have had to know sooner or later."

Joanna pushed her away. "But don't you see? She thinks that . . ."

"Shhh. It doesn't matter what she thinks, she's just fishing. That's her job. You didn't know about any of this. You had no way of knowing Jonas would react like that; so why would you want to hurt him?" She gave Casey a hard look.

Casey felt her face get hot. At the time she had told Jonas about the baby, it had seemed like the thing to do. Now, stated so baldly, it made her wince.

"I'm sorry," she said. "At the time it seemed that he had a right to know. His feelings over Billy Joe's death were so . . . I thought this news might make him feel better. I'm really sorry. But at any rate, as you must know, your child may very well be in line to inherit at least part of Jonas Lester's fortune."

Joanna dropped back down into her chair, and Arlene followed suit as Joanna said: "Well, I don't want or need Jonas Lester's money. I can take care of my baby myself."

"Joanna is going to sing again," Arlene said with pride in her voice. "She and Edgar decided. The band is staying together, and Joanna is going to finish the tour with them. After that, she'll take time off to have the baby."

"Again? Do you mean she's a singer? I didn't know that."

"Oh, yes, she was a singer before Billy Joe married her. That was how they met. She's quite good; but Billy Joe wanted her to give up her career. Now she has her chance again. They may come to hear the wife of Billy Joe Baker, but after they hear her, we hope that they will come again to hear Joanna Baker."

"I hope so too," Casey said honestly. She stood up. "Well, thank you for the delicious lunch, and I'm sorry if I upset you, Joanna."

Joanna nodded, then looked away. Casey turned to Arlene. "Arlene, remember those pictures of Billy Joe's boyhood buddies you showed me?"

Arlene nodded. "Oh, yes. I made out a list. I'll run upstairs and get it. But as I said, they are all old addresses. Probably most of the boys have long since moved." She rose and bustled out of the room.

Casey sipped coffee, looking across the table at Joanna. "Joanna, did you know any of Billy Joe's boyhood friends?"

Joanna shook her head. "Not that I know of."

Casey frowned. "I would have thought that he would have kept in touch with at least some of them."

Joanna shrugged. "His career kept him pretty busy. All I know is that he never mentioned to me that any of the men he knew were old friends from his boyhood."

At that moment, Arlene returned carrying a folded sheet of paper. She handed it to Casey. "Those are all the names I can think of. But even if you find them, I don't see how that will help you. Billy Joe knew these boys ages ago. As far as I know, he hadn't seen a single one of them in recent years."

Casey put the sheet in her purse. "Well, thanks anyway, for your effort. Joanna, don't forget that you will have to return to Phoenix until the investigation is over."

"I know," said Joanna, "but I don't see why. You know where I am." She lifted a hand dismissively, "I know, 'procedure'."

"That's right. Then I'll see you there," Casey said.

"Will you be coming with her, Arlene?"

Arlene shook her head firmly. "No, I won't. When I took Billy Joe and left Jonas I promised that I would never set foot in Phoenix again, and I haven't. I hate that town with a passion!"

CHAPTER EIGHTEEN

"I managed to track down one of Billy Joe's boyhood chums who still lives here in Nashville," Casey said into the receiver, "but I haven't talked to him yet except on the phone. He admits to following Billy Joe's career through the media, but he says that he hasn't seen or talked to him in years."

Josh said, "It would seem that Billy Joe really cut loose from his old friends when he got a taste of fame."

"I don't think that's exactly it, Josh. After all, people often drift apart when their lives go in different directions. I certainly haven't kept in touch with my high-school friends, for instance. People change, outgrow each other. You know how it is."

"I guess you're right. Anyway, the burning question is, will this guy come up with anything useful?"

Casey sighed. "Yeah. That's the question. It may be just a waste of time, but I feel I have to follow through."

"When are you going to see him?"

"Tomorrow. It's been a long day, and I need some sleep."

Josh's voice immediately changed. "Aw, babe. I'm sorry. I almost forgot what you've been through. What time are you seeing this guy?"

"He works at Twitty City, and I'm meeting him there in the morning, early."

"Then you'll head home?"

"Then I'll head home."

"Have all the band members, et cetera, returned to Phoenix?"

"All but Joanna, and she told me she'd be returning tomorrow, too. It turns out that she is a singer, and is going to finish out Billy Joe's tour. Edgar has changed the dates, and she will open in Phoenix." She smiled to herself. "I thought maybe you'd like to escort me to the opening."

Josh chose to ignore her remark. Instead he said, "How about Pace? Learn anything more about him?"

"Yes. Detective Woodson picked me up at the hospital this morning. He talked to Billy Joe's accountant yesterday, and the accountant said that he and Billy Joe had proof that Pace had been skimming. He even signed a statement to that effect. I'm bringing it back to Phoenix with me. The accountant said that Billy Joe intended to confront Pace while they were in Phoenix. He was going to offer Pace a choice — either to resign, and pay back what he had taken, or to face charges."

Josh grunted. "Well, there certainly is a motive for murder there."

"Yes, but it's a big step from there to being able to prove he did it."

"This Detective Woodson, is he any good?"

"I've already told you, Josh, he seems to know what he's doing. What more can I tell you? I've only seen the man a few times."

Josh grunted again. "Funny how you always seem to be bumping into good, quote, investigators out of town; like the one you met in Prescott, for instance."

Casey laughed. "Just lucky, I guess."

"Yeah, lucky," he said with a growl in his voice. "You just be sure you keep it on a professional level. That Prescott cop had a thing for you. A man can tell."

"Now just what is that supposed to mean?"

"You know what it means." His voice changed. "I almost forgot. Yesterday I dug up something that might be worth looking into. That soundman, Jack Stover, had a shouting match with Billy Joe about an hour before Billy was killed."

Casey relaxed, glad that the subject was being changed. "How did you learn that?" she asked.

"From one of the doormen. He dropped by the station late in the afternoon. I think he was spooked a little about us finding out about Lester getting by him, and wanted to get on our good side."

"Did he say why he hadn't mentioned it before?"

"Yeah. He said it slipped his mind; that he didn't think it was important until now. Anyway, he said he happened to be back by the dressing rooms, heard loud voices, and stopped to listen."

"Did he hear enough to know what the quarrel was about?"

"Apparently Billy Joe was threatening to fire Stover. The reason wasn't clear; but the door goon heard Stover say that if he was fired Billy Joe would regret it."

"And that's it?"

"That's it."

"I suppose you're going to question Stover?"

"Depend on it."

"Maybe you should wait until I get back with the accountant's statement before you talk to Pace again."

"I agree. What time is your flight tomorrow?"

She gave him the flight number and time of arrival.

"Okay!" Josh said. "Donnie and I will meet you."

"That will be nice." she said.

"I've really missed you, babe. I was just getting used to working in tandem with you."

"Your male ego is surviving?"

"Don't have one."

"Yeah, right. Good-bye, Detective."

"Is that all I get; good-bye, Detective? No terms of endearment, no love words?"

Casey smiled to herself. "Those can wait until we're alone, Detective. I'll see you tomorrow."

"You will," said Josh warmly. "Oh, you certainly will. Now you get some rest, babe."

Casey made an early start the next morning. After a quick breakfast, she drove the rental car out on the I–65, getting off at Hendersonville. A telephone call to Buck Dewey, Billy Joe's boyhood friend, had set up an appointment at nine. Dewey worked as maintenance supervisor at Twitty City, and she was to meet him there shortly after the place opened.

Although it was early, the parking lots at Twitty City were already filling, and people were lining up for the guided tour to the Twitty house and Conway's Showcase.

Buck Dewey was having a cup of coffee at the refreshment stand where he had told Casey to meet him. Dewey was a tall, rawboned individual of perhaps thirty, dressed in a tan jumpsuit. He wore a belt of tools around his narrow waist, like a gunbelt.

Keen gray eyes studied Casey intently as she introduced herself. "Glad to meet you, Miss Farrel. Buy you a cup of coffee?"

"Thank you, I'd like that."

They took their coffees over to an empty bench and sat down. Dewey fired a thin cigar, and leaned back. "Must be something real important to bring an investigator all the way back here from Arizona." His voice was soft, with a pronounced Southern drawl.

"As I told you on the phone, I'm looking into the murder of Billy Joe Baker."

"But that happened in Phoenix."

"His father was killed here in Nashville."

"His father?"

"Yes, didn't you read about it, or see or hear about it on the news?"

"I remember seeing something about some guy being murdered out near the airport, but his name wasn't Baker."

"It wasn't mentioned that Jonas Lester was Billy Joe's father?"

"Nope. Not that I saw."

Casey thought back. She hadn't seen a newspaper or watched television since Lester's death. Apparently the media hadn't discovered that Lester was the dead singer's father or they surely would be trumpeting the fact.

"So you never met Lester?"

Dewey shook his head. "Nope; only Arlene, Billy's mom."

"Did you go to Billy's funeral?"

He nodded. "Yep. Saw it announced in the paper, and thought I should, for old time's sake; even though I hadn't seen Billy in . . . oh, I don't know, several years anyway."

"So you didn't keep in touch?"

"Nah." He gazed off. "Billy's life went one way, and mine went another. Billy was on his way to fame and fortune, and me, well, here I am. Why would he want to pal around with the likes of me?"

"Did that hurt you?"

"Hurt me?" He looked at her again. "Reckon it did, a little, but I don't blame old Billy for that." He grinned. "We understand about show business here in Nashville. It takes a lot of time, and a lot of work to become famous; and sometimes there's just not enough time for everything."

Casey smiled. "Well, that's a very healthy attitude. But tell me, what about Billy's other old friends; do you know of anyone who was angry at Billy for moving on? Anyone who *did* resent Billy's success?"

Dewey was silent for a moment, thinking,

226

then shook his head. "Not that I know about; but then, I don't see many of them anymore either."

"Were you close to any of them besides Billy?"

"Uh . . . well, one, yes. Leland Thomas. He, me, and Billy used to pal around together. In high school they used to call us the Three Musketeers."

Casey nodded. "I think I saw a picture of you on the wall at Arlene's house — three boys on the steps, two with guitars."

"Yeah. I have a copy of that one too." He shook his head. "God, we were young. Young and full of dreams. Billy and Lee were going to become famous country-western stars, and I was going to be their manager. Well, at least Billy made it."

"How about Lee?"

"Well, he did all right for a while. He and Billy played together around town. Lee didn't have much of a voice, but he could sure play the hell out of that old guitar — even better than Billy. He was with Billy in that first band that Arlene and Billy put together."

"Did you ever go to hear them play?"

"Sure. We were still tight then. It was when they began getting gigs in other cities and states that we began to drift apart. I was working then, and there was a girl." He grinned sheepishly. "I married young, and we had a baby."

Casey nodded. "Natural enough."

"Yeah. I guess so. Anyway, it didn't leave me much time for running around after the band."

Casey smiled. "Well, maybe you chose the best path after all. Now Billy Joe is dead, and Lee? Do you know where he is?"

"I have no idea. Haven't seen or heard of him in years. I heard somewhere that he went down to Mexico."

"When was this?"

"I'm not sure. A few years ago."

"Do you know why he left Billy Joe and the band?"

"No idea at all."

"Do you know of anyone who might know where he is now?"

Dewey shook his head.

Casey tapped her pen on her knee. "That's too bad. I would very much have liked to talk with him."

Dewey shrugged, then stretched. "Well, for what it's worth, I don't think he'd know anything that could help you. From what I've heard on the grapevine, he hasn't been in touch with Billy since he left."

While Dewey was talking, Casey took her list from her purse, and looked at it. "What about Ray Parker?" she asked. "Do you happen to know where he is now?"

"Ray Parker. Last I heard, Ray went up to Montana to become a cowboy." He snickered. "Kinda funny, since when I knew him old Ray didn't know one end of a cow from another."

"Well, as you said, we all have our dreams," said Casey. "Was he close to Billy?"

"Nah. Not really. He left Nashville right out of High School and hasn't been back since, that I know of."

Casey refolded the list and returned it to her purse. "I really appreciate the time and trouble you took for me, Mr Dewey."

She held out her hand, and they shook.

"No trouble, Miss Farrel. As for the time, I felt that I could spare a little to help find the murderer of an old friend. I only hope that what I've told you will be of some use."

"It very well may be," Casey said.

"Well, I'd better get back to work then."

"Good-bye," Casey said, and watched him walk away into the growing crowd.

It was close to noon when Casey got to the outskirts of Nashville. She stopped at a fast food place and had a grilled chicken sandwich and a salad. Deep in thought, she scarcely tasted the food.

Afterwards, instead of heading directly for the airport, Casey drove to Belle Mead and Arlene Baker's house.

Arlene answered the doorbell with an expression of surprise on her face. "I thought you were returning to Phoenix today?" she said.

"I am. My plane leaves in a couple of hours; but there's one more thing I need from you, Arlene."

"What is that?"

"Those pictures on your study walls of Billy Joe in the old days, the ones with his friends. I know you treasure them and wouldn't let go of them but could I take them to a copy place? It should only take about forty-five minutes. I noticed a place not far from here."

Arlene hesitated for a moment, then nodded. She said slowly: "Well, I suppose so, although I can't imagine what earthly use they'll be to you."

She started for the stairs, Casey close behind her. In the study, Arlene began taking the pictures down.

Casey said. "Where's Joanna?"

"She took an early flight this morning," Arlene said over her shoulder.

"I thought that she was going to stay another day or so to keep you company."

"Edgar called last night. He wanted her to

come right away, so that she can rehearse with the band before they open."

"You're not going to the opening?"

"I told you. I never go to Phoenix."

"Yes, I forgot."

Casey could see tears in the older woman's eyes. "Besides, I need some time to grieve without any people around. I need time to grieve for my boy."

CHAPTER NINETEEN

The first thing that Casey saw when she exited the ramp into the terminal was her two men. The strength of her emotional response surprised her, as they came toward her, both smiling widely.

Josh gave her a warm hug, and Donnie, looking embarrassed, gave her hand a hesitant pat; however, the look on his freckled face told her how glad he was to see her.

"Did you guys miss me?" she asked.

Donnie nodded. "Josh isn't a very good cook," he said, grinning at Josh. "And Spot missed you too."

Casey smiled and ruffled his hair. "How about you, Detective," she said to Josh, "did you miss me?"

"You know darn well I did," he said gruffly, folding a large hand around her arm. "Let's get out of here."

As they started toward the baggage area he whispered in her ear: "Just wait until we're alone, and I'll show you just how . . ."

Casey reached a hand up to cover his mouth,

and whispered. "Shhh. Behave yourself!"

In a normal voice she said, "So, what did you guys eat while I was gone? Hamburgers? Pizza?"

"We had hot dogs once!" Donnie said.

"That was at the basketball game," Josh said. "I want you to know that I cooked regular meals for us: Lamb chops, steak, stew; and they were pretty good, no matter what the monster here says."

He gave Donnie a stage glare, and the boy grinned. "Well, I guess they weren't *too* bad," he said mockingly; "but not as good as the stuff Casey cooks."

Josh shook his head. "He's shameless. He'll do anything to get on your good side. Just remember that."

Casey looked down at Donnie, who gazed up at her with what he apparently considered to be an angelic look. God, she was glad to be back here with these two. She couldn't help it; she was having a real bad case of the Warm Fuzzies.

"I also want you to know," said Josh, squeezing her arm, "that at this very minute there is a savory tri-cut roast, with little red potatoes and baby carrots simmering in the slow-cooker."

"Mmmm. Good," said Casey. "I'm starving."

After they picked up her luggage and were heading out of the parking lot, Donnie said: "Have you decided anything about Spot?"

Casey's heart sank as she realized that she had completely forgotten the problem of the dog.

She sighed and said, "No, kiddo. I'm sorry, but I could hardly do anything about Spot while I was in Nashville. But it will work out. I promise."

Donnie settled back, for the moment content. Casey exchanged a look with Josh over the boy's head. It was very touching, Donnie's faith in her ability to make the world right for him; but it was also intimidating.

Now he looked up and said innocently, "Did you solve the murder while you were gone, Casey?"

Josh began to laugh, and after a moment Casey joined in. "No, Donnie. I'm not quite superwoman yet; but we're getting close."

"Speak for yourself," Josh muttered.

"Have faith, Detective," Casey said cheerily. "That's what you're always telling me."

"Yeah, but I've never worked a case before where there were a couple of hundred suspects. It makes a difference."

Donnie said seriously. "But haven't all the customers in the bar been eliminated?"

Casey and Josh exchanged glances. "Well,"

said Josh, looking down at the boy, "what have we got here, a budding detective?"

"That's what I'm going to be when I grow up. Just like you and Casey. I listen to what you guys say, you know."

Casey raised her eyebrows. "I guess you do, kiddo. I guess you do. I'll have to remember that, won't I?"

Donnie squinted up at her, suspicious that he was being made fun of, but not quite sure.

"Anyway, what about the Cardinals?" she said. "I thought you were going to be a football player, and join the Cardinals."

Donnie wrinkled his nose. "Ah, the Cardinals are never going to win a championship. What's the use?"

Casey hid a smile, and Josh said, "Have you ever thought that you might help them win? That would be something, wouldn't it? Besides, good football players earn a lot more money than cops, and they work better hours."

Donnie frowned. "But didn't you tell me that money wasn't important; that what was important was doing work that you liked?"

"My, you have been paying attention, haven't you?" Casey said. "What do you say to that, Detective?"

"Not much," said Josh.

"Then I'm going to be a detective," said Donnie, in a satisfied tone.

It wasn't until after they had eaten that Casey and Josh discussed the case. Like many men who had lived alone for a number of years, Josh — despite Donnie's teasing — was a decent cook. The roast tasted delicious, and Casey ate with good appetite.

It was growing late when they finished, and despite Donnie's pleas to be allowed to stay up, Casey made him go to bed. She knew that he wanted to hear about the case, but she wanted to discuss it alone with Josh. She was still feeling some effects of the blow to the head, and she didn't feel like dealing with the boy's interruptions and questions. She would talk to him about it later.

Donnie grumbled, but finally settled down. Casey and Josh cleaned up the kitchen, then took cups of coffee into the living room. The nights were growing too cool for them to be comfortable on the deck. As they settled themselves on the sofa, Josh said: "It's sure good to have you back, babe."

"It's good to be here," she said.

He squeezed her hand. "Can you stay the night?" he asked.

She hesitated. "As long as one of us gets up early enough to pretend that he or she slept on the couch," she said.

He groaned. "Aw, come on, Casey. The boy isn't stupid, and kids nowadays know everything."

She shook her head. "I don't care. I don't want to send him the wrong signals."

"You're a hard woman, Farrel; but all right. I'll get up in the cold dawn and come back to the couch. Okay?"

"Okay." She squeezed his hand.

He put down his cup. "You must be tired. Let's go to bed."

She laughed. "Not so fast, Detective. I haven't finished my coffee, and I want to talk to you about the case."

He sank back against the cushions. "Like I said, a hard woman!"

"So, did you talk to the soundman, Jack Stover?"

"Yeah, this afternoon."

"What did he tell you?"

"Well, he admitted to quarreling with Billy Joe that night. He said that Billy Joe had been in a foul mood, and had been drinking. Stover said he was late getting there and that Billy Joe was ticked off about it. Stover said that he was in a bad mood too. His wife is traveling with him on this trip, and she had been complaining about his having to work nights. She wanted him to quit and get another job. At any rate, both men were on short fuses, and when Billy Joe began to yell at Stover for being late, Stover flew off the handle and they went at it. Billy Joe threatened to fire him if he was late again."

Josh stirred restlessly. "Now that's hardly a reason to kill a man, is it? On the other hand, I've known people to have been killed for less." He spread his hands.

"And Lester? What reason could Stover have to take Lester out?"

Josh shrugged. "What reason would any of them have to kill Lester, except Joanna?"

Casey sighed. "Yes, the money, of course. As for the others, well, maybe Lester knew something that would incriminate Billy Joe's killer. Or maybe Lester was shot just to confuse us, to throw us off the track."

Josh shook his head. "As somebody once said, babe, it's a puzzlement. What did you learn in Nashville yesterday?"

Casey repeated what Dewey had told her.

"Do you think that it would be worthwhile to try to track down this Leland Thomas, and the cowpoke?"

"I don't know how much effort should be put into it," she said slowly; "but I would like to talk with them. I've got a feeling that there is something we don't know, something . . ."

238

Josh snickered. "*Something?* How about a lot of things, babe?"

She reached over and punched his arm. "You know what I mean, Detective. Call it a hunch, if you must; but remember that you were the one who told me to always follow my hunches."

"Yeah," he said. "I know. But what I didn't tell you was that they don't always pan out. A couple of years ago, I sat down and worked it out. The way I figure, I've only solved about thirty percent of my cases by following my hunches."

"Well, my percentage is better than that, well over fifty percent."

Josh hooted. "So how many cases have you had? Half a dozen, maybe?"

"The number doesn't matter."

"I suppose it's that fabled woman's intuition?"

"So what are you saying, Detective? That with men it's hunches, with women, intuition? Define the difference for me!"

"Aw, come on, Casey." He waved a hand at her. "How did we get into this?"

Casey laughed. "How do we ever get into these arguments?"

"I prefer 'discussion,' " said Josh, settling back onto the sofa. "So, let's brainstorm a little here. What have we got so far? In my estimation the two strongest suspects are still Jo-anna Baker and Edgar Pace."

"I'd go along with that."

"Using the classic triad, motive, means, and opportunity, they certainly had the strongest motives for wanting Billy Joe dead; and they also had opportunity. As far as Lester's death is concerned, Joanna would seem to be out in front. I can't see how Pace would benefit, unless, as you say, Lester's murder was just a red herring."

"Yeah. So, what's next? Tomorrow I think I'll run Leland Thomas' name through the computer and see if I can run him down. Maybe the cowboy too. How about Pace? When do we brace him with the accountant's statement?"

"I think the sooner the better, and I think we should do it together."

"Together? Okay." She stretched, and as she did so, Josh pulled her into his arms.

As his arms went around her, his mouth descended on hers; and Casey felt her blood heat, as arousal sparked along her nerve ends. She felt as well as heard his warm whisper in her ear: "God, that feels good. I've sure missed you, babe."

Casey sighed, and leaned her head against his chest. "Me too," said softly, thinking that maybe, just maybe, being married to this big, kind, infuriating man wouldn't be so bad after all. She made no protest as he led her into the house and down the hallway toward his bedroom.

Casey was at her office early the next morning. She was going through the pile of mail that had accumulated during her absence when the phone rang. She picked up the receiver.

"Farrel!" Bob Wilson barked. "My office. Now!"

With a sigh, Casey complied.

When she entered his room he looked up and frowned. "Well, back from your vacation, Farrel?"

Casey took the chair before his desk, determined not to let him get to her. "You have a question, Bob?"

"I sure do!" He waved a piece of paper at her. "The Opryland Hotel? You couldn't find someplace cheaper?"

Casey took a deep breath and let it out slowly. "Well, Motel 6 was full, and I thought I might as well be comfortable. If there's any problem, I'll pay the difference out of my own pocket. Satisfied?"

He snorted. "Not by a damn sight. You let Jonas Lester be killed right in front of your face. How do you think *that* is going to look in the papers? We're going to look like fools."

Casey bit her lip. "It wasn't exactly in front of my face, Bob. I was out cold at the time."

"Yeah. Some cop! I ought to take you off the case."

"Then why don't you? If you will recall, I didn't want it anyway; and now that Lester is dead . . ."

He raised a hand. "No, you don't get off that easy. Besides, if I took you off the case it would only make us look worse."

Casey nodded. That was what he was worried about of course; the fact that *he* might be made to look foolish. He had an ego the size of a football field.

He slammed the paper down. "So, did you learn anything in Nashville that might offset any of this?"

She gave him the details. When she was finished, he shook his head. "Not a damn thing!" he said. "You might as well have stayed here."

"I don't think so," she said. "Sergeant Whitney and I believe that the two murders are connected. Maybe something will come up in the new case that will help us here."

"Doesn't seem likely. Nashville will be handling Lester's death."

"Well, I've established a useful contact in a Sergeant Woodson; and he's promised to keep me informed. I'm sure he'll work with us."

Wilson grumbled under his breath.

Casey stood. "Is that all? I have my report to write."

He looked at her, eyes narrow. The anger Casey had been controlling boiled to the surface. She leaned forward and put her hands on the desk. "Look, Bob. If you aren't happy with my work, if you want me out of here, just say so. If you can't work with me, why don't you fire me?"

Wilson's eyes widened, and his mouth opened. Without giving him a chance to reply, she swept out of his office.

Back in her own office, she was still trembling with anger. After taking a few minutes to calm down, she attacked the papers on her desk, expecting the phone to ring any second — Wilson handing her walking papers.

The phone remained silent. Her mail read, she turned to the computer on her desk, and began typing her report.

Halfway through, she swiveled away from her desk, picked up the phone, and punched out the number of Harvey Woodson in Nashville.

She was relieved to find Woodson in. "Casey," he said, "glad to hear from you. What's up?"

"Nothing here. Any new developments there?"

"We-ell, not really. We're still canvassing the hotel employees and the guests on Lester's floor; especially those who had a late check-out."

"Have you got the autopsy report yet?"

"Yeah, it's on my desk now."

"Any surprises?"

"No. Death by gunshot. Oh, there *was* one thing; Lester had a bad heart. Maybe the killer went to all that trouble for nothing."

"Maybe the killer couldn't wait. How about the gun?"

"Nothing helpful there. It was reported stolen in a burglary about two weeks ago. My hunch is that the killer bought it on the street."

"Just like the gun in our case here. It was stolen too."

"Pretty coincidental, huh? Anything at your end? What did you find out from Billy Joe's old pals?"

"I'm just making out my report now. I'll make a copy and fax it to you. It's against task force policy, but I'll do it anyway. I'm mad at my boss right now."

"Good! That you're sending the fax, I mean. If anything pops up here, I'll let you know."

As Casey replaced the receiver in the cradle, it rang, startling her. Gingerly, she lifted the receiver again. "Hello?"

"Hi, babe!"

She let out her breath. "Josh!"

"I called Pace's motel. He wasn't in, but they said that this evening he would be at Nashville West; that's the club where Joanna and the band are rehearsing. I'm going to try to catch him there. Can you meet me?"

She thought for a moment. "What time?"

"About five-thirty."

"Five-thirty is fine. Will the sitter be able to stay with Donnie?"

"I've already called her and told her we'd be home late. She said there was no problem."

"Very efficient, Detective. Okay. See you at five-thirty."

Casey hung up the phone again. She wasn't looking forward to the confrontation with Pace, but it had to be done. She wondered how he was going to react.

CHAPTER TWENTY

Nashville West, located on Camelback, had a little more class than the Okay Corral. For one thing, the parking lot was paved, and the building was newer. A sign was already in place, "Opening Tomorrow Night: Joanna Baker, Widow of Billy Joe Baker."

The club was usually dark on Monday nights, but, because of the rehearsal, several cars were parked in the parking lot. Casey parked as close to the entrance as possible.

As she opened the front door to the club she was greeted by a blast of music. Only the lights above the stage were lit, and Casey stopped just inside the door to let her eyes become accustomed to the gloom.

Joanna Baker stood at the mike on stage, a sheet of music in her hand. She was wearing a pair of jeans and a loose, Western-style shirt with the tails hanging out.

Seated at a table about half-way down the room were several people. Casey walked toward them, and as she drew near she recognized them as Josh, Edgar Pace and

Michelle Tatum. Josh was talking to Pace, who stared morosely at the table top. Michelle, wearing granny glasses, leaned over an open notebook, scribbling busily.

As Casey approached, Josh looked up and smiled. "Good. You're here."

Pace did not look up, but Michelle glanced up and nodded.

"You'll have to excuse me. I'm going over a song I just finished for Joanna."

Suddenly the band fell silent, and Joanna said into the mike: "This is a new song, written by Michelle Tatum, for this, my opening performance. It's called 'The Two Time Blues.' "

Behind her the band swung into the opening chords, and Joanna began to sing:

"Worry every morning,
Worry every night,
Worry every minute that that man's not
   in my sight,
Oh, I walk the floor,
Till I wear out my shoes, oh yeah!
'Cause I got the blue time,
Double crossin' two-time, blues."

As Casey listened to the rest of the song, she thought that, as a singer, Joanna didn't seem likely to fill her dead husband's shoes.

Her voice wasn't bad — it had an appealing, husky quality — but she lacked Billy Joe's stage presence, that ability to grab an audience and hold them. Still, she hadn't performed in public in some time, and should improve with practice. The song was good. Not country-western, but real blues; still, with the country sound behind it, Casey supposed it could be categorized as "crossover."

When the song was finished, Michelle said ruefully. "She's going to need some work."

"But at least you get credit for the music," Casey said.

Michelle grinned. "And she's paying me well too. More than Billy ever did."

She broke off as Joanna stopped singing and turned to face the band. As she talked to the men, Toby Green left the stage and hurried up front to the bar. In a moment he came back by the table, tearing the wrapper from a pack of cigarettes. At the same moment, Joanna left the stage and approached the table. She and Green reached the table at almost the same moment.

Josh said, "Mr Green?"

Toby Green skidded to a stop and stared at Josh in evident consternation.

"Toby, you know that Jonas Lester was killed the night before last."

Green nodded nervously.

"Can you account for your whereabouts between seven and eight o'clock that night?"

"Why ask me that?" Green bleated. "I didn't kill him."

"I didn't say you did. Just answer the question."

Green's face was very pale, and he moved his weight nervously from one foot to the other. He swallowed. "I was in my motel room, lying down, from around six until we all left for the airport. I wasn't feeling so good."

"You seem to get sick a lot, don't you, Toby?" Josh smiled slightly. "I suppose you don't have anyone who can confirm your alibi?"

Green shook his head. "No, I don't. I didn't know I was going to need an alibi."

"You never know when one might come in handy," Josh waved him away.

Green left, almost running, and Joanna, who had been waiting impatiently, said, "I'm taking a short break. Come along, Michelle, we need to talk about this song."

Michelle rose to her feet, gathered her papers, and the two women turned to go. Edgar Pace rose as if to follow, but Josh raised a hand. "Mr Pace, would you please stay? I didn't want to mention it in front of Miss Tatum, but we need to talk with you."

Pace appeared surprised. He looked after

the departing women, then sat down again, frowning. "What is it now? Are these questions ever going to end?"

"Not until we find the killer, or killers," said Casey.

"I presume you know about Jonas Lester's murder?" Josh asked.

"Yes, of course. It was in all the papers, and Arlene called me."

"On the night of the murder, what time did you leave Nashville?"

"I caught a late flight."

"Just how late?"

"We took off a few minutes before midnight."

"Then you were still in town when Lester was killed?"

Pace frowned. "Just what are you suggesting?"

"I'm not suggesting, just asking," Josh said. "Please answer my question."

Pace sighed aggrievedly. "Well, the answer is obvious, isn't it? If I didn't leave Nashville until almost midnight, I must have still been there. Really!"

Casey said, "How about the others? Do you know what time they left?"

"I don't know why you're asking me, but yes, they flew back on the same flight, except for Joanna."

Josh leaned forward. "And just where were you during the time in question?"

Pace hesitated. "Let's see. As I recall, I was eating dinner." His features assumed an exasperated expression. "I wasn't keeping a record, you know. There was plenty of time until my flight left."

"Did you eat alone?"

"Yes. The others were staying at a different motel, farther from downtown."

"Where did you eat?"

"At a fast food place, a block or so from my motel. I wasn't very hungry."

Josh stared at him, hard. "I don't suppose anyone there would recognize you?"

Pace shrugged. "No reason that they should. The place was nearly empty, and those kids they have working there never really look anyone in the eye. I'd have to say the chances are slim that they would remember me.

"But this is ridiculous, you know. What reason on God's green earth could I possibly have for killing Jonas Lester?"

"I'm not sure," Josh said. "But I can think of a reason that you might want Billy Joe out of the way."

As Pace glared at him angrily, Josh removed the signed statement of Billy Joe's accountant from his pocket and slid it across the table.

Warily, Pace picked it up, and read it. As

he did so, the color drained from his face.

When he finally looked up, his eyes were dull. He said slowly: "I know that everybody says this, but I was going to put the money back, honestly. I wouldn't rob Billy Joe, or Arlene. I only meant it to be a loan."

Josh made a dismissive gesture. "I don't care about that. That's between you and Billy Joe's attorney. I'm only interested in the murders; and that," he pointed at the paper, "looks like a pretty good motive for wanting Billy Joe out of the way."

Pace winced as if struck. "Maybe I deserve that," he said with resignation; "but what about Lester? I had no reason to want him dead."

Josh shrugged. "Billy Joe talked to Lester just before he died; maybe he told him about you. Maybe after Billy Joe's death Lester threatened you."

Pace's face reddened. "Why, that's ridiculous! It's nothing but conjecture. You're bluffing. You haven't a bit of evidence!"

Josh smiled grimly. "Not yet, but we're working on it. Just don't leave town."

Pace stood, glaring at Josh. "I have no intention of leaving. I may have borrowed some of Billy Joe's money without permission; but I've killed no one. Look I'm putting a show together here, if you'd care to notice. And

I might add, earning the money to pay back what I owe. Now, if you will excuse me."

Head high, he strode away. Casey stared at his retreating back as Josh said, "Well, what do you think?"

Casey sighed. "I'm just not sure. We know he's an embezzler, but a cold-blooded killer? I just don't know. And he's right, you are bluffing. You haven't really got anything on him, at least not anything concrete."

Josh opened his mouth, then closed it, for Michelle Tatum was approaching the table. She smiled at them coolly, then resumed her seat, laying her papers and pen down on the table.

"Well," Casey said amicably, "did you work it out?"

Michelle nodded. "Yes. No real problem. Joanna just wanted a line or two of the lyrics changed. At least Joanna isn't as hard to work with as Billy Joe was."

Joanna was now back at the mike, and the band began another song; an oldie that Hank Williams had made famous. Casey thought that she did a better job this time; maybe because she was more at ease with the familiar melody than she had been with the new material.

Josh fidgeted all during the performance, and when Joanna was finished, he turned to

Michelle, who had gone back to her writing.

"Miss Tatum," he said. "I understand that you and the members of the band took the late flight back from Nashville on the night that Jonas Lester was killed?"

Michelle looked up, impatiently. "Yes. That's right."

"Can you tell me where you were during the period from seven to eight P.M. that night?"

She frowned. "Let's see. I had a quick dinner around six or so. After that, I was in my room, packing."

"Did you see anyone during that period?"

"No, not after I went to my room."

"Did you have a rental car?"

"Sure. I had to get around while I was there."

"What time did you turn it in?"

"When I got to the airport, about eleven fifteen."

"Then between dinner and your arrival at the airport, you could have easily driven to Lester's hotel; and no one would have been any the wiser."

She laughed, softly, derisively. "I could have, yes, but I'd need a reason, wouldn't I? The only time I ever saw Lester was at Billy Joe's funeral."

"We figure that the two deaths are connected."

Michelle shrugged. "So? I told you in Phoenix that I had no great love for Billy Joe; but that's not usually considered grounds for murder. And as for Lester, as I said, I didn't know the man."

Josh took a sheet of paper from his pocket. "This is a list of Billy Joe's boyhood friends. Does either of these names mean anything to you?"

He handed the paper to Michelle. She looked at it and handed it back. "Not a thing. Now, if you're through with this nonsense, I have work to do here."

"I'm through," said Josh. "For the moment."

Michelle returned to her work, and Josh exchanged glances with Casey over the woman's bent head. He shrugged, spreading his hands.

On stage, Joanna had started in on a new song, "Honky Tonk Woman." She seemed to be gaining confidence as she went along, and this time she sounded good. The plaintive melody and lyrics suited her husky voice.

The sound of Josh's beeper turned Casey's head. "I'd better call in," Josh said, and headed for the pay phones near the entrance.

He came back in a moment, but did not sit down. "I have to leave, Casey. They need me at the station. I've done about all I can here, anyway."

Casey looked up at him. "I think I'll stay a while. I want a few words with Joanna, and I don't want to interrupt her rehearsal. I'll stick around 'till she's finished."

Josh shrugged. "See you later then."

"Okay." She watched him as he walked toward the entrance, then turned and veered back. "Have to make a pit stop first," he said.

From the stage Joanna said, "The band is taking a short break, Michelle. Can we go over that music again?"

Michelle looked up. "Sure," she said. "Be right there."

She gathered her music and started toward the stage. Casey sat on alone. All of the band members, and Michelle and Joanna, had disappeared now. Soon Josh emerged from the men's room, gave her a wave, and went out through the front doors. Casey turned to watch him. As the doors opened and closed, she could see that it was now dark outside.

Josh emerged from the nightclub, and stopped for a moment so that his vision might adjust. It had been dim inside the club, but none of the outside lights was on, and the parking lot was darker than the inside of a whale's stomach.

Cheap bastards, he thought; somebody in charge must have known a rehearsal was taking place here tonight, so why couldn't they have left at least a *few* lights on?

He started toward the area in which he had parked his car, wishing, in passing, that he had parked closer, his mind on the complexities of the case.

On the edge of his consciousness, Josh heard the engine of a car coming up behind him. Thinking the driver was looking for a parking slot, he didn't look around. He plunged his hand into his pocket for his keys, only then realizing that there was something wrong.

As Josh turned, he heard the car's engine rev, and realized what it was. The driver was driving without lights!

CHAPTER TWENTY-ONE

Inside the club, Casey's thoughts, also, were fully engaged with the case. She had the uncomfortable feeling that she was missing something, something vitally important. Still alone in the big room, she decided to use the time to go over the chronology of the case, event by event.

Casey closed her eyes, noticing how quiet the room was; but even as she thought this, she heard the roar of an engine and a squeal of brakes from outside. Her eyes flew open. Who would be racing around the club parking lot? It must be kids.

She tried to gather back her thoughts, but a sense of unease prevented her from doing so.

Abruptly, Casey got to her feet and started for the entrance, almost running by the time she reached the doors. Outside, she stopped, confused by the darkness, looking one way, then another, for the car making the noise. There was no engine-roar now, but she could hear a car idling.

Looking in the direction of the sound, she saw the pale shape of a white Cherokee, just like her own.

As she approached it, she experienced a sense of shock. It *was* her own. But that was impossible. Groping in her purse, she found her keys. She looked up again at the car. The driver's door stood open, and the vehicle was empty. She leaned in, groping for the ignition, and, finding a single key, turned off the motor.

"What the devil's going on here?" she said aloud.

Straightening, she stepped back and pushed the door shut. It was then that she saw the figure on the pavement a few feet away. She approached cautiously. It was a man, lying prone, a tall man . . .

Recognition came with a cold wash of panic. It was Josh!

Tentatively, Casey touched his throat. The pulse under her fingers was weak and erratic.

Hearing voices behind her, she stood, looking back toward the club. Several of the band members stood looking in her direction.

"Somebody call 911," she shouted. "Tell them an officer is down and needs assistance. Tell them to send an ambulance. And tell them to hurry!"

The ambulance and two patrol cars arrived

only moments later, but to Casey, staring down into her lover's unconscious face, it seemed much longer. As Josh was lifted into the ambulance, she stood watching, indecisive. Should she go with Josh to the hospital, or talk to the people in the club? One of them, she was certain, had tried to kill Josh.

"Is he likely to regain consciousness soon?" Casey asked one of the medics.

The man shrugged. "Hard to say. He's banged up pretty bad. Even if he comes to, he probably won't know what's going on for a while."

In the end, it was Casey's deep anger that caused her to remain behind. Someone apparently had declared war on cops. First it had been she who had come close to being killed, in Nashville, and now this had happened to Josh.

Casey stood watching as the ambulance pulled out of the lot. As she started to turn into the club, she spotted someone she knew driving into the lot. She waited until he parked. In the driver's seat was Roscoe Barrows, a homicide officer who often worked with Josh.

He slid out of the unmarked car, a man of about fifty, overweight, with the rheumy eyes and florid complexion of a heavy boozer. Despite his unreassuring appearance, Josh had told Casey that Barrows was a good cop, street-wise and savvy. She was glad to see him.

"Casey." He walked over to her, his small, dark eyes sympathetic. "What went down here? I understand Josh was shot?"

Casey shook her head. "No. You received wrong information. He wasn't shot, but he was badly hurt. Someone ran him down with my car." She indicated the Cherokee.

"Do you have any idea who the driver was?"

She indicated the club with a jerk of her head. "Somebody inside there now, I'm positive."

He glanced at the club entrance, then back at her. "Maybe you'd better fill me in a little here before we brace them."

Leaning tiredly against the Cherokee fender, Casey briefly sketched in what had happened, including some of the pertinent details about the Baker case.

When she was finished, Barrows nodded. "I see. So you're pretty sure this attack is tied in with the Baker case."

She nodded. "I'd stake my life on it."

"One thing puzzles me; the fact that the perp used your car. You in the habit of leaving your key in the ignition?"

She shook her head. "No way. My keys are right here in my purse. The perp evidently made a copy; and that, by the way, could tie him into Lester's death."

Barrows looked puzzled. "How do you mean?"

"Well, I was sapped when Lester was killed. The perp took my purse. He, or she, could have made the copy at that time. Later, my purse was found. Intact."

Barrows looked skeptical. "Seems to me your killer was looking pretty far ahead."

"Well," Casey said ruefully, "he — or she — has been pretty far ahead of us so far. And maybe the key wasn't taken for this specific incident. They could have taken it to be used as needed, so to speak, in case a situation occurred in which it might be useful."

Barrows nodded. "Yeah. I guess that's possible. How badly is Josh hurt?"

"The medic wasn't sure, only that he had a broken leg and probably fractured ribs, as well as head injuries. He said they wouldn't know about internal injuries until he was examined at the hospital. I'm going there as soon as we're through here."

"Speaking of which, I guess we'd better get to it."

Barrows started for the club entrance and Casey followed him in. The interior lights had been turned on, and visibility was better now. The stage was empty, and the band members, as well as Pace, Joanna, and Michelle Tatum, were seated around a table, looking glum. Someone had raided the bar, and all had drinks in front of them, except for Joanna.

Joanna saw Casey approaching. "Is it true, Casey? Was Sergeant Whitney run down outside?"

"All too true, I'm afraid."

"Who did it, some drunk?"

"No." Casey took a deep breath. "It wasn't a drunk. I'm afraid it had to be one of you. Probably the same one who killed Billy Joe, and his father."

A collective gasp came from the little group at the table, and Edgar Pace banged the table with his fist. "Goddamnit, are we to be blamed for everything? Is there no end to this?"

"I don't know about 'we', Mr Pace, but one of you, at least, is cold-blooded killer. If you really want to put an end to all this, then help us uncover the person responsible."

Michelle said, "But how do you know it wasn't someone who just drove into the lot?"

"Because they used *my* car," Casey said grimly. "Someone had a key made for it."

She indicated Roscoe Barrows. "This is Detective Barrows. We'll be working together while Sergeant Whitney is recovering."

She glanced a question at Barrows, and he nodded. "If you don't mind, Casey, for now, since I'm new to the case, I'll just listen, but

you might tell me who these people are."
Quickly Casey introduced him to the people at the table.

"Now," she said. "It's like this. Josh was run down during your break. None of you were in sight when I heard the commotion and ran outside. I need to know where all of you were at that time. Joanna?" She looked closely at the other woman. Joanna's face was pale, and she looked tired.

"I was in the dressing room in back."

"Alone?"

"Well, yes, most of the time."

"I thought you and Michelle were going to go over some music?"

"Well, we were, but I had developed a nasty headache and I couldn't concentrate; so I took a couple of aspirins and lay down for a moment instead."

Casey looked at the songwriter. "Michelle? How about you?"

Michelle looked thoughtful. "After I left Joanna, I went to the john. I was in there until I heard a commotion and came back in here."

"Anyone else come in while you were there?"

Michelle smiled faintly. "Hardly. Joanna was lying down and I guess you were outside. After all, it *is* the ladies room!"

"So it is," Casey said in a dry voice. "Pardon

264

me for a moment."

She turned away, walking over to the uniform leaning against the wall. In a low voice she said, "Officer, would you do something for me? Check and see how many exits there are in this building, will you?"

He nodded. "Certainly, Miss Farrel."

As the officer moved toward the back of the room, Casey returned to the table.

"Now, about the rest of you. Mr Pace?"

Edgar Pace looked more mournful than ever. "I'm afraid I have no alibi, Ms Farrel. The club owner has an office in the back and he said I could use it to catch up on some work. I was there the whole time."

"Then nobody saw you there?"

He shook his head. "I didn't see a soul."

Casey sighed inwardly and looked around the circle of faces. "How about the rest of you?"

They all exchanged looks.

Jack Stover, the sound man said, "I was tinkering with the sound equipment the whole time. Some of the guys must have seen me. I know several people passed back and forth, but my attention was on what I was doing." He smiled weakly. "Of course a sound man is pretty much like a piece of furniture. No one takes particular notice of something or someone who's always there."

Casey nodded. "Anybody else?"

Wesley Keyes said, "I needed some air and a smoke." He held up a half-smoked cigar. "I must have been outside for about ten minutes."

Casey's gaze settled on him. "My Cherokee was parked around to the side. Did you notice it?"

Keyes shook his head. "Nope. There's a vacant lot behind the club, and I was out there."

Casey looked at Toby Green, who immediately began fidgeting. "Mr Green?"

"I was in the men's room."

"The whole time?"

His face reddened. "Yes."

Wesley Keyes laughed. "Old Toby is still having throne trouble, so you can probably believe him."

The rest of the band members more or less alibied each other; they had been having coffee in a little room backstage, but each had, at one time or another, left the room for a few minutes.

Casey gave a sigh of exasperation. None of them had a firm alibi. The field was wide open.

At that moment the uniformed officer returned and she gave him her attention. "Three entrances all told, Miss Farrel," he said. "One large one in the back, for deliveries; the one in front; and a small side entrance

266

just opposite where your Cherokee was parked."

"Were the back and side entrances locked?"

"Nope. Both have dead-bolts on the inside, but they weren't thrown."

"Thank you, Officer," Casey said with a nod, and turned back to the people at the table. "That's all of the questions I have for now. You may return to your rehearsal."

Pace said bitterly, "It's a little late now for that!"

"And I'm not in the mood for any more rehearsing, anyway," said Joanna. "May we leave now?"

Casey said, "If you like."

Wesley Keyes leaned across the table. "Is it true, what I've always heard, that cops work much harder to solve a case when another cop is the victim?"

A sense of dread seized Casey. During the process of questioning these people she had almost forgotten that Josh was lying in the hospital. Now panic washed over her, leaving her weak. If anything were to happen to Josh . . . No. She didn't even want to think of it.

Before Casey could gather her suddenly shattered thoughts to reply to this question, Roscoe Barrows leaned on his hands on the table, thrusting an angry face at Keyes. "I'll answer that, friend. I'll put it this way; if Sergeant Whitney dies, police will be swarming over you people like flies on shit; and we won't let up until the killer is found!"

Keyes leaned back, hands in front of his face. "Whoa there, partner! It was just a simple question."

"Well, you got your answer; and I'll even give you the reason. Every day of our lives we cops deal with the slime of the earth, people without morals or ethics; some of them ready to kill without compunction, or even reason. Our job is difficult and dangerous enough without giving scum the idea that they can kill cops and get away with it. That's why we pay particular attention to cop killers. Understand?"

Barrows straightened and turned to Casey. Seeing the stricken look on her face, he took a step toward her. "Damn, Casey, I wasn't thinking," he said in a low voice. "I'm sorry. But I'm sure that Josh will be okay."

"I'm sure he will," she said in as steady a voice as she could muster. "But I think I'd better get over to the hospital and see for myself."

CHAPTER TWENTY-TWO

Hurrying down the hospital corridor, Casey took Donnie's hand and pulled him along toward the elevators. On the way, they passed a flower and gift shop. Donnie held back.

"Casey . . . Ain't we going to buy Josh flowers or something?"

"Aren't, not ain't," she corrected automatically. She felt a strong surge of affection for the boy. At times he could be so thoughtful; flowers for Josh had never occurred to her. "I think that's a very good idea."

Inside the shop Donnie said, "What kind of flowers does he like?"

Casey smiled slightly. "I haven't the faintest idea. Josh probably doesn't know one kind of flower from another."

In the end, the decision was easy. Donnie spotted a football-shaped planter holding a healthy looking ivy, and the choice was obvious.

Donnie insisted on carrying the plant to the elevator and down the hall to Josh's room. The door stood open. Casey held Donnie back, peering into the room, which held two beds. One was empty; Josh was in the other, his right leg in a cast that was supported by a sling.

She urged Donnie into the room. Josh's eyes were closed, but as they approached the bed, he opened them. He had a drowsy look, and it took a few moments for recognition to dawn in his eyes.

"Hi, babe," he said weakly. "And hey, Donnie!"

Donnie held up the plant. "See what we brought you, Josh?"

Josh smiled weakly. "Now that was thoughtful of you." His gaze moved to Casey. "Whose idea was it?"

"I never lie," Casey said. "It was Donnie's."

Josh's smile widened. "Well, it's much appreciated."

Casey reached for his hand and grasped it in hers. "We're a fine pair, aren't we, Detective? I was slugged on the head in Nashville, now look at you. Sorry I couldn't get here sooner, but I had to stay and see if I could learn who ran you down; then I had to pick up Donnie."

Josh gestured vaguely with his free hand. "Don't sweat it, Casey. I was pretty much out of it until just a few minutes ago."

"What's the diagnosis?"

"Leg broken in two places, two cracked ribs

and a minor concussion from where my head thumped the concrete. A few other bumps and bruises." His smile was wry. "Aside from that, I'm fit as a fiddle."

Casey shook her head. "You're obviously going to be laid up for quite a while."

He grimaced. "So I'm told. Hell, the ribs have to heal fully before I can even hobble around on crutches. It looks like I'm pretty much out of the picture, babe. The department will assign another detective, but he'll be new to the case. I guess you'll have to carry the ball."

Casey squeezed his hand. "Barrows answered the call."

Josh brightened. "Barrows? That's great. He's a good man, and you know him. It could be worse."

Casey smiled grimly. "Don't I know it." She was thinking of one or two of the Phoenix detectives with whom she had had a less than ideal working relationship.

"But back to you, Detective. I don't suppose by some miracle you caught a glimpse of whoever it was that ran you down?"

"Hell, no. It happened too quickly. I heard the roar of a motor behind me, snatched a quick look, saw a big sucker of a vehicle coming at me, and tried to jump out of the way. Too damned late, I don't need to add."

Casey winced. "You aren't going to like this, but that big sucker of a vehicle was my Cherokee."

"*Your* Cherokee? How the hell did that happen?"

"The only thing that seems logical is that whoever killed Jonas Lester, and took my purse, made an impression of my car key. It's the only solution that makes sense."

His look was intent. "Did you question everyone who was at the rehearsal? It had to be one of them."

"I know, and yes, for all the good it did. They were scattered all over the club, outside and inside, and no one has a fool-proof alibi. It could have been any one of them. What I can't figure out is, why?"

"Maybe I was getting too close to something or somebody, and they wanted me off the case?" Josh tried to sit up. Donnie sprang to help him.

After a moment of struggle, Josh grunted in pain. "Never mind, sport. I don't think it's worth the effort. Just push the pillow down a little lower."

When he was comfortable, Casey said, "For whatever reason, it must have started back in Nashville, when my purse was taken. As Detective Burrows said, the killer was thinking far ahead."

Josh stared at her thoughtfully. "Were your house keys on the same ring as the car keys?"

Casey's eyes widened. Her voice was faint when she answered. "Omigod, yes! I've been so busy that I didn't even think about that."

Josh sighed. "You'd better have your locks changed, babe."

"It's a little late tonight to do that. I'll tend to it in the morning."

Josh looked skeptical. "I think that it would be a good idea if you and Donnie spent the night at my place. I'd feel a lot better if you would."

"That might not be a bad idea. Donnie?"

"Yeah. That's a great idea. Spot is still there, and old Mr Ralston might get sore if we bring him back home."

"Yes, there is that." Casey hesitated, thinking for a moment. If she was in danger at the apartment, it meant that Donnie would be at risk as well. Even if the locks were changed, anyone determined enough could still get in. She said, "Any idea how long you'll be in the hospital, Josh?"

"The doc said two or three days."

"With your leg in that cast, and the broken ribs, you're going to be flat on your back even when you're home. You'll need someone to take care of you. Maybe Donnie and I should plan on staying with you till you're on your feet again; that is if you don't mind?"

Josh's grin clearly expressed his feelings. "Mind? I think it's a great idea."

Donnie's grin was wider than Josh's. "We can watch football together, Josh," he said happily.

"Right, sport." With difficulty Josh reached out and gripped the boy's shoulder, then sank back onto the pillow. He looked pale and exhausted.

"We'd better go, Josh," Casey said. "Let you get some rest." She leaned down and kissed him on the lips.

"You'll keep in touch with me about the case?"

"I'll give you a full report every night."

"And you be careful, babe. We're dealing with some kind of nut-case here."

"I'll be careful."

The next morning Casey drove Donnie to school, then stopped off at her apartment to pick up clothing and personal items for the boy and herself.

As she lugged the bags out to the Cherokee, Ralston, the superintendent, spotted her and came trotting over.

"Miss Farrel! Taking a trip?" His face wore a look of alarm. "Not moving out, are you?"

"No, no," Casey said. "We're just moving

in with an injured friend for a few days. I wouldn't move out without telling you."

He looked relieved. "That's good. I was afraid, the dog and all . . ." He gestured vaguely. "I'm sorry about that, but I really do have to consider the other tenants."

"I know, Mr Ralston, I know," she said testily. "I've been out of town on a case, and I haven't had time to decide what to do about Spot; but I will."

Driving away from the apartment, Casey knew that she was going to have to do some serious thinking about the situation, but not now! Right now, the unmasking of the Honky-Tonk killer was the top priority in her life. Donnie would understand.

In her office, Casey half-expected to see an urgent memo from Bob Wilson demanding her presence in his office; but there was none.

She turned on her computer and called up the data she had compiled on the case. Starting at the beginning, she scrolled through the material, every fact of the case unrolling before her eyes. The feeling that she had missed something important came back to plague her. Some fact she had overlooked, maybe, or some fact she had read wrong. Or maybe just a flash of insight that had come and gone so quickly that it hadn't registered in her consciousness?

Finally, Casey sat back with a sigh. Nothing

in what she had seen on the screen had triggered a response. From experience, she knew that it would come to her eventually. Whatever it was might not lead to an instant solution, but it was usually enough to begin unravelling the elusive threads that led to the core of the mystery.

She turned to the telephone and punched out the number of Nashville Homicide, and asked for Detective Harvey Woodson. She was informed that he was out, but was due back shortly. Casey left her name and number.

Fifteen minutes later the phone rang. "Hello?"

"Casey?"

"Hi, Harvey. Thanks for calling back."

"Always have time for you, Casey. What's up?"

"Something happened here last night. I thought I should fill you in." Quickly, she told him what had happened to Josh.

"And you think the killer is the person who ran him down?" Woodson said thoughtfully.

"Darn near sure of it. That's one reason I called. If the perp is the same, it means that Jonas Lester's killer is now here in Phoenix."

"So you're telling me to relax, leave it in your capable hands?"

"Well, not exactly. Don't close the file on

it. There are some things I'd like you to do for me there."

"Such as?"

"Those two missing childhood friends of Billy Joe, have you found out anything about them?"

"There's not much on Leland Thomas. After he went to Mexico he simply disappeared. But Ray Parker, the one who wanted to be a cowboy, well he became one sure enough. He's working on a ranch outside of Cheyenne, and swears he hasn't been back to Nashville since he left. He also swears that he has never set foot in Arizona. His boss says that Parker was moving some cows to winter pasture at the time Lester was murdered. I'd say that pretty much ruled him out."

Casey sighed. "I didn't hold out much hope in that direction anyway."

"Your partner, Sergeant Whitney, is he going to be okay?"

"Well, he'll be out of action for some weeks."

"Give him my best, will you? I know what it's like to laid up in the middle of a case."

"Thanks, I will."

"And thank you for calling, Casey, and for keeping me up to date. If anything breaks at this end, I'll give you a ring."

"Same here, Harvey. Goodbye for now."

Hand still on the phone, Casey thought for a few moments, then picked up the receiver and punched out the number of her uncle in Second Mesa.

After a few rings, the phone was picked up on the other end and Claude Pentiwa's deep voice said, "Yes?"

"Hello, Uncle."

There was a brief silence before he said, "Oh-ee-e! I am happy to hear your voice, *Nessehongneum.*" Her uncle always addressed her by her Hopi name. "How are you, Niece?"

"I'm fine, Uncle."

"And the boy?"

Each time Casey visited the reservation with Donnie, Claude and Donnie became closer. Although not a demonstrative man, her uncle couldn't hide his affection for the boy.

She said, "Donnie is fine. Growing like the proverbial weed."

Claude grunted. "And you, are you still hunting the killers of the white men?"

Casey smiled to herself. Claude never changed. An educated and sophisticated man who had spent considerable time in Hollywood and the great cities of the world, he chose, when it suited him, to present himself as "The Noble Savage". Now that he had returned to his roots on the mesa, he was an activist on behalf of his people, and in this he was sincere.

She answered his question as she always did: "Of course. It's my job, Uncle."

"It is not a job for a woman, especially not for a Hopi woman."

"I'm only half Hopi, Uncle." She immediately regretted her remark. Claude Pentiwa did not like to be reminded that she was half white. She hurried on before he could speak, telling him of the murders she was trying to solve. She knew he would have no interest in the case, but she chattered on to cover her embarrassment.

When she was finished he was silent for a few moments. "It would be better for the Hopi that white men be allowed to kill each other off," he said. Then, "Remember, *Nessehongneum,* that things are not always what they seem to the outer eye."

After they had said their good-byes, Casey sat puzzling over what he had said. She was accustomed to his often puzzling aphorisms; yet Claude Pentiwa often revealed a startling prescience about events and people.

But what on earth could he have meant by that remark? What bearing could it possible have on the deaths of Billy Joe Baker and Jonas Lester?

CHAPTER TWENTY-THREE

The next morning, Casey had breakfast at Denny's with Roscoe Barrows. It was well past the early morning rush and the place was almost empty. Barrows got them an isolated booth in one corner.

When the waitress, a buxom blonde of indeterminate years, came to take their order, Barrows and she joked back and forth, making it clear that he was a habitué of the place.

Casey had run a couple of miles that morning before taking Donnie to school, and she was hungry. She ordered orange juice, coffee, a large stack and, after a moment's hesitation, a side of ham. Usually, she kept her breakfast menu on the modest and simple side, but there was something about eating breakfast out that triggered her appetite. Well, since she was eating late, she wouldn't want any lunch.

Casey sat back as Barrows ordered orange juice, bacon and scrambled eggs, and sourdough toast. "And keep the coffee coming."

The waitress smiled. "Sure thing, Ross."

As the woman walked away, Casey said,

with raised eyebrows, "Ross?"

Barrows got an embarrassed look. "I hate the name Roscoe. It sounds like someone just out of the hills."

"Oh, I don't know," Casey said. "I think Roscoe is kind of cute."

"You might, but I don't."

"Well then, I'll call you Ross — unless you prefer Mr Barrows?"

He grinned. "God, no. That makes me sound like my father."

"You should hear my Indian name," Casey said. "It's *Nessehongneum*."

Barrows whistled softly. "Now there's a mouthful. I didn't know you had Indian blood, Casey."

"Half Hopi," Casey said, "on my mother's side."

Barrows hesitated. "Does it present any problems?"

She shook her head. "None that I haven't been able to handle. Of course, it probably helps that it was my father who was white, so I have a conventional last name. And my features are fairly ordinary."

Barrows cocked his head. "Well, I wouldn't exactly say that, Casey. You're a very pretty woman, you know."

"Well, thanks for those kind words, Detective; but what I meant was that I don't look noticeably Indian. People generally seem to think I'm Italian, or a light-skinned Latina. At any rate, I've never experienced any real prejudice because of my race, only because I'm a woman."

"Well, I have the feeling you could cope with even that. In fact, I get the impression that you could cope with just about anything, Casey."

"Not everything," she said with a shrug. "This case, for instance. I'm far from coping with it."

"That's why we're here." Barrows was clearly just as happy to change the subject. "And I want to clear up one thing right at the start. You've been working this case for some time and it's all new to me, so I'm not going to charge in and take over."

"That's nice of you, Ross," Casey said and meant it. Some cops of her acquaintance certainly would have done, simply because she was a woman.

"I had a long talk with Josh," Barrows continued, "and he's pretty much filled me in. He also told me that you are one hell of an investigator."

Casey smiled. "Well, Josh has been known to exaggerate, but I think I know my business. So, he told you where we were heading?"

"Yes. He said that the two of you have narrowed the suspects down to several possibilities: Billy Joe's manager; Billy Joe's wife; the song writer — what's-her-name; Toby Green, a band member; and Jack Stover, the soundman. He said the other band members were on stage when Billy Joe was shot."

"That about covers it; unless it was someone out of left field. I don't think that's too likely, after Lester being killed. There has to be a tie-in."

"So you're convinced the two murders are connected?"

"Almost positive. All the main suspects were in Nashville at that time, and none have firm alibis."

Barrows nodded. "And Josh said the strongest motives belong to the wife and business manager. Pace, because he had been embezzling funds from Billy Joe, and the wife for Billy Joe's estate; but what motive would the others have?"

"Toby Green was about to lose his spot with the band because of his constant illnesses. I know that doesn't seem like much of a motive; but also he doesn't seem to be wrapped too tight. He used to have a drug problem; says he's clean now, but . . ." She shrugged.

"As for Jack Stover, the soundman, he and Billy Joe had what has been described as a violent argument just before the performance that night; and God knows, more than one killing has been committed in the heat of anger."

"But if it was one of those two, wouldn't that make hash of your theory that the same perp killed both Billy Joe and Jonas Lester? Why would either of those two have a reason to kill Lester?" Casey shrugged. "Who knows? To confuse the police, maybe — though I admit that's really reaching."

Barrows leaned forward. "Have you thought about this? What if two killers were working together? One killed Billy Joe, then the other killed Lester in Nashville?"

Casey sighed. "It's possible. Anything is possible. But I flat out don't believe it. As Josh would say, it complicates things too much."

Barrows smiled. "Occam's Razor," he said.

She thought a moment. "The rule that says that if you have several possible solutions to a problem, the simplest is more apt to be right?"

He nodded. "Just so. Ah, the food."

Casey looked up to see the waitress approaching with their food. Her stomach growled.

When the edge had been taken off their hunger, Barrows sat back and sighed. "That was good. Now, so where do we go from here?"

Casey took a sip of coffee. "Well, I have some work to do at the office, and then I want to talk to the two doormen at the Okay Corral. I also want to talk to Stover. Josh has already talked to all of them, but maybe if I come at them from another direction, they might drop something."

She put down her cup. "I've been thinking," she said. "You know that they say that the usual motives for murder are revenge, love and jealousy and money? Well, there's another motive just as strong. Fear!"

Barrows looked interested. "You think fear might be the key?"

"What I think is, once we learn the motive here," she said with a smile, "we'll have our killer."

Casey arrived at the Okay Corral shortly before opening time, hoping to catch the two doormen before they got busy. She found both men at the bar, having coffee.

Casey approached the two men, showing them her card. "I'm investigating the murder of Billy Joe Baker," she said.

The men were alike enough to be twins. Both were broad, muscular, well over six feet, and dark haired. They looked at her with the same blank eyes set in similar pasty faces. One took her card in a beefy hand, peered at it suspiciously, then handed it to the other.

The first man said sullenly, "We've already been raked over the coals by one cop. Enough is enough."

Casey smiled sweetly. "And you are?"

"Ben Twilling."

Casey turned the smile on the other man. "Joseph Sutton," he mumbled. She wondered if he was the one who had spoken to Josh about Stover. She didn't want to ask, in case he hadn't told his pal about it.

In the face of so much testosterone, Casey decided that she would catch more flies with honey, so she kept her tone light.

"Oh, I'm not here to talk about Mr Lester. I just thought that since you two are professionals, and used to this kind of scene, you might have noticed something that the general audience missed."

She increased the wattage of her smile, and tried to appear non-threatening. It seemed to work; both men relaxed noticeably.

Casey opened he briefcase, took out a sheet of drawing paper and spread it on the bar. "This is a rough sketch of the room," she said. "Here . . ." she stabbed her finger at the three tables situated near the back of the room, "At these three tables were seated four people that night. Edgar Pace and Joanna Baker at one; Michelle Tatum at the second, and Judy Lloyd

286

at the third. Do you know any of these people by sight?"

Twilling shook his head. "Nah."

Sutton said, "I know Mr Pace."

Casey recalled Pace's story of his movements that night. "Pace told us that just before Billy Joe was shot, he left his table and came up front to the telephone. Did you notice him?"

The men exchanged looks, and Sutton said: "We were both at the door. Some people were trying to get in, and we were busy keeping them out. The place was packed to capacity. The law says how many people we can have in here." He added virtuously, "And we try to obey the law."

"Yeah," Twilling said, "we both had our backs to the room when the singer was shot. We didn't even know anything had happened until people began to scream."

"Then you wouldn't have noticed if any of the other three left their table shortly before the shot was fired?"

"Nope," Sutton said.

Twilling looked at Casey earnestly, the effort showing in his eyes. "You have to understand something here, lady. To us this is just a job. We've been working here two years now. All these singers become boring as shit after while, excuse the expression. We're here to man the door, collect the cover charges, and to keep out people who try to sneak in. We don't pay much attention to what goes on on stage."

Casey sighed. "I understand. So neither of you noticed anything unusual that night."

"Nah," Sutton said. "Just like we told that other cop."

"Well, thanks anyway," Casey said. A waste of time she thought; a big fat waste of time.

Turning away, she walked down to where the three waitresses stood at the end of the bar. They fell silent at her approach and eyed her warily.

Casey held out the sketch which she still held in her hand. "I'm investigating the death of Billy Joe Baker," she said. "Were any of you working on the night he was killed?"

They nodded in unison. They were all wearing name tags: Cheryl, Rona and Bonnie.

"Anyone else working that night?"

Bonnie said, "There's another girl, Mary Sue. She's off tonight."

Casey said, "At the time of the murder, where were you all located?"

Bonnie smiled. "Right where we are now. We're not supposed to serve drinks during the performance when we have a headliner performing. Most of them have it in their contracts. It distracts the attention of the audience."

"What about *your* attention?" asked Casey.

"Not sure what you mean." It was Bonnie again; apparently she had elected herself spokesperson.

"I just spoke to the two doormen, as I'm sure you saw." Casey indicated the two men with a jerk of her head. "They said they were busy at the door, and that they don't pay much attention to what's going on on stage. Is it the same for you?"

Cheryl started to giggle, and Bonnie said: "You mean the B-boys?"

"B-boys?"

"Yeah. Booze, broads and bullying. That's all they care about."

Cheryl grinned. "The Steroid Twins," she said. "That's what the bartender calls them. He says the steroids have messed up their brains — that is, what brains they have."

"But we *love* the music," Bonnie said. "It's one of the perks of the job."

"So you watch the performers? Were you watching when Billy Joe was shot?"

All three nodded.

"And did you see anything unusual before that, anything at all?"

Rona spoke for the first time. "Maybe I did. I mean, I'm not sure . . ."

289

Casey was instantly alert. "What did you see?"

"Well . . ." Rona hesitated. "It probably doesn't mean anything. I mean, I never even thought of it when I talked to the other cops; but now that I think about it . . ."

Casey urged, "Tell me, please. Let me be the judge of whether or not it's important."

"Well . . . just as Billy Joe came on stage, before he even started to sing, I saw this guy in the back get up and walk across the room. I thought it was strange that someone would do that just as Billy Joe was about to let loose. Then he went into the restroom alcove, and I thought that he just had to go real bad and couldn't wait, so I forgot about it."

Casey laid her sketch on the bar. "Here's a sketch of the room as it was that night. Show me where you think this person you saw was sitting."

Rona studied the sketch with a frown, finally picking it up and turning around with it so that the drawing would correspond with the layout of the room. Then her face cleared. "Yes! Over there!" She pointed a long-nailed finger to the right — the area in which Pace, Joanna, and Michelle had been sitting that night.

Excitement bubbled in Casey. She said, "This person crossed toward the restroom alcove, walking between you and the stage?"

Rona nodded, her hair bobbing. "That's what he did, yeah."

"Did you see this individual come out, or stand in the alcove?"

"No, nothing like that. When I saw he had gone into the restroom alcove I forgot about him. Billy Joe had started to sing, and I was watching him."

Casey glanced at the two other women. "How about you two? Did either of you notice this man?"

Cheryl shook her head, and Bonnie said: "I sure didn't. I was watching Billy."

"Rona," Casey said, "you keep saying 'he'. Are you sure it was a man? A lot of women in these places wear jeans or trousers."

Rona hesitated. "Well, no, not for sure. I wasn't paying all that much attention. It just *seemed* like a man. You know."

"Walked like a man, you mean?"

"Yeah, I guess so. Like I said, I wasn't consciously paying attention."

"Did you notice his size? Was he tall?"

She shrugged. "I don't know. Sort of medium, I guess. I don't recall him being real big."

Casey studied the sketch in relation to the room, trying to visualize it dark and crowded with people. It would have been difficult to pinpoint the gender of anyone wandering around, much less recognize them, particularly with the added distraction of Billy Joe coming on stage.

She folded the sketch and returned it to her briefcase. "And that's all any of you saw?"

The three nodded.

"What about this other waitress, Mary Sue? Do you think she could have seen anything?"

Bonnie said, "I doubt it. She certainly never mentioned it, and she idolized Billy Joe. She was antsy for him to come out."

"Could I have her address?" Casey had her pad and pen out and she jotted down the woman's address and phone number as Bonnie gave it to her.

"Thanks," she said. "Thanks to all of you for your help. I appreciate it."

Leaving the women, she talked to the two bartenders. Like the doormen, they had no information. One of them had been in the employee's restroom; and the other had used the break to have a cigarette in the storeroom.

But Casey was cheered by what the waitress, Rona, had told her. She left the building, and stood for a moment beside the Cherokee, thinking. She wanted to talk to Jack Stover, the soundman, but it was late now; the band and Joanna would be performing. She had left Donnie with the sitter again, and should be picking him up about now. Originally, they had planned to visit Josh in the hospital this evening, but she had called Josh just before coming to the club. After listening to her report of her busy day and the planned trip to the nightclub, Josh had discouraged her from coming. "I'm fine here, babe," he had said. "I'd probably be asleep by the time you could get here, and you need a good night's rest. You guys go on out to the house after you're finished, and I'll see you tomorrow."

"To hell with it!" she said aloud. She'd done enough for one day, and she had found a lead, albeit a slender one.

When Casey and Donnie drove up toward Josh's house perched on the bank of a deep gully in North Phoenix, Casey noticed that there was a light on in the front room. She went tense. "Kiddo, we didn't leave a light on this morning, did we?"

Donnie frowned. "I don't think so, Casey. You told me to always check."

His frown deepened. "Casey, do you think . . . ?"

"I don't know," said Casey.

Reaching for the glove compartment, she removed the small automatic that she kept there. "You stay in the car until I check," she said to Donnie.

As she got out, Donnie said, "Be careful, Casey!"

She didn't reply. In her mind was Josh's warning that the killer might come after her next. But how could anyone have learned that she was staying with Josh?

She approached the house warily, ears straining for the least sound. As she tiptoed up the steps, she heard the familiar sound of the TV going inside.

Soundlessly, Casey tested the door; it was unlocked. Taking a deep breath, she kicked it open, gun pointed, her eyes raking the room.

"Jesus!" a voice boomed. She pointed the gun in the direction of the sound, and saw Josh, his face pale, staring at her from a wheel-chair placed opposite the TV.

Her heart slamming against the walls of her chest, she lowered the gun.

"Jesus!" said Josh again, his color returning. "You scared the hell out of me."

Casey took a deep breath. "Likewise, I'm sure. Why didn't you tell me you were coming home? I could have shot you."

"Yeah." A look of pride crossed his face. "Yeah, and you have no idea how much better that makes me feel."

She looked at him angrily. "What in the devil do you mean by that?"

He wheeled the chair toward her. "I mean

I'm proud of the way you handled it. Like a real cop. If I'd been a perp, you'd have gotten the drop on me."

He frowned. "Of course, you really should have called for back-up."

Casey slipped the gun into the pocket of her jacket. "For God's sake, Josh; you cause all this, and all you can think of to do is lecture me? Why didn't you let me know you were coming home? You know how touchy things are."

He looked abashed. "I'm sorry, babe. The doctor didn't come in till late this afternoon, and he told me that since I have someone to look after me, I could go home. I didn't mean to spook you."

She turned, as Donnie came running past her, crying out as he saw Josh. Josh hugged him awkwardly, smiling over the boy's head at Casey.

She closed and locked the door, then crossed slowly to stand looking down at the big detective.

He said, "You look a little beat."

"I am."

"Get anywhere today?"

"Well, I've found what may be a lead; but it's still one step forward, three steps sideways, and two steps back."

He grinned. "The Cop's Dance, babe."

"Well, I wish they'd change the music," she said tiredly.

"Sometimes *you* have to change the music," he said with a sympathetic nod. "Only way you can get anywhere."

CHAPTER TWENTY-FOUR

Casey was busy at her desk the next morning when her door opened without warning, and Bob Wilson walked in.

She leaned back in her chair. "Didn't your mother ever tell you that it is polite to knock?"

He bared his teeth in a vulpine grin. "I'm the boss, I don't have to knock. I just finished reading your latest report on the Baker case. It doesn't seem to me that you're making a hell of a lot of progress, Farrel."

"I'm making progress."

"Well, not enough. Not nearly enough! I want this case solved. I want the killer of Billy Joe Baker and his father behind bars."

"Getting some pressure from the VIPs, Bob?"

"Never mind that," he made a brushing motion. "I understand that your cop friend is laid up for a while."

Casey nodded. "Yes, he was run down two nights ago, broke his leg — among other things. He'll be house-bound for a while."

"Same perp, you think?"

"In my estimation, yes."

"Have they assigned someone else to the case?"

"Yes. Roscoe Barrows. Do you know him?"

He nodded. "Slightly. Good man. Look, the media has been on my ass for a press conference. So I've scheduled one this afternoon at three, in the press room. I want you there, Farrel."

"Me?" Casey said in dismay. "Why! What happened to your policy that only you make statements to the media?"

"This is a one-time-only thing." He stared at her with displeasure. "All right, if you must know; they know that you are the investigator on the case, and they will probably want you."

A sneer twisted his thin lips. "You're the media darling, aren't you? Just be there, Farrel, and be damned careful what you say."

Cameras flashed, and the red eyes of TV cameras swung balefully in Casey's direction as she entered the Press Room at three o'clock on the dot. Questions were hurled at her from every side as she made her way to where Bob Wilson stood at the podium. Wilson pounded for quiet, to no avail.

Relative quiet finally ascended after she stood beside Wilson, who said: "This conference, as you all know, concerns the Baker ho-

298

micide. I have a short statement to read, and then we'll be open for questions."

The statement, however, was not short. It also conveyed no real information being what Casey liked to call Bureaucrat Bilge, a lot of fancy, non-specific words that sounded lucid, but in the end told nothing that any relatively intelligent adult could not have garnered from reading the newspapers. She wondered why he wanted her to be here.

When Wilson finally finished the statement, the questions resumed. Wilson fielded them with evasive answers that soon had his audience angry and frustrated. Casey saw that he was starting to sweat.

Finally, the crime reporter from the *Arizona Republic* said, in exasperation, "Why not let Ms Farrel answer the questions? She's the one working the case."

Wilson raised his hands. "All right. I'll allow it this one time only. But, as you know, all media statements issued by the task force are channelled through me so don't take this as a precedent."

A voice from the center of the crowd shouted: "Give us a break, Wilson!"

Bob Wilson flushed an angry red and stepped aside reluctantly, allowing Casey to take his place.

The questions came fast and furious. Casey

handled them calmly, answering as truthfully and frankly as she could, holding back only those facts that would harm the investigation if they were made public.

The *Republic* reporter got her attention. "Casey, can you tell us if you're close to nailing this Honky-Tonk Killer?"

Casey frowned. "Honky-Tonk Killer? How did you come up with that one?"

The reporter grinned. "I have an eleven-year-old son who is in the same class as your son, Donnie. He got the name from him."

I'm going to have to have a firm talk with that young man, she thought grimly; now the media was going to jump on the name and run with it.

"My son has a vivid imagination," she said composedly. "As for knowing how close we are to nailing the killer, well, we have several strong suspects, and I hope that we will soon have the killer behind bars."

"The usual 'strong suspects'," one reporter said. "The usual crap."

Casey's temper flared. The media often tried her patience. A lot of them had all the charm and warmth of circling sharks looking for blood in the water; and many would not have hesitated to put that blood there themselves. She fixed the woman who had sneered with a cold stare. "Look, I'm sorry if my holding a few facts back so that we can solve the case gets in the way of your getting a hot story; but you know the rules. We can't tell you anything that would jeopardize our investigation."

The woman flushed, and Casey wished that she had kept silent. No doubt the woman's next article would deal unkindly with her. Well, it was just too bad; she was just about sick of being what Wilson nastily referred to as a "Media Darling".

Abruptly, she nodded to Wilson and moved away from the podium. Her boss stepped in and closed the session with a few unctuous words.

As the press corps filed out, Wilson said waspishly: "Honky-Tonk Killer! Thanks a whole heap, Farrel; that phrase will be in every paper and on the air before sundown."

Casey stared at Wilson. He really was a weasel. She said calmly: "You called the press in, Bob, not me. Besides, I'm sure they will mention your name a few times too."

Late that afternoon, as Casey was preparing to leave the office, her phone rang. She looked at it, debating whether to answer or just scurry out.

Duty won. She snatched up the receiver. "Yes?"

"Casey?" It was Josh. "Glad I caught you. You know, I've been a busy boy today. I was getting bored out of my skull sitting here; but luckily I brought my files home and I've been fooling around with the computer, running all the names through again. Guess what I found?"

"Josh," she sighed. "I haven't had what you might call a good day. I'm in no mood for guessing games."

He ignored her impatience. "I don't know why I didn't see this before. It seems that Toby Green is pretty handy with a pistol. He's won a couple of sharpshooter medals. How about them apples, babe?"

Casey was silent for a moment. Maybe she was just tired. Maybe her brain was suffering from overload, but she did not find this information terribly exciting.

"Well, say something, damnit!"

"I don't know if it means much, Josh. So, he's good with a pistol. That doesn't mean he's our shooter."

The excitement faded from Josh's voice. "Trust you to dump a bucket of cold water. At least it's worth exploring."

"Oh, I'll explore it, all right. I am heading out to Nashville West tonight anyway. I want to rattle Stover's cage a little, and I might as well include Toby. I'm just leaving now to

302

pick up Donnie. I'll drop him off with you, then head for the club."

"What about dinner?"

"I'm not up to cooking . . ."

"You don't have to cook. Just stop by the chicken place, or some such."

She said grumpily, "This makes a good excuse for you and Donnie to eat fast food. I'll bet you two could exist on that junk forever!"

"Depend on it," Josh said cheerfully.

Casey arrived at Nashville West about a half hour before the first show was to begin. She found all the band members as well as Joanna, Michelle Tatum, and Edgar Pace, in a small staff lounge in the back of the building. The musicians were playing around with their instruments, and everyone had soft drinks or coffee from the machines.

As she came in, Wesley Keyes cowered back against the wall in mock terror. "Watch it, people, the fuzz is here!"

Toby Green put down his guitar and started out of the room. Casey barred his way. "Stay, Mr Green. I have a few questions."

Michelle Tatum asked, "How is Sergeant Whitney, Casey?"

"He'll live, no thanks to one of you."

Joanna said, "How can you say that? You don't know that for sure."

"I'm sure enough." She turned to Toby Green. "I see you're still with the band, Mr Green. I thought you were leaving?"

Toby flushed and moved from one foot to another. "I . . . that was before . . ." His face took on a stricken look.

"Before Billy Joe was killed?"

"I didn't mean it like that! Besides, I probably won't be going on the road when the time comes."

"Mr Green, we've just learned that you're an expert pistol shot. In fact, you've won a couple of medals."

His mouth fell open. "That was years ago! Do you mean that because of that you think I killed Billy Joe?"

"Well, it would take a better than average shot to hit a man dead center with a handgun from halfway across the room in bad light."

"I never killed him, I swear!" Green wailed. "I haven't fired a handgun in years. Just ask anybody."

"We'll do that."

He hopped from one foot to another. "I have to go. Please."

Casey waved dismissal, and he bolted from the room. She looked round at the others who had all been listening avidly. Ordinarily, she wouldn't have questioned a suspect in front of others, but she had wanted to shake them all up a little.

Joanna said reproachfully, "You shouldn't have given poor Toby such a bad time. The poor guy is frightened enough as it is. He's too timid to kill anyone."

Casey shrugged. "One thing I've learned as an investigator is never to accept people on surface appearances. It can be very dangerous."

"Joanna's right," Michelle Tatum said. "I can't imagine Toby as a killer."

"On the other hand," said Wesley Keyes, "how many times do you read in the papers about some guy who's wiped out a whole family and all of his friends and relatives swear that the guy wouldn't kill a fly?"

Casey said, "Have any of you ever seen Toby fire a pistol?"

"Oh, yeah, I've seen that," Keyes said with a nod. "Back in Tennessee when we were much younger; back when Billy organized his first band. On weekends we'd all go out to a shooting range outside of town and bang away. Jack, you remember that, don't you?" Keyes glanced over at Stover.

Stover drew back under the impact of Casey's look. "Yeah, I was there a few times."

Casey frowned. "I'm a little confused here. I was under the impression that this band didn't go that far back?"

"Oh, it doesn't," Keyes said with a grin. "Like I said, that was Billy's first. It disbanded after less than a year. Billy put several groups together before he became really successful."

"So, you used to go shooting together? Was Billy a good shot?"

"Darn good, as I recall."

"Arlene encouraged him," Joanna said. "She's a crack shot herself, and she thought Billy Joe should learn how to handle a gun."

"It's funny how men's stories of their exploits improve with age," Michelle said. There was a touch of a sneer in her voice. "Billy was only a passable shot."

"That ain't true," said Keyes. "I said he was good, and he was, wasn't he Jack?"

Stover answered sullenly, "Yeah, that's the way I remember it."

Keyes grinned. "Don't mind old Jack — he's just pissed cause he was the worst shot of the bunch. Couldn't hit the side of a barn with a scatter gun."

"Well, I never liked it much, shooting, that is. I only did it because Billy ragged me into it."

Casey turned to him. "Did he rag you about a lot of things?"

He gave her a cool look. "I don't know what

you're getting at, but no. He didn't."

"You know," said Wesley, "all this talk about the past is making me sentimental as hell. Those were pretty good days, when you think about it. We didn't have much — no money, no real prospects — but we had a hell of a lot of expectations. It seemed like everything was possible then.

"Some of Billy's old buddies from school used to come out with us once in a while, and after we practiced, we'd sit around and talk about the future and what we hoped for." He shook his head. "God, we were young."

Casey felt a stir of excitement. "Just who were these old buddies?"

Wesley scratched his head. "Let's see if I can remember their names; it's been years since I've even thought of them. One was Dewey, yeah, Buck Dewey. And the skinny one . . . that was Lee Thomas. Jack, do you remember the third guy?"

Stover said, "Parker. Ray Parker."

"Yeah. That's it."

He looked at his watch. "Well, folks, it's show-time."

He aimed a sardonic look at Casey. "That is, of course, if we have your permission, investigator?"

Casey, suddenly realizing how weary she

was, waved a hand. "Go ahead. I'm through here. For now."

As the performers filed out, Michelle Tatum lingered behind. "You staying for the show, Casey?"

"I don't think so. It's been a long day." She looked at the woman curiously. "Do you attend all the performances, Michelle?"

"When I'm working on the music I do."

"But aren't the songs all written?"

Michelle laughed throatily. "Often songs are re-written and changed a number of times, and some of them are never really finished." She waved a hand and followed the others out of the room.

As Casey got into the Cherokee, she thought over what she had learned here tonight. So, Billy Joe and some of his band members had once practiced shooting together, and Billy Joe's "Musketeers" had occasionally joined them. There wasn't that much there, so why did that fact seem so important? And it was important, her gut told her so. There was a missing piece, she knew it. If she could only find it . . .

Shortly before one o'clock the telephone jarred Casey out of a sound sleep. She groped for the receiver and said groggily, "Hello?"

"Casey, this is Ross. Toby Green is dead."

Casey came fully awake. "Murdered?"

"It looks like suicide. I think you'd better get down here right away."

"I'm on my way."

CHAPTER TWENTY-FIVE

Casey made it to Nashville West in twenty minutes. The club was dark, but several police cars were parked in front, their roof lamps flashing whirls of light across the face of the building. Casey screeched to a halt and hurried toward the entrance.

A uniform barred her way. "You can't go in there lady. Police business."

"I'm Casey Farrel," she flashed her card. "Ross Barrows called me. I'm working with him."

"Oh, sure, Ms Farrel. He told me to expect you." The officer stepped aside. "You'll find him through the last door down the hall."

Several uniforms were clustered at the end of the corridor, smoking and chatting. When Casey identified herself, she was allowed inside the room.

There were a half-dozen men in the small room, which was an office. The air smelled sharply of cordite, fresh blood and tobacco, bound together with the flowery scent of gin. Trying not to breathe too deeply, Casey looked around. There was a large desk in front of the window on the far side, with a computer on it. Since the room was swarming with detectives and police technicians, Casey assumed that Green's body was in here, but she didn't see it. She felt a stab of dismay. Surely they hadn't already removed him?

Ross Barrows, standing at one end of the desk, turned, saw her, and started across the room. Reading the look on her face, he said, "No, Casey, the body hasn't been removed yet; I wanted you to see it first." He beckoned. "Over here."

Casey followed him, moving around to the end of the desk, and saw Toby Green. His face lay on the computer keyboard. His eyes were open and staring; a bullet hole in his right temple had leaked blood onto the computer keys. His left hand dangled down, and his right hand was curled on the desk. There was a pistol in his right hand, the muzzle only inches from the bullet hole in his forehead. An empty glass, on its side, and a half filled bottle of gin rested by his right elbow.

As the familiar feelings of sorrow and anger rose in her — along with her stomach contents — Casey fought to keep control, looking at everything carefully, trying to memorize the details. The gun, she noticed, was a thirty-eight automatic.

Looking up at Burrows, who was studying her sympathetically, she said. "A thirty-eight."

"Right," said Barrows. "A not unusual choice of weapon."

"I know," said Casey. "It's what was used on Billy Joe and on his father."

Barrows smile expressed satisfaction. "That's not surprising, since it appears that Green here is our murderer."

Casey looked at him unbelievingly.

He pointed to the computer screen, which Casey could not see from her vantage point. She moved around behind the body.

There was a short message on the screen. It read:

"May God forgive me for my sins,
I killed poor Billy Joe.
My sorrows can't be drowned by gin,
I think it's time to go.

Toby"

Casey said, "So you think it's suicide?"

Barrows sighed. "And you don't? Come on, Casey, there's the gun in his hand, the hole in his head — complete with powder burns — and he left a note. What more do you want?"

Casey read the message over again, and frowned.

Barrows said, "Pretty much a confession, wouldn't you say?"

Casey looked up. "It might be, but it's an odd one. Why do you suppose it's written in rhyme?"

Barrows shrugged. "He was a musician, wasn't he? And most of them fancy themselves song-writers of sorts. It seems to me that he might well have chosen that way to sign off."

"That's true," Casey said reluctantly. "And he was drunk, or I suppose he was. So you're going for suicide?"

"I don't think that will be up to me," he said with a faint smile. "Besides, we're working on this together, and I can see that you have doubts. Mind telling me what they are?"

Casey moved away from the body. "Well, first, someone could have gotten him drunk, then put the gun in his hand and held it to his head. If he was drunk enough, it wouldn't have been hard."

Barrows nodded. "True. That's a not unreasonable scenario; but they would have had to type the note first, because they sure couldn't have done it after."

Casey nodded. "They could have done that."

Barrows sighed. "You don't think you're reaching here? After all, the evidence seems pretty much cut and dried."

"It just doesn't feel right," said Casey. "Can you estimate the time he was shot? And who found him?"

"The club closed at one o'clock. One of the bartenders was still here, doing some cleaning at the bar. He thought everyone had gone, then he heard a shot in the back, at 1:21. He grabbed a pistol-grip shotgun from under the bar and went to look. He found Green's body, and called us."

"So enough time elapsed for the killer to escape out the back before the bartender made it back there?"

"If there *was* a killer. Why do you think anyone would want to kill Green? What's the motive?"

"I'm not sure," Casey said slowly, "but I think I have an idea."

One of the men approached Ross. "Ross, can we remove the body now?"

Barrows said, "I think so — Casey?"

She said, "Sure, go ahead."

When the body had been zipped into a body bag and taken away, Casey moved around to where she could see the computer screen, and jotted down the message there.

"Well," said Ross, "I guess that's all there is here."

Casey nodded. "We'll have to talk to Billy Joe's crew again. The best time would prob-

314

ably be before they go on tomorrow night, when they'll all be together."

Barrows looked doubtful. "That is, if one of them doesn't skip. Do you think we should wait that long?"

"I don't think that will happen, Ross. If the killer hasn't run by now, it isn't likely to happen. I believe our perp is pretty arrogant. I think he, or she, is convinced that he has us all fooled."

Barrows shook his head and sighed. "Well, as far as I'm concerned, he wouldn't be too far off the mark."

When Casey got back to Josh's place, a light was on in the living room, and Josh was sitting before the television. He was sound asleep, his head resting on his chest. She watched him for a moment, smiling softly. Tiptoeing past him, she switched off the set.

Josh came awake with a start. He blinked at her. "Jesus, babe, you startled me!"

She stroked his cheek. "I'm not used to having someone wait up for me, particularly a man in a wheel chair. I don't know whether to be pleased or upset."

He captured her hand. "You ran out of here in such a rush . . . The telephone woke me, but you'd already answered and hung up. I heard the front door slam, and I called out, but you were already gone. I've been worried as hell. What happened?"

"Sorry Josh. I didn't know you were awake, and I was in a hurry."

"So, what was it?"

"We have another body."

He frowned. "You mean it's connected to the Billy Joe killing?"

She nodded. "Toby Green."

He rubbed his eyes with his hands. "Jesus, that poor schmuck. How did it happen?"

Casey told him the details. He frowned. "And you think it wasn't suicide? I'm sorry Casey, but this time I don't understand where you're coming from. Green was unstable as hell. If he is our perp, and he thought we were getting close, suicide might have seemed the easiest way out. You said he was extremely upset when you questioned him last night."

"It just doesn't feel right, Josh. I know that's not exactly legal proof, but I've learned to trust my feelings. I'm convinced that the killer is still out there, laughing at us."

Josh shook his head. "Casey, Casey. You know better than to form a theory, then try to find facts that fit it. But that's what you've done, haven't you? I don't know why I'm surprised; you never were orthodox, babe."

"Well, neither are you," she retorted. "And that is not what I'm doing."

He yawned suddenly. "Look, I'm wounded here, and not up to these late hours. I'm going back to bed."

She patted his shoulder. "Me too. I have a strong feeling that I'm going to have a very busy day tomorrow."

Casey did indeed have a busy day.

After dropping Donnie off at school, she went directly to her office, where the first thing she did was type Toby Green's message or the message that she was supposed to think was his — into her computer.

Then she sat back and read the message again. Why had he written it in rhyme? Was it supposed to be a few lines from some country song? If so, it seemed to her rather imaginative; something of a light, mocking sign-off. The thing was, she couldn't really see Toby Green as being the type of man to write such a thing.

She read the words again. Her thoughts jumped back and forth as she opened her mind and let bits and pieces of information come to her. A remark from Wesley Keyes: "Billy Joe was straight as a ruler about sex . . . As for sex between men . . . Well, you can imagine." The information she had gathered last night while interviewing the band members; the talk about the target shooting back in the

317

old days. Her uncle, Claude Pentiwa's words: "Remember, *Nessehongneum,* that things are not always what they seem to the outer eye."

Reaching into her purse, she pulled out her notebook and re-read carefully the notes she had taken during her interrogation of the band members last night.

Then she opened her desk and pulled out the prints of the photos she had gotten from Arlene.

When she was finished, she reached for the telephone and punched out Josh's home number. He answered on the first ring.

"Josh," she said. "Can I ask you to do something? I'll be working on the problem as well, but I need some help, and Barrows is busy on this new case."

"Fine, lay it on me, babe," he said eagerly. "Anything to keep me occupied."

She told him what she needed.

"It may not be easy," he said dubiously.

She smiled into the phone. "A really smart detective once told me that 'Good Detective work is never easy.' "

"I should learn to keep my big mouth shut," he grumbled. "You're good at turning my own words back at me. I'll get right on it. You going to be in most of the day?"

"I'll be here until I find out what I need to know."

"What if you're wrong?"

"I've been wrong before. If I'm wrong this time, you'll tell me about it, won't you, Detective?"

"Depend on it!"

For the rest of the day, Casey kept her nose in the computer. There were few interruptions. Ross Barrows called shortly past noon with the preliminary autopsy report on Green. There was nothing unusual or illuminating. He had been killed by a .38 caliber slug to the brain, which had come from the gun in his hand; a blood alcohol content high enough to stun a horse; no identifiable prints except Green's; no signs of force on his body. About what Casey had expected.

Barrows said, "Still think it's murder?"

Casey said quietly, "Yes. More than ever, and I think I can prove it."

"Prove it?"

"Yes. Just two more pieces, and I'll have the picture."

"Well," he said doubtfully, "what do you have?"

"I'd rather not say yet, Ross. There's still a chance I'm wrong; but I hope to wrap it up before the day is over. Let's meet at Nashville West tonight when our suspects are all together."

He laughed. "Come on, Casey, not the climactic facedown with all the suspects present?"

She laughed also. "I know how it sounds, Barrows, but I think it's the best way to handle it. Okay?"

"Okay." He was still laughing as she hung up the phone.

Two hours later she had it. "Got you, sucker!" she said triumphantly.

CHAPTER TWENTY-SIX

Casey leaned back, staring at the screen. She had a headache, her neck muscles felt like lengths of stiff cable, and she felt she was on the verge of going blind from staring at the computer screen.

Inside, she felt wonderful. She was certain now that she had uncovered the identity of the person who had killed Billy Joe Baker, Jonas Lester, and Toby Green.

As if on cue, Josh called. "You're right, Casey," he crowed. "I just confirmed it. Casey Farrel, intrepid investigator, strikes again."

"I know," she said somewhat smugly. "I just confirmed it myself."

"You know, it's hard to believe; really out of left field. What put you on to it?"

Casey leaned back in her chair. "I'll tell you the details later. Right now, I have to pick up Donnie at school and drop him off with you; then I have to go on to Nashville West. I should get there about the time 'The Entourage' as you put it, arrives."

"Now, Casey. You're not going alone?"

She sighed. "Of course not. Barrows is meeting me there, and the department is sending a couple of uniforms who'll wait outside."

"Good."

"You can't really have thought I'd barge in there without any backup?"

"I never know *what* you'll do, babe. Unpredictable, that's you."

"Another case of the pot calling the kettle names. Listen, I need one more thing; I need a good sketch artist."

"Brad Powell. The department uses him all the time."

"Would you call him and find out if he can see me in about an hour?"

"Sure, babe. No *problema*."

Casey winced at his accent. "I'll be here for about another half hour. Call me back and let me know."

"I'll be back to you in about fifteen minutes."

It was well after seven when Casey drove the Cherokee into the parking lot at Nashville West. Briefcase banging against her leg, she hurried inside.

She found Ross Barrows at the bar, talking to the club manager. He looked up as she approached. "Casey, I was beginning to think that you weren't going to make it."

"I got delayed. I'll fill you in later. Are all of them here?"

"The last one arrived ten minutes ago."

"Good."

"Did you find what you were looking for?"

She grinned. "I found it."

"Is it hard evidence, enough to nail our perp?"

She hesitated. "Not exactly; but it's strong, Ross, enough to give a powerful motive, and that's what's been missing from this case. Several people have possible motives, but nothing really compelling!"

They walked for a moment in silence. A few feet short of the open door to the lounge, Barrows stopped her with a hand on her arm. "So you're not going to tell me?"

Casey smiled. "Don't you like surprises?"

"No, I don't, damnit!" he said harshly. "This is not a game we're playing here, Casey."

She looked at him seriously. He was a good man, and she didn't want to upset him, but she wasn't quite as positive as she acted — and what if she came a cropper? No, it was better if he didn't know what she was doing until she did it.

She put her hand on his arm. "I'm sorry, Ross, but I need the element of surprise, and I think it's better if you don't know what

I'm planning to do."

He stared at her. "Well, you'd better be right, Farrel. I thought I knew what you were doing, but right now I feel like somebody in one of those Peter Sellers movies."

They went into the room. All the members of Billy Joe's entourage were present. It was a glum group Casey faced.

Even Wesley Keyes made only a weak attempt at levity. "It's the fuzz again. Why am I surprised?"

Edgar Pace was obviously drunk. He peered at Casey belligerently. "Why are you bothering us again? Surely now that Toby has confessed, you have your killer? Why don't you leave us alone?"

"Because Toby Green is not the killer," Casey said firmly. A dead silence greeted her words.

"How can you say that?" said Joanna. "It was in all the papers this morning. Toby committed suicide because he couldn't live with what he'd done. He left a note."

Casey shook her head. "No. The note was written by whoever killed Billy Joe, Jason Lester — and Toby Green."

Silence fell again. They exchanged looks as Casey placed her briefcase on the table, opened it, and took out a blow-up of one of the pictures from Arlene's wall. "I have a picture here that I'd like all of you to look at. I want to know if any of you recognize this young man."

She handed the picture first to Ken Woodrow. He shook his head and passed it down the line, to Edgar Pace, who also shook his head, passing it on to Joanna Baker.

Joanna hesitated, frowning. "The face is sort of familiar, but no. I don't think so."

She passed the picture on to Wesley Keyes. Keyes studied it a moment, then nodded. "Sure. This is one of Billy Joe's high school friends."

He looked up at Casey. "Last night we were talking about the old days — when we used to practice our shooting. This is one of the boys that used to join us, Leland Thomas."

He handed the picture to Stover. "Right, Jack?"

Jack studied the picture and nodded. "Sure is." He looked up, "What does it mean?"

Casey took the picture from him and handed it to Michelle Tatum. "Michelle, do you recognize this?"

Michelle's face was expressionless. She handed the picture back to Casey. "No, I'm afraid I don't know him; but then, as I told you, I didn't know Billy Joe back in those days."

Casey nodded. "That's right. That's what you said. Well, how about this one?"

She took another picture from the briefcase, and held it up so that all could see. It was a sketch, well done, realistic, and obviously a likeness of Michelle. Wesley Keyes said, "What the . . . ?" There was a general rustle of reaction.

"Here, let me see both of those," Edgar Pace said, rising from his chair.

Casey held up both pictures side by side at chest height. The likeness was unmistakable.

"I gave the photograph to a police artist," Casey said, "and asked him to take that face and portray the individual as a woman with shoulder-length straight hair. This is what he came up with."

The babble of voices nearly drowned out her last words. She was watching Michelle Tatum, whose face was still blank.

"That's ridiculous," Michelle said calmly. "What is the point of this?"

Casey did not reply, but said, "Three years ago, Michelle, or Leland, you went down to Juarez, Mexico, where you stayed for a year. During that time you were a patient of Dr Ramon Ruiz, who performed a sex-change operation on you. You came back to this country as Michelle Tatum, determined to forget your past, or most of it. This is all documented, by the way."

Michelle swallowed, staring straight ahead, as gasps and exclamations of astonishment echoed in the room. She closed her eyes, then opened them, and glared around the room. "So what? So I'm a transsexual, it's not that unusual. What has that got to do with anything? I have a perfect right to do what I want with my body."

Casey placed the pictures on the table.

"That's right, Michelle, you do. But that's not what this is all about, is it? Or perhaps it is."

"What does that mean?" Michelle said tersely.

"It means," Casey said softly, "that you killed Billy Joe, and Jonas Lester, and Toby Green."

"I killed nobody." Michelle shook her head from side to side. When she looked up, her face was twisted with emotion. "I loved Billy Joe. I know I said that our relationship was only business, but I lied. I loved Billy Joe, and he loved me too . . ."

Her next words came in a whisper. "For a while."

Casey nodded. "And that was your motive. When you finally came to him as a song writer, Michelle Tatum, he had no idea of who you really were. It had been a long time since he'd seen Leland Thomas, and he certainly didn't connect you two.

"From what you just said, I gather you eventually had an affair and then somehow he found out who you really were — maybe you even told him. At any rate, when he found out that the woman he had been sleeping with was a man . . . well, Billy's homophobia was well known. I imagine that he took it pretty hard. What did he say to you?"

Michelle leaned forward, tense as a coiled rattlesnake. Her eyes flashed hatred at Casey. "He told me . . ." She broke off, realizing what she was admitting.

The room had gone very still. All eyes were on Michelle. She looked slowly around the room, then suddenly seemed to collapse inward, as if all passion had leaked out of her. Her voice was dull: "He told me that he loathed me; that in doing what I did I had made myself into a monster, a nothing! That I wasn't a real woman, and I sure wasn't a man. He said I must be crazy to do such a thing and that he would never forgive me for what I had done to him. He told me to get out, and that if he ever saw me again he'd beat me to within an inch of my life."

She took a deep, shuddering breath.

"He shouldn't have said that. I did it all for him, because I loved him. I always had, ever since we were in school together. Of course nobody knew. I acted as butch as the rest of them. There were so many times I wanted to tell him how I felt; but I knew how he felt about sex between men." She paused. "So later, when I could afford it, I had myself made into a woman."

She lowered her head. "But even after he finally made love to me he still had other women. So . . . I told him. I thought if he knew what I'd done for him . . ."

"And then he turned on you," Casey said gently, "and so you killed him."

Michelle looked up. "Yes. I had to, don't you see? I'd given him everything — my songs, myself — and he hated me."

She looked pleadingly around at the accusing faces. "If he wouldn't love me, what I had done was all for nothing! Nothing!"

She broke off, looking down at her lap where her hands were clenching and unclenching.

Casey said, "And Jonas Lester, why did you kill him?"

Michelle lifted her head and gave Joanna Baker a fierce glare.

"Because I wanted you to think that *she* did it, the bitch. She had Billy, but she didn't really care about him. She didn't make him happy. I wanted her to suffer. Since she would be the one to inherit both Billy Joe's and his father's estates I figured you'd suspect her. And I didn't like him. I knew about how he had treated Billy and Billy's mother."

"And why Toby?"

Michelle closed her eyes. Her face was white and lax. She didn't answer.

"Tell me if I've got this right," Casey said. "It was misdirection again. You knew how unstable Toby was, and you were there the other evening when I questioned him about being a crack shot, and he broke down. You thought that made him look guilty, and it did. Since we didn't seem to be going to arrest Joanna, you decided that he would be an even better scapegoat, so you asked him to meet you here, after the club closed, and you took him to the office. Is that right?"

Michelle nodded, but did not open her eyes. When she spoke, her voice was barely audible. "I got him drunk, typed the note, then put the gun in his hand and helped him pull the trigger." She gave a slight shiver. "He was the hardest, because I didn't hate him . . ." Her voice trailed away. She shook her head.

"I shouldn't have written the note that way, should I? I thought it was funny at the time, like a chorus from a bad country-western song; but it wasn't what Toby would have done, was it?"

"No," said Casey, "it wasn't."

Joanna's voice, harsh and angry, broke the ensuing quiet. "You killed all those people for no more reason than because Billy Joe dumped you? My god, Michelle, you must be insane!"

Michelle came off her chair screaming, "You bitch! You got Billy Joe when it should have been me! I could have made him happy if he had let me. You never did."

Leaping from the chair, she ran at Joanna. Casey stepped in her path. "Now Michelle, calm down. You don't want to . . ."

Michelle transferred her venom to Casey. "And you! I wouldn't have had to kill old man Lester and Toby but for you. You just never would give up!"

She reached out clawed fingers to rake Casey's cheek. Too late, Barrows seized the woman's wrists, but Michelle, with maniacal strength, pulled herself free.

Barrows grabbed her again, this time not underestimating her muscle power, wrapping her in his big arms. In his grip, Michelle's body whipped and thrashed wildly, then suddenly collapsed. He brought her arms behind her back, and Casey heard the click of handcuffs.

As Barrows read Michelle her rights, Casey

turned away. From her purse on the table she took several tissues and dabbed at the bleeding scratches on her cheek. Michelle's stinging accusation rang in her mind. Was *she* partly to blame for the deaths of Jonas Lester and Toby Green? Were her actions, or lack of action, responsible in any way?

Joanna Baker approached her cautiously. She asked timidly, "Is it all over now?"

Casey nodded. "Yes, it's over, Joanna . . ."

The club manager stuck his head in at the door, interrupting her. "It's show-time, people." He turned back down the hall.

Joanna said, "Is it all right?" She gestured at the door.

Wesley Keyes walked up behind her. "Of course it's okay, honey. The show must go on, right, Casey?" He smiled and winked. "That's show business."

He made a sweeping gesture with his arm, and the others began to gather their things. They left the room one by one. Edgar Pace was the last to go. He went looking back over his shoulder at Michelle, a stunned look on his face.

Michelle was again seated in her chair, Barrows right by her side. Now, he backed up to Casey, not taking his eyes off his prisoner. He said in a low voice, "You were lucky, you know that? What you've got, it proves that

Leland Thomas and Michelle Tatum are the same person, but there's no hard evidence to prove that he, or she, or whatever, killed those people."

Casey smiled wanly. "I think I could have made a good enough case for an arrest; and I think I could have proved opportunity; but sometimes direct confrontation pulls the cork on people, so I took a chance."

He raised his eyebrows. "And what if she hadn't spilled her guts?"

Casey smiled, "Then I would have had you arrest her, and started to scurry like hell to find something else that linked her to the crime."

"Well, I'd better get her down to the station, and book her."

Casey watched as he crossed to Michelle and gently prodded her to her feet. At the door, he turned back and gave Casey a wave.

Casey, feeling the let-down now, gathered her things. As she walked out, through the darkened club, she saw Joanna on stage at the mike, singing the song she had been working on with Michelle.

Keyes was right, she thought; the show must go on. That's show business.

CHAPTER TWENTY-SEVEN

By the time Casey got back to Josh's house in North Phoenix it was after three in the morning.

She found Josh and Donnie both asleep on the couch in front of the television, where a very old movie flickered on the screen. Josh had his bad leg propped up on a kitchen chair, and Donnie was curled up beside him. The room was dark except for the light from the screen.

In repose, Josh's face looked almost as young as Donnie's. Casey stood looking at them both for a moment, filling herself with the sight of them, then placed a hand on Josh's shoulder. He opened his eyes.

"Uh, Casey!" He looked at his watch. "Jesus, it's after three! Why didn't you call?"

She gave him a kiss on the cheek. "I've been a little busy, Detective. What's Donnie doing up so late?"

"He got up to get a drink of water about two hours ago, and wanted to know why you were so late. Then he wanted to wait up for

334

you, so I said okay. Besides . . ." He gestured. "You can see that he's hardly 'up'."

Their voices roused Donnie. He sat up, scrubbing at his eyes. "Casey!" he cried. "Did you catch the bad guy?"

Casey smiled, and reached to ruffle his hair. "Yeah, sport, I got the bad guy," she said dryly, "in a manner of speaking." She moved over to the end of the couch, and switched on the table lamp.

As she faced around, Josh exclaimed. "What happened to your face?"

Her fingers went to the scratches. "Well, the bad guy got a little out of hand at the end."

Josh frowned and his face darkened. "He scratched you? The son-of-a-bitch! What kind of a man scratches?"

Despite her fatigue, Casey couldn't help but smile. "A rather unusual kind of man, I guess you could say."

Josh glared at her. "For God's sake, woman, tell me what went on before I go crazy. You can be the most infuriating . . ."

She raised a hand. "Now, now, Detective, don't get impatient. Ah, where to begin?"

"How about the beginning, that's usually a good place — at least, that's what you always say."

"Yeah," said Donnie expectantly.

She gave them the chronology, step by step, soft-pedalling the sexual aspect of Leland Thomas's change into Michelle Tatum. She had always tried to be truthful with Donnie, and answer his questions honestly; but she didn't know exactly how much he knew about such things, and she didn't want to confuse him. Still, the whole thing would be blazoned over the news tomorrow, and he should be prepared.

When she was finished, Josh sighed, rather enviously, she thought. "I wish I could have been there with you, kid. God, I really wouldn't have pegged Michelle Tatum for the job. I thought that she was cold, and calculating — remember?" Casey nodded. "But I really didn't think she could be the killer. What first made you suspect her?"

Casey said: "It was a lot of little things; but the one thing that brought it together was what she said when I was talking to the band members about the old days, when the boys used to go shooting. Keyes and Stover both said that Billy Joe had been a good shot. Michelle said that he had been mediocre at best; she was rather nasty about it. The thing is, how could she have known?"

Josh nodded. "Right. When we interviewed her she said that she had known Billy Joe for a comparatively short time, and that their relationship was strictly business."

Casey grinned. "Exactly! Then it all began to come together, why the boy in that picture on Arlene's wall had seemed familiar; why Michelle had been agreeable to letting Billy take credit for her songs; why Billy had started to drink . . ."

"Yeah," Josh said. "I guess he must have been pretty shaken up when he found that he had . . ."

Casey pinched his arm, and shot a quick look at Donnie, who was listening with total attention.

"Yeah," Josh finished sheepishly. "I can see what you mean."

"Wait!" Donnie said. "What do you mean?"

"I'll explain the rest of it to you later, kiddo. You've got the story now, so I think it's time you got back to bed."

Josh said, "Right, pardner. Time to hit the hay, snuggle down, crash, hit the mattress . . ."

Casey threw up her hands. "Enough! We'll see you in the morning. But first a hug."

Grinning, Donnie gave Casey a big hug. She hugged him back, cherishing the feeling of his thin arms around her neck. Josh got his hug too, then the boy reluctantly disappeared down the hall.

Casey leaned back against the couch, and

sighed. "Well, I guess I'd better get to bed too. How about you, Detective?"

Josh blinked. "I'm wide awake now." He put an arm around her and pulled her close. "So Casey Farrel, our fearless crime fighter, has done it again. I'm proud of you, babe. But you had some luck. If Tatum hadn't broken, it would have been a lot harder."

"I know that," she said a trifle smugly, "but she did!"

"So, are you feeling good about it?"

She squirmed around to face him. "I'm not quite sure, Josh. Do you know what Michelle said to me before we took her in? She said that I was to blame for the deaths of Lester and Toby Green, because I kept pushing, and so she was forced to kill them."

He snorted in derision. "Don't be ridiculous, Casey, don't let her lay that on you. *She* killed those people, you didn't. Don't even begin to think you're responsible; that way lies madness."

She sighed. "I know you're right, but still . . ." She shook her head. "I guess I'm just down. There's always a rush when you solve a case, but there's always a let-down afterward."

He smiled gently. "Don't worry, babe. There'll be another case along all too soon. It's the life of a cop."

"Well, I hope it's not all *that* soon," she said with a sigh. "I've got to get busy finding another place for us to live where we can keep Spot."

"What you should do is buy a little house, then you'd have no problem keeping a pet."

Casey sighed again. "I know. I've thought about it, but I just don't have the down payment yet."

"I've been thinking about that," he said diffidently. "As I've told you, since my divorce I've had nothing to spend my money on. I can easily afford to lend you enough for a down-payment. No strings, no hassle; a simple business deal, all very legal with a contract and everything. What do you say?"

Casey looked up at him speculatively. "No strings? No pressure to marry you? Nothing like that?"

"Absolutely none. Depend on it. What the hell!" He spread his hands. "If I wanted to keep the pressure on, I'd do whatever I could to keep you here with me. Why would I loan you the money to buy your own house?"

She stared at him thoughtfully. "You know, Josh, you continually amaze me. Just when I think I have you figured out, you change directions on me."

He grinned. "The secret of my charm, babe."

She nodded in sudden decision. "All right, I'll take you up on it. It will solve my most pressing problem." She yawned widely. "I'm going to have to go to bed."

"Me too."

He reached for the crutches beside the couch and awkwardly began to lever himself up.

Casey rose and took a step toward him. "Can I help?"

He motioned her away. "No. I have to learn to do it myself. You're not going to be around every minute."

She shook her head in amusement. He looked at her mischievously. "But I will take a good-night kiss, if anyone offers."

Casey stepped close to him and put her arms around his neck. The kiss was warm and deep, and if she had been less tired, and Josh less disabled, would have led to bed all right, but not to sleep.

"Goodnight, Detective," she whispered.

"Goodnight, babe."

She was halfway across the room when he spoke again, "Casey?"

She faced around. "Yes."

"You know that my other offer is still open too; as of now anyway. But it may not be open forever."

"Is that a threat, Detective?"

"No, not a threat, but it's something you

should think about."

Casey felt the cool touch of a brief unease, but smiled.

"Oh, I do think about it, Detective, all the time. If I decide to marry you, Josh, you'll be the first to know. Depend on it."

The employees of THORNDIKE PRESS hope you have enjoyed this Large Print book. All our Large Print books are designed for easy reading — and they're made to last.

Other Thorndike Large Print books are available at your library, through selected bookstores, or directly from us. Suggestions for books you would like to see in Large Print are always welcome.

For more information about current and upcoming titles, please call or mail your name and address to:

THORNDIKE PRESS
PO Box 159
Thorndike, Maine 04986
800/223-6121
207/948-2962